THE HOUSEWIFE ASSASSIN'S FOURTH ESTATE SALE

JOSIE BROWN

A BOOK BY

SIGNAL
PRESS

Library of Congress Cataloging-in-Publication Data is available upon request

Cover Design by Andrew Brown, ClickTwiceDesign.com

Trade Paperback ISBN: 978-1-942052-81-4

V041919

Praise for Josie Brown's Novels

"This is a super sexy and fun read that you shouldn't miss! A kick ass woman that can literally kick ass as well as cook and clean. Donna gives a whole new meaning to "taking out the trash."

—Mary Jacobs, *Book Hounds Reviews*

"The Housewife Assassin's Handbook by Josie Brown is a fun, sexy and intriguing mystery. Donna Stone is a great heroine—housewives can lead all sorts of double lives, but as an assassin? Who would have seen that one coming? It's a fast-paced read, the gadgets are awesome, and I could just picture Donna fighting off Russian gangsters and skinheads all the while having a pie at home cooling on the windowsill. As a housewife myself, this book was a fantastic escape that had me dreaming "if only" the whole way through. The book doesn't take itself too seriously, which makes for the perfect combination of mystery and humour."

—*Curled Up with a Good Book and a Cup of Tea*

"*The Housewife Assassin's Handbook* is a hilarious, laugh-out-loud read. Donna is a fantastic character–practical, witty, and kick-ass tough. There's plenty of action–both in and out of the bedroom... I especially love the housekeeping tips at the start of each chapter–each with its own deadly twist! This book is perfect for relaxing in the bath with after a long day. I can't wait to read the next in the series. Highly Recommended!"

—*CrimeThrillerGirl.com*

"This was an addictive read–gritty but funny at the same time. I ended up reading it in just one evening and couldn't go to sleep until I knew what the outcome would be! It was action-packed and humorous from the start, and that continued throughout, I was pleased to discover that this is the first of a series and look forward to getting my hands on Book Two so I can see where life takes Donna and her family next!"

—*Me, My Books, and I*

"The two halves of Donna's life make sense. As you follow her story, there's no point where you think of her as "Assassin Donna" vs. "Mummy Donna', her attitude to life is even throughout. I really like how well this is done. And as for Jack. I'll have one of those, please?"

—*The Northern Witch's Book Blog*

Novels in The Housewife Assassin Series

The Housewife Assassin's Handbook (Book 1)

The Housewife Assassin's Guide to Gracious Killing (Book 2)

The Housewife Assassin's Killer Christmas Tips (Book 3)

The Housewife Assassin's Relationship Survival Guide (Book 4)

The Housewife Assassin's Vacation to Die For (Book 5)

The Housewife Assassin's Recipes for Disaster (Book 6)

The Housewife Assassin's Hollywood Scream Play (Book 7)

The Housewife Assassin's Killer App (Book 8)

The Housewife Assassin's Hostage Hosting Tips (Book 9)

The Housewife Assassin's Garden of Deadly Delights (Book 10)

The Housewife Assassin's Tips for Weddings, Weapons, and Warfare (Book 11)

The Housewife Assassin's Husband Hunting Hints (Book 12)

The Housewife Assassin's Ghost Protocol (Book 13)

The Housewife Assassin's Terrorist TV Guide (Book 14)

The Housewife Assassin's Deadly Dossier (Book 15: The Series Prequel)

The Housewife Assassin's Greatest Hits (Book 16)

The Housewife Assassin's Fourth Estate Sale (Book 17)

The Housewife Assassin's Horrorscope (Book 18)

Burying the Lede

In newspaper parlance, to "bury the lede" (pronounced leed) means the news article doesn't start with the most salient point of the story. Instead, it is buried behind secondary and less important facts.

Even off the written page, when it comes to life events, some of us conveniently quote-unquote bury the lede.

Example #1: Your husband tells you, "I saved forty dollars on our new big screen TV!" Then, when the credit card bill arrives, you find out he paid twice your agreed budget.

Example #2: Your husband tells you, "I watched the ballgame with some pals." But he doesn't mention that the gathering took place at the local Hooters.

Gentle Reader, in the future, feel free to insist that he states upfront and unequivocally the particulars: who, what, where, when, and how of the whole story.

However, should your mandate somehow slip his mind, feel free to bury some lead (pronounced led) in his backside!

JUST AS IT'S ABOUT TO CLOSE, I LEAP INTO THE WILSHIRE GRAND Center's only high-speed elevator that caters to its VIP guests.

Doing so in a short, tight skirt and four-inch heels makes it a grand feat indeed: one that's not lost on the two others along on this ride—a tall, blond man, mid-forties, in a bespoke double-breasted suit and a plump, bespectacled woman ten years his senior.

As I nod primly, the man smothers a smirk but continues to gaze appreciatively at me. The woman's cheeks flush. She feels my shame.

Ah, perfect.

Until we reach our floor, I'll ignore her. At the same time, I do my best to hold the man's attention.

I'm proven successful when his head tilts as he catches the faint scent of Clive Christian No. 1, released when I pull off the silk scarf tied loosely around my neck. He is tall enough to get a peek-a-boo view beneath the plunging neckline of my cream-toned silk blouse, where my black lace demi-bra does much more than lift and separate. My breasts are thrust forward like zeppelins heading into combat. With my left hand, I pull back an errant tendril of my auburn wig, allowing him to take note of my singleton status.

It works. Through the elevator's mirrored doors I watch as the man's grin widens.

The woman sees it too. But when our eyes meet her glare proves that she's on to my little act.

A soft chime indicates we've reached our floor.

"Good day," I say with a smile then lick my lips slowly.

The man murmurs, "Good day, indeed."

The woman rolls her eyes. As she stalks down the hall to her room, she mutters, "*Ich habe sowas von die Nase voll!*" Whipping out her keycard, she opens the door and slams it behind her.

I don't know if she meant to address him or me. From his

2

sly wink, I realize that he couldn't care less, so I guess I should feel the same way.

Ever the gentleman, he allows me to exit first.

Ever the lecher, his eyes will stay on my bum while I stroll down the hall toward my room.

Just as my hotel keycard penetrates its near-field zone, I hear him pass me on the way to his room next door. I look up, feigning surprise. "Good night, neighbor," I tease.

He nods and smiles as I enter my room.

Because my contact lenses also give eyes to my Acme tech-op team, my boss, Ryan Clancy, had a front-row seat to my little meet-and-greet. After I shut the door, he declares in my earbuds, "Perfect. Within the hour Ernst will be knocking on your door for a cup of sugar."

"He'll get more than he bargained for," I promise.

Ernst's last name is Bakker. He's a partner in Wagner Klein, a German law firm that has a small Los Angeles office on the twenty-ninth floor of this mixed-use complex. The law firm's clients include Russian oligarchs and ministry officials, many who use shell companies set up by the firm to launder dirty money through real estate investments in America's poshest communities: Beverly Hills, Manhattan, and Boca Raton, to name a few.

A month ago, the CIA assigned my covert ops organization, Acme Industries, the mission of infiltrating Wagner Klein and stealing its clients' digital files. Once the Russians' U.S. assets are identified, the American government will then confiscate the properties as part of our Russian sanctions initiative.

Easier said than done. Although the firm's general correspondence takes place through a cloud-based provider with a formidable firewall, Wagner Klein keeps its client files in an onsite Apache server that has no network connection and is protected by a Faraday shield. It also has enough static content to make it thus far impenetrable. Within the law firm, only one administrator has internal security: Ernst. The formal verification needed to open this Pandora's box is literally in his hands.

More accurately, just one finger: his right thumb.

Acme would have had greater success if it had somehow infiltrated the firm. But unfortunately, this satellite office of three lawyers considers itself fully staffed with one receptionist, three assistants, and a paralegal: the woman who was in the elevator. Her name is Wera Schäfer.

To deter an after-hours break-in, the firm's thick steel exterior door can only be opened with a digital scan of its employees' thumbprints.

Since Plan A—planting an operative inside the firm—is impossible, it's time for Plan B: Ernst must fall in lust with me.

It helps that he has only recently moved to Los Angeles and spends many a lonely night in the building's rooftop bar, whiling away his sorrows with expensive Scotch and whatever women he can coerce into accompanying him to his hotel suite. From what our Acme mission team has seen and heard, he likes them friskier than the wife he left behind in Munich.

My husband, Jack Craig, isn't thrilled that Ernst has a rough bedside manner. And since Jack is also my team's leader, he's here in my hotel room.

He lies on the king-sized bed, staring intently at the television screen. It's tuned to one of the several closed-circuit channels set up within the building. Our mission's tech-op, Arnie Locklear, hacked the security cams. Then, dressed as a telephone repairman, Arnie was able to get miniature surveillance cameras in Wagner Klein's offices as well as Ernst's hotel room.

I can tell by Jack's scowl that he's witnessed my not-so-subtle elevator foreplay then he switched to the hall feed in time to catch my *sotto voce* salutation to Ernst. Now he watches as my target restlessly paces his hotel suite.

Jack attempts a smile as he waves me over.

As I drop to his side, I close my eyes. No need to get the rest of our team hot and bothered as I greet Jack with a slow, searing kiss.

When I open my eyes, Jack is smiling. One mission accomplished.

I now turn toward the TV. Ernst is watching his set too. A naughty history lesson is taking place on a porn channel. In it, a naked guy in a horned helmet is ravishing a woman who wears even less: a dog collar attached to a chain. Right now the dude is jerking it.

"Is he supposed to be a Viking?" Arnie asks.

Jack snickers. "Your guess is as good as mine."

Ernst is jerking something too, and quite vigorously.

Ryan must also be watching because he chuckles. "Yep, he's primed."

"I'll say," Jack mutters. "Maybe it would have been easier to arrange a temporary illness for one of the office staff. That Wera woman looks as if she could use a vacation."

"My German is rusty so there was no guarantee he'd have hired me," I remind him.

"Oh, I'm sure Ernst would have figured out a way to get you on his 'staff,'" Jack retorts. "Maybe he'd have offered to give you private German lessons—and a dog collar."

"Now, now, children," Ryan chides us. "Donna's certainly piqued his interest, so let's wrap this up tonight." He and Arnie sign off.

Jack still looks worried. Time to change the subject. "What did Wera say when she stalked off?"

"She told Ernst that she was fed up with him," Jack explains.

Speaking of the devil, we're interrupted by Ernst's ecstatic groan.

I laugh. "That certainly took long enough."

After taking a moment to catch his breath, Ernst snatches the kerchief out of the breast pocket of his jacket and wipes himself clean.

I shudder. "I don't blame Wera in the least for being disgusted with him."

"What we saw was just the entr'acte." Jack rolls his eyes. "From what he emails prospective dates on Tinder, he's under the assumption a couple of tugs a day strengthens his staying power."

"Not if he's drugged," I counter.

"Good point." Jack rises from the bed. Reaching for his tux jacket hanging on a chair, he adds, "And off to work I go."

I pick up his bowtie from the dresser. Placing it around his neck, I vow, "Everything will go as planned."

"Famous last words," he retorts.

This time, when he pulls me in for a kiss, my eyes are wide open and so are his.

Seduction is a part of our job. Still, that doesn't mean we like it.

FROM SEVENTY-THREE STORIES ABOVE STREET LEVEL IN THE ROOFTOP bar of the Wilshire Grand Center, on a cloudless indigo night, you feel as if you can reach up and touch the stars.

Ernst is more interested in groping my breasts through the plunging neckline of my lace mini-sheath.

Because we're in public and I'm a lady, I giggle as I slap away his hands—a clear hint that he hasn't earned that honor just because he bought me a couple of mojitos.

Sure, I'm playing hard to get now. But eventually, I'll allow Ernst to sweet-talk me into his room. Sometime during the inevitable love tussle, he'll pass out cold, thanks to a roofie slipped into his drink.

As Ernst snores like a babe, I'll take his security card along with a replica of his thumbprint and enter Wagner Klein's offices. With the help of Arnie, I'll infiltrate the firm's data files. Despite the slight smirk on his face, the bartender is not amused by Ernst's public pawing. That's to be expected since he's Jack.

My husband's way of showing his displeasure is to pulverize a lemon with an ice pick. No doubt he wishes he were hacking the grin off Ernst's face.

Ernst signals Jack for another round. Jack is more than happy to accommodate him. With some sleight-of-hand, he's made sure that Ernst's Macallen 18 neat will knock him out within fifteen minutes.

Time for me to make my move. After Ernst takes a swig of his drink, I lean in and put a lip lock on his neck. He doesn't mind at all. As I come up for air, I purr, "Oops! I just gave you a hickey!"

"*Hee-kee? Vhat ees that?*" His tongue is already fuzzy.

"You know, a bit stronger than a kiss. A *really* hard suck." To make my point, I demonstrate on my thumb. "How 'bout I do it to you again, only somewhere less, er... public?"

Ernst must get the point because he laughs hysterically. But this time when he gropes me, he knocks his glass to the floor. As the glass shatters, Ernst chortles even louder.

Jack's eye catches mine. I know what he's thinking. Did Ernst finish enough of his drink for it to take effect?

I shrug as if to say, hard to tell. In any event, time to go before whatever amount made it into Ernst's system wears off.

Those around us crane their necks, curious to see what all the fuss is about.

Wera is here too, at the far end of the bar. Despite her

attempts to ignore us, her disapproval of her boss's behavior is etched in her deepening scowl.

As Ernst stumbles to his feet, Jack growls, "Should I put this on your room's tab, sir?"

Ernst nods slowly and fumbles in his pocket for his hotel keycard. When he finally finds it, he tosses it down on the marble counter.

While Jack charges his room, I keep Ernst occupied by nuzzling his neck. Finally, Jack hands me the card. "Time to get sleeping beauty home."

Ernst staggers to his feet. So that he doesn't do a swan dive off the roof, I prop him up by placing his arm around my shoulder.

He takes that as permission to pat my ass.

I tamp down the urge to grab his errant arm and jerk it out of its socket by wrenching it straight out to the side then behind him. Instead, I pull Ernst even closer and tweak his nipple through his shirt.

The things I do for flag and country.

By the time we reach Ernst's hotel room, he's too cross-eyed to place his key card close enough to the door's near-field lock. Instead, he waves it at the ceiling.

"Here, let me help you," I coo.

Ernst nods. He may be having a hard time focusing, but that doesn't stop him from gagging me with his tongue. I guess I should be happy that he only licked one of my cheeks before finding my mouth.

"Yuck!" Arnie whispers through my earbud. "Well, at least he's having a great time. The minute you enter his room, I'll switch the feeds in both the hallway and the elevator to show them as empty. That way, you can slip out."

"Marvelous," I whisper as I shove Ernst through the door.

He lands face down.

Oh, dear.

On the bright side, it'll be easy enough for me to take a putty imprint of his right thumbprint, from which I'll create a fake skin. Once inside, I'll go to Ernst's office, where I'll use the skin once more to access his computer and the necessary files.

All in a night's work.

Too bad Jack and I have to skedaddle the moment we have the goods. Our room's tub is to die for—figuratively, that is.

I TAKE THE ELEVATOR DOWN TO WAGNER KLEIN'S OFFICES.

"The hall feed shows that it's empty," Arnie assures me.

The fake skin sheaths my thumb. When I get to the door, I place it on the security screen.

And a red warning sign blinks:

PLACE FULL HAND—ALL FINGERS, AND PALM—FLATLY ON THE SCREEN, AND LOOK STRAIGHT AHEAD.

I hiss, "Arnie, what the hell?"

Through my lenses, he too sees my dilemma.

"Um...sorry, Donna!" he responds. "It seems they've installed a different security system since I planted the webcams. This one calls for full palm and retinal scans."

"Tell me something I *don't* know," I grumble. "Maybe Jack can fling Ernst over his shoulder, and we can prop him up somehow."

"Jack has his hands full," Ryan interjects.

"Oh yeah? What's more important than helping me get inside Wagner Klein?"

"He's...er...entertaining."

"And what's that supposed to mean?"

"When Wera let it slip that she was going back down to the office to finish some filing, he felt it was time to turn on the charm."

In other words, I'm on my own.

I never knew Jack's German went beyond a few phrases. Apparently, they're the right ones to keep the lonely spinster occupied.

I hop back into the elevator. The sooner I grab Ernst, the quicker we can get out of there.

ERNST IS HEAVIER THAN HE LOOKS. IT TAKES ALL MY MIGHT TO LUG him halfway down the hall.

Then I hear the ping of the elevator and laughter.

Afraid of what some hotel guests will think when they see us, I hoist Ernst against the wall. But the only way to keep him there is to lean against him. As he begins to topple over, I raise a knee to anchor us. So that it looks as if we're in an embrace, I fling his arms over my shoulders and grind my mouth into his.

When the couple sees us, their giggles stop. Still, they snicker as they walk to their room.

In German, I hear my husband whisper, "*Sie sollten ein Zimmer bekommen!*"

"*Er ist ein schwein,*" Wera scoffs. "*Es scheint, er hat sein Speil gefunden.*"

Jack roars with laughter.

Out of the corner of my eye, I watch as he follows Wera into her suite.

One way or another, I'll make Jack come clean with what they said.

Ernst stirs. At least part of him. *Ewww!*

I leap away, cursing under my breath as he crumples to the floor.

No time to lose. I grab Ernst by the legs and drag him into the elevator.

THE PALM SCAN IS EASY. HOWEVER, GETTING ERNST'S HEAD propped up level with the retinal scanner is a more laborious task. I do it by grabbing his hair, only to have it come off in my hand.

So, those thick luscious curls were a toupee?

Figures. If I weren't so tired, I'd laugh.

THANKFULLY, THE DOOR OPENS WITH A CLICK. ONCE AGAIN, I drag Ernst, this time down the long, polished hall to his office.

It's a minimalist's dream.

A phone is the only thing on his massive post-modern mahogany desk. No pen, no paper, nothing else except for a good-sized chunk of stone. It boasts a plaque declaring it's a piece of the fallen Berlin Wall.

There are also two post-modern chairs and a closet.

"The computer is in there," Arnie insists.

I use the finger skin to unlock the closet's door. I do the same with the computer's thumb scanner.

Yes, it clicks into operating mode.

"Where to from here?" I ask Arnie.

After an endless series of commands, Arnie finally declares,

"Now, put in your thumb drive, hit download, and we're golden!"

Done.

I slip the thumb drive into a hidden pocket on my dress, and not a moment too soon, since Ernst is moaning.

Damn it!

By the time I turn around, he's opened his eyes. Seeing me, he smiles—

Until he realizes where we are.

I run out of the closet toward the hall.

Angered, Ernst staggers to his feet and charges at me. But before he can catch his breath, I pick up one of the chairs and fling it at him. He grunts when it wings his shoulder, but it barely slows him down. A high sidekick catches him in the gut, and he doubles over. Once again, I hightail it for the door, but he lunges at me, toppling me to the ground.

Ernst grabs me around my waist then slams me against the floor-to-ceiling window. "Even at twenty-nine stories up, the architect thought a bit of fresh air would be appreciated." Ernst flips a lever. The large window flings open.

I find myself leaning out over six lanes of Wilshire Boulevard traffic. From this height, even the slightest breeze sounds as if you're in a wind tunnel.

I struggle, but Ernst has his full weight against me. "Beg for your life," he hisses in my ear, "or, with one shove, you're gone —*whoosh*! Just like that!"

"Go to hell," I spit.

He hoists me higher through the window.

I close my eyes, but I refuse to cry or speak, let alone beg.

A hard slap to my ass accompanies Ernst's laugh. "Your untimely demise can wait, *ja*?"

He grabs me by my hair and jerks me back into the room.

Apparently, he won't let me deny him the one thing he has craved all night long.

Ernst drags me to the desk. Heaving me onto it, he then shoves me down so hard that I hit the back of my head. I'm too stunned to move but I must. As he unzips his fly, I bend my legs. Then, with all my might, I kick him in the gut.

He slams into the wall.

I scramble off the desk, but he's already charging my way. I have to find something—*anything*—I can use as a weapon:

The Berlin Wall.

With both hands and all my might I swing the jagged chunk of concrete against Ernst's skull.

Dazed, he drops to his knees.

Instinctively, his hand reaches for his wound.

Big mistake.

Ernst gazes at the warm, thick blood on his fingers. Already, some of it has flowed onto his white shirt and turned it a bright scarlet.

He staggers to his feet, but he's too dizzy to do anything but go backward—

Through the open window.

By the time I reach it, his body is hurtling downward at such a high speed that a second later the cars below are screeching to a halt.

Then, silence.

Except for the wind.

I get the hell out.

As I enter the elevator, Arnie whispers, "His office had one heck of a view of the Hollywood sign! But I tell you—from that height, I got vertigo!"

"You and me both," I mumble. As the elevator rises, I feel as if my heart is going to burst.

I head to a different suite on another floor of the hotel. Abu

Nagashahi, another Acme operative, has already moved my things into it. He reserved the previous room under an alias. He'll check out as soon as he's done scrubbing away anything that might tie Jack or me to the room.

Arnie has already erased me from any and all hotel security footage. Jack turned in his notice this morning.

The moment I get into my new hotel room I upload the intel to Acme's server.

Then I throw up.

Vertigo finally kicked in.

WHEN JACK FINALLY COMES INTO OUR ROOM, HE'S WHISTLING. HE doesn't seem at all surprised to see me there. Yes, our bags are packed, but I lie on the bed in my robe.

Jack points in the direction of Ernst's suite. "How's sleeping beauty?" he asks.

"Clean up on Aisle Five," I declare. "Well, more like a splatter on Wilshire Boulevard."

Hearing this, Jack raises a brow.

"Long story," I admit. "But not half as interesting as yours, I'll bet."

"I doubt that." He flops down on the bed beside me. "You know, Wera hated him and everyone else at Wagner Klein. From what she intimated, she knows the law firm has dirty hands." He shakes his head. "She's no friend of the Russians. Too much history between her people and theirs."

"With what she suspects, why didn't she go to the Feds?"

"She was afraid of being deported: not to Germany, but Russia. According to her, 'The U.S. Government has been infiltrated at the highest level.'"

"How did you loosen her up?" As if I didn't already know.

Propping himself up on one arm, Jack faces me. "I hit her hot button, alright." He points to the television remote control and presses a button. We're on the premium network that plays around-the-clock live soccer. "The true saving grace was that the *Bundesliga* was playing! Dortmund versus Leipzig. She's a Zig'ger, of course." He chuckles. "Otherwise I'd have had to find another way to, um, detain her."

"I doubt it would have been a rousing game of chess." I roll on top of him. "Wera will be disappointed when she finds out you've turned in your notice. By the way, what did she say when she saw Ernst and me in the hallway?"

"What any woman might: she called him a pig." He smiles. "On the other hand, I simply suggested that you two get a room."

"Ugh! Hardly!" I declare. "I'm glad to be done with this mission."

"Really?" Jack shrugs. "I've got to admit there's something I'll miss about it."

"Oh?" I coo. "Do tell."

"This place has a lot of heavy tippers!" He pulls a wad of greenbacks from his pocket.

I laugh. "I'm sure Ryan will think of some way to make it up to you."

"Frankly, I was hoping for a different sort of compensation and certainly not from Ryan."

I bat my lashes. "Such as?"

Actions speak louder than words. Jack scoops me up in his arms and takes me into the bathroom. Apparently, the sunken tub had piqued his interest too.

But I've beaten him to the punch. The Jacuzzi jet stream is gurgling. Candles flicker around it. And because I've added a couple of bath bombs, the scent of roses fills the air.

Jack puts me down and pulls the sash on my silk robe.

Noting his satisfied grin, I untie his tux bow and toss it away. Then I unbutton his shirt and pull it off. When I unzip his pants, I have reason to smile too.

Once again, I find myself in Jack's arms. He steps into the tub and eases me into the water.

Does watching a sudden death make one delirious for life? I think so. It's why my lips thirst for Jack's.

And why the mere thought of him fills my eyes with tears.

And why my heart swells with joy whenever he is in sight.

I run my palm over his skin to reassure him that nothing is as important as him and me, both now and forever. My tongue moves to his earlobe, the cleft in his chin, his nipple. My fingertips follow: stroking lightly, probing gently.

Jack groans as he tries to hold back the urge to reciprocate. He knows his time will come soon enough.

When, finally, I move on top of him, he is more than ready to enter me. Still, he holds off. He gets too much joy from my gratification.

He doesn't disappoint. Even with his eyes closed, he remembers all my pleasure points. After putting me on my hands and knees, he moves his mouth from my neck to the small of my back. He cups my breasts before stiffening my nipples with his tongue. His fingers prod gently and deeply before opening me.

Enraptured, I moan as he finally enters me. He gasps, delighted when I tighten around him.

In no time, all our sensations are synchronized to his thrusts.

Lust is that timeless interval between longing and penetration. Each piercing jolt brings anticipation. All pulsating sensations take your breath away. Every second must be savored, its memory stored away for those times when our lives are deadened by acts of inhumanity: those of others.

And yes, our own.

At least, at this moment, I think only of the here and now: the sky-high ecstasy, the deep-down bliss, and the all-enveloping love I share with my husband.

Only after we crash back down to our reality do I remember:

Tonight, I killed a man.

Even before his fall, Ernst's life was already ebbing from his body. Still, this doesn't make me feel any better.

A spy must kill or be killed. The stakes are always high, and the odds are invariably low.

A successful mission must be savored. It too is an act of lust.

So, why am I crying?

Gently, Jack wipes away my tears, shushing me all the while.

"It was that good, eh?" He's teasing, of course.

I'll never tell him how bad it might have been.

Instead, I vow, "Always."

2

Citizen Journalism

When untrained members of the public take to social media to report news, we hail their efforts as citizen journalism!

If enough people see an article and it resonates with them, it catches the zeitgeist like an electric charge zapping dry kindling. Enough reposting on Instagram, SnapChat, and Facebook, along with a plethora of re-Tweets, and mainstream media will notice too.

First, the poster must capture the story with eloquence. Can this be done with a simple photo and caption, or in two hundred and eighty characters? A resounding yes!

Next, the story must resonate with readers. To do so, it must leapfrog videos of piano-playing cats and clumsy dance moves. Think natural disaster, or inspiring moment, or (yes, sadly) act of terrorism. We are in awe of the first. Our heart fills with joy at the second, and we cry at the last. In any regard, our emotions are stirred.

Finally, you must accept this new reality: you are the camera. You are the logical answer to the hypothetical question: If a tree falls in a forest and no one is around to hear it, does it make a sound?

Without us to bear witness, it never happened.

"HEY, SO GUESS WHO'S THE NEW EDITOR OF THE *HILLDALE HIGH School Signal*?" our son, Jeff, announces.

Jack glances up from his iPad, where he's reading today's *Washington Post*. "Are you trying to tell us that congratulations are in order?"

"If it earns me an extra pancake, heck, yeah!" Jeff nods toward the stove, where I stand watch over a griddle filled with hotcakes.

Jack tousles Jeff's hair. "Wow! I'm proud of you, son. These days, the Fourth Estate needs all the help it can get."

"We're studying the U.S. Constitution in history class," Trisha informs us. "Freedom of speech is written into the First Amendment. But I don't understand why they call journalism the 'Fourth Estate.'"

When I look up to reward Trisha with a smile, I have to stifle my gasp instead. Her make-up is as polished as a supermodel's and as thick.

Oh…no.

Jack catches my eye. With a cough and a shake of his head, he warns me away from confronting our youngest daughter in front of the rest of the family.

I nod and turn away. I realize I have to give Trisha some leeway now that she's in the fifth grade. Still, our under-standing was that meant clear or pink lip gloss or nail polish, not carte blanche access to her sister's make-up case. Or worse yet, mine.

Jack's able to keep a straight face when he turns to address Trisha. "Historically, the three branches of our government—Legislature, Executive, and Judiciary—were considered the First, Second, and Third Estates. Because news organizations have acted as a check on all three of the branches, they've become known as the Fourth Estate."

"Unlike Russia or China, which only have state-sanctioned media, and are really mouthpieces for those governments," Jeff adds.

"But not all of our news outlets do a good job." My aunt, Phyllis, points out. "They have to take advertising, so sometimes they don't go in-depth in telling people the whole story."

I don't know if she's scowling because of her feelings about the media or because of her homemade green juice: a concoction of almond milk, pulverized kale, frozen berries, and a handful of carrots.

And yes, it tastes as bad as it looks. She drinks it as part of her new "live forever" regimen. My guess is it won't even last as long as the Thigh Master that's collecting dust bunnies under her bed.

"And some news outlets don't fact-check either," Jeff concedes. "A lot of TV and radio so-called news shows are a bunch of talking heads who shout blather at each other and call it news."

As I place a serving platter stacked tall with bacon on the table, I ask, "So, what are your plans for the paper, Jeff?"

"Hard news only," he assures me. "True investigative journalism! And our teacher advisor, Mr. Franklin, says I'm fully in charge of editorial decisions, including who gets on staff."

Mary, our eldest, looks up from her texting, with the love of her life, I presume: Evan Martin, who is now a freshman at UC Berkeley. "Wait! You convinced Mr. Franklin to make *you* the editor? But you're just a freshman!"

Jeff leans back on the banquet with a satisfied smile. "He knows talent when he sees it. I guess my social studies paper convinced him I was the right person for the job. I wrote about how commercialism has ruined journalism and scored an A-plus-plus."

Great grades are my crack. I fold my fingers into a heart and send it to Jeff with a kiss.

"Mr. Franklin agrees with me that, from now on, we publish only in-depth articles that are fact-based and fact-checked."

"*Booooring*," Mary grumbles without even looking up. "Trust me, Jeff. Without a society page or gossip column or anything that features the students themselves, no one will read the darn thing!"

Her brother shakes his head. "Sure they will, if we tackle issues that are important to them."

Mary snorts. "Oh yeah? Like what?"

Jeff's brow creases. "Well…for example, instead of just reporting that the gym got tagged this week and quoting Coach Everett as saying it's a disgrace."

"Coach Everett's exact words were that it was a damn disgrace, and if he finds out who did it, he'll beat the kid to a bloody pulp," Mary reminds him.

"How do you know?" Jack asks.

Mary snickers. "Because he bellowed it during my first-period volleyball class. Everyone in the gym heard him, so Jeff will have plenty of sources to fact-check."

"If I were already the editor, the *Signal* would have quoted him exactly," Jeff responds. "Not only that, I'd have sent a reporter to track down who did it."

"And the poor sap would have gotten spray-painted by the taggers," Aunt Phyllis retorts.

Jeff shrugs. "Journalism is a dangerous profession. But it shouldn't stand in the way of the truth! The students have a right to know things, like what really goes into our cafeteria food and why the student parking lot has more expensive cars than those in the teachers' lot."

"That's because Hilldale parents spoil their children," Aunt Phyllis argues. "Anyone under the age of twenty-one shouldn't be driving a brand spanking new Mercedes, Porsche, or Lexus."

Jeff nods fervently. "Exactly! And for that matter, if teachers were paid decent wages, they wouldn't be driving ten-year-old second-hand cars. Hey, did you know that some of them are still paying off their student loans?"

"I don't think Hilldale High students want to hear you preach about how good they've got it," Mary counters.

"If they aren't aware of economic issues now, they'll soon be facing them," Jeff says. "How much do you think college will cost by the time you're there? Or me? Or Trisha?"

"Well now, there goes my breakfast," Jack mutters.

Mary waves her bacon at him. "See? My point exactly! Who wants to read about horrible things? You should make the paper fun!" She leans back languidly. "Look Jeff, if this newspaper makeover of yours is going to work, you're going to have to put honey on that gruel. What say I make it easy for you? If you like, I'll be glad to be your lifestyle editor."

Mary is offering to help Jeff?

As my eyes go to our eldest child, my spatula misses its opportunity to catch the pancake I've just catapulted into mid-air. One of our dogs, Lassie, is the beneficiary. Snatching it before it hits the ground, she's out the dog door with her booty.

Our other dog, Rin Tin Tin, looks hopefully at me.

I shake my head. "Nope, sorry."

Mournfully, he whines as he follows her out.

Jeff is smart enough to be suspicious too. "Why would you do that?"

Mary shrugs. "If my college transcripts are going to stand out, I'll need a few more electives." Mary bats her eyes at me. "And who knows? Maybe it'll help me earn a scholarship so that our parents won't have to shell out so much next year."

"If you really want to help out, take a weekend job at the mall," I suggest.

Mary nods. "Okay, sure. But I can be the *Signal*'s style editor too. In fact, I'll bet the Hilldale Mall would love it if the *Signal* showcased some of its couture and accessories."

Jeff holds out his hand to Mary. "You're hired."

They shake on it.

"I can recruit Babs and Wendy to help me with features. And since most students read the *Signal* online, we'll produce feature videos and a weekly fashion podcast too!" Suddenly, Mary's face brightens with a new thought. "Hey, I'll bet some of the merchants would show their appreciation by supporting the *Signal* with ads! If it becomes a revenue source for the school, I'm sure Principal Stewart will appreciate it."

Jeff frowns. "Commercializing the paper puts us at the beck and call of our advertisers. What if they balk when we run something controversial?"

I hand out plates stacked high with pancakes. "What do you mean by 'controversial'?"

Jeff thinks for a moment. "Like, if I point out some store policy that isn't great for our students."

"It might make them consider a different policy," I reason.

My son nods slowly. "I guess you're right. The press can't be afraid to call it as it is."

The pancakes are gone in no time. As the children rise from the table, I notice Trisha's skirt. It's too tight and too short. And when her sweater swings open, it reveals a shirt cropped high above her belly.

What is happening here?

Jack's eyes follow mine and grow big when he sees the subject of my shock and awe.

Just then, our cell phones hum in unison. He's still in shock, so I reach for mine first to review the most recent text message:

Overdue book! The Firm —Hilldale Librarian

I'M SURE JACK GOT THE SAME WARNING. IN TRUTH, IT'S A CODED message from Acme, letting us know that there is some unfinished business with our last assignment. We'll need to get to the office as soon as possible.

I point to Mary. "You and Jeff will take my car to school. Since Dad and I have an errand, we'll drop Trisha at her school."

Mary nods and grabs my car key fob from its hook.

Aunt Phyllis picks up her gym bag. "Can you can drop me at my hot yoga class? I'd walk, but I don't want to get sweaty before I get there." She sniffs an armpit.

Mary puts her arm around her great-aunt. "Of course! Hop onboard our magic carpet."

"Which always drives at or below the speed limit," I remind her.

Mary and Aunt Phyllis roll their eyes at me.

Jeff picks up his backpack as well as hers and heads for the door. "On the way, we'll discuss some ideas for feature pieces."

Mary nods. "Great idea! *The Signal* will be cutting edge! Sensational graphics, in-the-moment trend analysis, thought-provoking essays..."

It's rare that my children have found common ground, so yes, I'm doing a happy dance in my head. Granted, they won't always agree about the goal or the process, but through this collaboration, their respect for each other will grow. I couldn't be happier...

Well, yeah, maybe I could. As soon as I figure out how to

broach the topic of middle-school-appropriate make-up and clothes with Trisha.

The conversation starts now.

Thank goodness Jack is here to support me.

"*SERIOUSLY*? YOU'RE MAKING ME *WASH MY FACE*?" TRISHA IS incredulous.

"With all the makeup you're wearing, one would think you're about to walk the red carpet!" I exclaim.

"Everyone wears it like this." Trisha's head shakes as she folds her arms at her waist.

I guess she realizes it's the only way to keep me from staring at her bellybutton.

Wrong.

I point upstairs. "And when you finish, change into a top that covers your midriff and a skirt that covers your thighs! Have you forgotten that your school has a dress code?"

"Everyone dresses this way," she says indignantly. "Why shouldn't I?"

"You mean to tell me that everyone at school breaks the rules?" Jack is bemused by Trisha's audacity.

"Yeah, sort of. If I keep my sweater buttoned, who's to know the difference?"

I raise a brow. "Your skirt is still much too short."

"To get noticed, you have to *stand out*."

I take her other hand. "Honey, there are good ways to stand out and there are bad ways. Getting called out for inappropriate dress won't earn your teachers' respect."

Trisha holds her head high. "I'm a straight-A student! My teachers should never judge me on what I wear, but what I do or say."

I'm speechless.

"She has a point," Jack murmurs.

"Nope. Not if she gets expelled," I hiss back. But my tone with Trisha is firm and loud: "We've always been proud of you for your hard work and dedication to your studies," I assure her. "And you're right. Your teachers should only judge you on your merits. Not just your academic record, but as you put it, your actions and your words as well." I look her in the eye. "So, Trisha, I ask you: What message are you trying to send to those whom you want as friends?"

"That I fit in." She scowls stubbornly. "I'm the only girl in my class who doesn't wear mascara or blush or eye shadow or eyeliner!"

"I find that hard to believe," I declare.

"Oh yeah? Just look!" She pulls out her phone. A moment later she's showing me a photo. In it, Trisha is ganged together with three other girls.

She's right. Their face paint is thick, their skirts graze their upper thighs, and when their cardigans are open, their blouses are tied high on their abdomen.

One of the girls at the end has her arm extended to snap the selfie of their identical poses: mouths are pursed, exaggerating the natural plushness of their lips. Each girl's right hand is extended in a gang signal.

Jack's eyes grow large. He doesn't say anything. Instead, he bites his lip to keep from laughing.

On the other hand, I'm trying to hold my temper. "Who taught you that hand gesture?"

"Madison's brother, Curt. He says it's really gangsta."

"Oh, I'll say it is," Jack responds. "Honey, if you do that to the wrong person, they may hurt you."

"But…it's just a joke!" Trisha sighs as she rolls her eyes. "It's something you say if you want to be snatched."

"That's our point!" I exclaim. "We don't want you snatched!"

"Obviously!" She puts her hands on her hips, as if ready to do battle. "Mom! Dad! Madison has finally noticed me! And now that she wants me in her squad, I've got to up my game! Otherwise, they won't respect me!"

"Which one is Madison?" I ask.

Trisha points to the girl holding the camera. Her blond hair has dark roots: a deliberate ombre dye job. She also has a small tat on her wrist that proclaims BARELY VIRGIN.

Oh, great.

I force my voice into a gentler tone. "But Trisha, you've just said that respect shouldn't be based on how you look; that what really matters is how you act, and whether you keep your word and others' respect."

"You're twisting my words to make your point!"

Another text pings both mine and Jack's cell phones. This discussion must end *now*.

I point to the stairwell. "No arguments, Trisha! Now, put on an appropriate top and skirt. Otherwise, you're grounded from all extracurricular activities and no cell phone, iPad, or computer." My tone says it all: I am not kidding around.

Trisha storms upstairs.

DURING THE DRIVE TO SCHOOL, TRISHA IS SILENT.

When we pull up, Jack turns to face her. "Look, kiddo, maybe you and your mom could go on a shopping spree after school. You've certainly earned the right to some new clothes."

"Why bother? Mom wants me to stay her little girl forever!" She slams the car door and stalks off.

Jack sighs. Seeing the sad look on my face, he shakes his head. "You know she didn't mean that."

"Yes, she did." Frustrated, I shake my head. "And you know what? She's right. She is my little girl. If I could, I'd freeze time. Life is too precious to waste a moment of it. We've both been to the precipice, and by the grace of God, we were pulled back. We should cherish every moment with the children."

"You did nothing wrong by insisting that she follow school policy." Jack strokes my cheek. "She just wants a little independence. It's part of growing up."

I wipe away a tear. "I don't mind that as long as Trisha doesn't...well, as long as she doesn't grow up *too* fast."

"Whether she does or not may not be in our control," he reminds me. "Even under normal circumstances, a child's innocence is never assured."

Of course, he's right.

Even before Trisha's birth, our family wasn't "normal." Thanks to my dead and buried ex-husband Carl's duplicity, I just didn't know it.

"There was a time in my life when I thought I'd never experience the joys and trials of parenting," Jack admits. "Sure, it's not always fun. But I wouldn't trade the experience for anything in the world."

His confession earns him an eye roll. "Wait until Trisha turns eighteen then tell me how you feel."

For just a second, his smile turns upside down. But his kiss tells me that he's more than ready for the challenge.

Together we'll get through it. And so will she.

WE WALK INTO THE ACME CONFERENCE ROOM TO FIND A WOMAN kneeling in front of Dominic Fleming, one of Acme's operatives. He has his back to us, but from what we can see, this comely lady's hand is high between his legs.

Jack snickers. "Well, this has got to be good…"

Apparently, our opinions differ on the matter.

This sight stupefies other members of our team, specifically, Arnie and Abu. On the other hand, our ComInt op, Emma Honeycutt, is busy scanning a video on her computer screen. Like me, she finds Dominic's sexploits less than impressive.

Ryan is still in his office, on the phone and pacing the floor. Oh, joy. I can't wait to see his reaction to this scene.

It isn't until we walk around Dominic and his friend that we notice her astounding beauty. The woman holds a cloth tape measure that stretches up from the floor. Looking up adoringly at Dominic, she purrs, "My, that's quite an inseam you have, sir."

He grins down at her. "Impressive, I know."

His smile widens when he sees us. "Ah! Here's the old boy now! Jack, if anyone needs a new suit, it's you. And Seamstress Simone is just the person to wrap you in luxury to which you'll soon grow accustomed." He strokes the cuff of his shirt admiringly. "Let me tell you, she's quite a flocker! I can vouch for the fact that her finger press is, er, the tightest I've ever felt."

"You don't say," I growl.

I look down at Simone's open sewing box. Amid all sizes of needles, thread, and fabric samples she's got a large darning mushroom. If Dominic keeps up the sewing puns, I'll be tempted to put it where the sun don't shine.

As if reading my mind, Jack quickly assures him, "Thanks, but no thanks. I'm an off-the-rack kind of guy."

Dominic sighs. "Sadly, it shows. Ah well…" He winces when Simone's fingers graze his crotch. "Gently, dearest! One must handle the family jewels with the utmost care."

Emma rolls her eyes. "Don't be so coy, Dominic. Your testicles have seen more action than most porn stars."

Instead of being miffed, Dominic swells with pride.

I look over Emma's shoulder at her computer screen. "What's this? Reconnaissance for our next mission?"

Emma's cheeks turn crimson. Guiltily, she shakes her head. "Um…no. I…Well, Nicky started toddler preschool today, and I thought I'd check in to see how he's doing."

The scene on her screen would melt any parent's heart: a dozen toddlers, sitting in a circle, are singing "Itsy Bitsy Spider" with their teacher.

I move in for a closer look. "I don't see Nicky. Where is he?"

Emma's finger taps the corner of the screen, where Nicky sits in the lap of another teacher. Despite her attempt to engage him in the song, he is crying.

"It's natural for him to be a little forlorn. It is his first day of school and all," I remind her.

"I know…but…I feel *as if I've abandoned him*." A tear rolls down Emma's cheek.

"Em, it may take a few days or even a week, but he'll adjust as long as you keep telling him that he's having fun making new friends. And as you can see for yourself, he's in capable hands." I smile encouragingly. "I think it's great that the preschool has a webcam system. I'm sure the parents find it soothing."

"Yeah, um…about that…" Emma bites her lower lip. "To be honest, it's not their webcam. I sort of set it up after hours." She puts a finger to her lips. "Please don't tell anyone, especially not Arnie! He'd laugh at me for being such a…such a *mom*."

"Cross my heart," I promise. "First and foremost because it's illegal *and* unsanctioned! If Ryan finds out, he'll have to fire you."

Emma nods sadly. "I know. I'm so sorry, Donna! But, I just

couldn't bear leaving Nicky without some way to watch over him."

"Emma, listen, I understand thoroughly. Still..." I think for a moment. "Hey, why don't you offer the preschool a free webcam system? Pitch it as a way to make the parents feel secure. If you do it at the next parents-and-teachers gathering, I'm sure they'd jump at it, especially if the other parents are just as cautious."

Emma attempts a smile. "You're right. In fact, there's a potluck tomorrow night." She kisses her fingertips then places them over her little guy's image on the screen. "I'll turn it off the moment I get him home."

We both snap to attention when we hear the door open.

Ryan rushes in, but he stops short when he sees Seamstress Simone, who is now measuring Dominic's waist. Why she feels the need to stand practically breast-to-chest with him is beyond me.

Apparently, Ryan feels the same way. His growl is incomprehensible when he sees them.

Dominic turns pale.

Seamstress Simone knows better than to turn on the charm. Instead, she tosses her tape measure into her sewing kit and scurries out the door. Through the glass window, we see her being escorted out by two security guards.

Before Dominic can explain, Ryan barks, "You're lucky we don't have time to get into why you presumed it would be a smart idea to bring nonclassified personnel into our conference room. However, Mr. Fleming, if Acme is compromised, you'll find yourself being hauled off to a black site wearing nothing but an ill-fitting orange jumpsuit. *Do you hear me?*"

Dominic nods solemnly and sits down.

"Good." Ryan nods, satisfied. "Everyone, please take a seat. We've got a crisis in the making."

3

Backgrounder

The information within an article that provides context and history to a current news story is called "backgrounder."

You and I create our own backgrounders. For example, yours may include loving parents and the collie that pulled you to safety after a flood. This backgrounder explains why you are an animal lover and have five kids of your own.

Or perhaps you had a cute-meet in a frozen yogurt parlor with your future husband who turned out to be a serial killer. In this case, an aversion to both fro-yo and husbands is understandable.

Should your backgrounder include experience as a professional assassin, no need to let that particular scalded cat out of the bag. Just make something up!

And, if someone should dig up the truth? Bury it—along with the researcher who found out your dark little secret.

"BESIDES THE COVETED STATESIDE RUSSIAN ASSET LIST, THE Wagner Klein mission netted the CIA something else of interest." As Ryan clicks a button, the far wall in front of us becomes a floor-to-ceiling screen.

Immediately, a map of the world appears.

A logo on the map proclaims:

Hart Media Corporation

"Hart Media is another client of Wagner Klein. Not only has the German law firm been setting up offshore bank accounts for this media conglomerate in the BES Islands—that is, Netherlands Antilles—it appears that some of the transfer of funds were held, jointly or prior, in accounts controlled by one of Russian President Putin's straw men: Kirill Sokolov."

"Why would the Russians be paying a news network?" I ask.

Emma snickers. "You mean, other than its propaganda mouthpiece, RT America?"

Ryan isn't laughing. "The CIA is asking the same question. And Hart Media isn't just any media company."

Blue stars shimmer over specific major metropolitan areas: Paris, Rome, London, Tokyo, Sidney, Rio de Janeiro, Berlin, Amsterdam, Madrid, Johannesburg, New York, Los Angeles, and Washington, D.C., to name a few.

"Randall Sinclair Hart is the sole owner of the largest news organization in the world," Ryan announces. "His company owns newspapers in eleven world capitals. Additionally, it has a total of five newspapers in the United Kingdom, and three in Germany. It also has dailies in the top ten major U.S. markets and another thirty secondary markets."

The screen now morphs into a montage of banners from the company's various publications.

"Hart Media's content is not only syndicated to sister publications but to smaller media companies all over the world," Ryan continues.

Red and gold stars appear on the map. Most of these are clustered in capital cities or large urban metro areas.

"Today, Hart's media empire includes television and radio stations too," Ryan explains.

The map's graphic is now under the sheer gold net that seems to be coming from a tiny orb circling the Earth.

"Then, a decade ago, Hart Media bought the controlling interest in a Hong Kong-based satellite broadcasting network," Emma adds. "Afterward, it purchased another satellite outright —one that's based here in the U.S. Through these assets, it has created a news reporting organization that is second to none in the world."

Ryan nods. "Any news story Hart Media deems worthy for a broader audience is pegged for in-depth development before being distributed more widely, with country-to-country translations. Invariably, though, the stories are slanted to appeal to a populist audience. No matter where the articles appear, the message is always a nationalist one: country first and foremost."

The screen now shows a photo that looks as if it was taken from a corporate annual report. A tall, square-shouldered man in his mid-eighties with thick graying hair stands in the center. A woman and a man, both in their thirties, stand on either side of him.

"Randall has two older children from his first wife, Marie Lange, whom he divorced two decades ago. Hart's children run different portions of his empire," Emma explains.

Just like their father, they wear power suits. They share his florid features, his square-cut jaw, and his long, straight nose. And like his, the camera picks up the disdain in their brittle expressions.

A digital spotlight appears on the man to Randall's left. "Harold Hart runs the newspapers and radio divisions," Ryan continues. "He allows his division directors to do the heavy lifting. He'd much rather be out on the golf course. He will do anything to please his father, except for one thing: he has a penchant for dipping his pen into the company inkwell, something his father abhors."

I've run into his type before. The son feels he can't compete with a financial titan of a father. He'll end up with his father's largesse anyway, so why bother?

But if his sister is competing for daddy's favor, he's exploitable. I'm sure Ryan feels that's where I come in.

Honeypot 'R' Me.

I watch as the spotlight now rolls to Randall's daughter. "Charlotte Hart heads up the radio, film, and television entertainment divisions. Beyond television shows and movies, her domain also includes any live television broadcasts, such as the upcoming International Nuclear Disarmament Summit," Emma points out.

Ryan nods. "She's considered a stickler for detail and is very much a daddy's girl. She has never married, although she's come close a couple of times. Sadly, her fiancés seem to meet with fatal accidents."

Yikes! I hope Jack isn't assigned to entice her.

Emma adds, "She's renowned for her flamboyance and mercurial nature. She loves hobnobbing with celebrities, and even appears regularly on the network's internationally syndicated show, *Good Morning Hartland!*"

The next photo shows Charlotte standing proudly on the morning show's set.

"Is that a misspelling in the name?" I point to the title, where the word heart now excludes the letter E.

Emma shakes her head. "Nope. It's just a bit of subliminal

sleight of hand. The show is a folksy combination of personal interviews, entertainment features, and news. One moment a celebrity is making a favorite recipe with the morning team, the next the hosts are clucking their tongues at a current event that doesn't seem 'all-American.'" Emma makes air quotes. "Their happy talk always has a populist slant." Involuntarily, she glances at Jack. Blushing, she turns back to me. "And President Chiffray is the most frequent piñata for their barbs."

Jack grins at this. He doesn't mind watching Lee squirm. I guess it lessens his ongoing disgust of Lee's infatuation with me.

"On the other hand, they fawn after the First Lady. The hosts' latest political rants are that POTUS isn't tough enough on quote-unquote bad guys. But they never elaborate on who they mean."

"He can start with FLOTUS," I grumble.

Lee Chiffray's wife, Babette, was too close with too many members of the Quorum, the international organization known to finance terrorist cells all over the country. Its titular leader, Eric Weber, is now deceased. After discovering that Carl Stone, my first husband, had infiltrated the Quorum, Eric recruited him as a triple agent. Since Trisha's birth, this has been my cross to bear.

Ryan glances sharply at me, but he knows better than to engage me on the topic. Instead, he shrugs. "Randall's advanced age has Vegas bookies and Wall Street brokers taking bets as to who will be his successor." Ryan nods toward the family photo. "Both kids make no bones that they want the job."

"So right now, the winner is a toss-up," I surmise.

"Randall is past eighty. He must be grooming a successor. If the heir and the spare aren't in on the Russian connection, eventually the new CEO will have to be informed. That's where Acme comes in."

With a flick of a switch, the screen goes dark. Ryan faces us. "We guess that the Russians loaned Randall the money he needs to grow his empire. In return, he may be laundering money for certain Russian officials."

Arnie's cough easily passes for *"Putin!"*

Ryan finally cracks a smile. "Our mission is to infiltrate the company, find any money trail that affiliates it with Russia, and discover just how many executives on the management team know about it. It may just be Randall. Or, it may be several members of the family. If so, and if one is willing to cut a deal with State Department prosecutors and implicate the others involved, it will be a feather in the CIA's cap, not to mention Acme's."

We nod solemnly.

"By tomorrow, Arnie will be planted in Hart Media's tech division. From there, he'll hack the company's database and Acme's financial forensic team can go to work."

Arnie gives him a thumbs-up.

"Dominic's cover is that of vice president of a major British bank that already has a seat on Hart Media's executive board, and just in time. The company's monthly board retreat takes place in a few days. There, he'll be able to hobnob with the family and other key members of the management team."

Dominic frowns. "What? My cover isn't that of on-air talent?"

"Sorry, no," Ryan says firmly. "Randall's daughter is single and she has a wandering eye and for that matter, hands. This time you'll put to use your celebrated talent in the area of social engagement. But you're right. Hart Media is always on the lookout for overseas journalists. Which brings me to the Craigs."

He turns to Jack and me. "In Hart Media's smaller foreign offices, reporters are expected to do triple duty. They not only write newspaper articles but also provide audio and video reportage. Acme has already devised rock-solid print and broadcast resumes for 'Grant Larkin,'" he points to Jack, "and 'Gwendolyn Durant.' If we're lucky, Hart Media will hire both of you. In fact, Hart Media has an immediate need for reporters in its Moscow satellite office. Recently, its staff of three quit. They received better offers from news organizations located in their home countries."

Jack raises a brow. "How convenient."

"Truly a shame." Ryan's sly grin gives away his role in this development.

"It's not going to be easy to fake a journalist's background. And, except for that horrific reality show, we've done a great job of staying off-camera, for good reason," I remind him.

Spooks aren't supposed to be heard let alone seen.

"Emma and the ComInt team has pulled a year's worth of broadcast footage from small news services all over the world: organizations that use freelance journalists, what they call 'stringers.' From these news pieces, they've dummied up news-paper articles under your bylines with datelines from all over the world. If anyone searches, your bylined articles have already been placed online." He hands us binders filled with ComInt's handiwork. "As for the radio broadcasts and televi-sion clips needed to build your portfolio, you'll memorize these scripts, which support the archival footage that Emma's team has pulled. Then, after a few alterations guaranteed to make you camera-ready and unrecognizable, we'll put you in front of a green screen, where you'll repeat the news stories as if you were the original reporters."

Jack nods slowly. "I guess it's worth a try."

"But, Ryan, what happens when we're given a *real* news assignment?" I ask.

"Your articles and soundbites will be written for you by Lamar Crenshaw. His journalistic chops are legitimate: he worked for the Department of Defense before joining us. After this meeting, he'll go over the basics with you. It boils down to encapsulating the who, what, where, when, why, and how."

"You make it sound easy," Jack retorts.

"You've had harder assignments, believe me."

It's Ryan's way of saying, *Shut up. It's a done deal.*

By his sigh, I guess Jack realizes this too.

"Besides, you're a shoo-in," Ryan insists. "It helps that you know some Russian, Jack. And your fluency in French and German will also be an asset." Ryan turns to Abu. "And your facility for languages makes you a shoo-in as 'Grant' and 'Gwendolyn's' cameraperson. In that position, you'll assist with any tech or cleanups."

Abu smiles and nods. "Great! With broadcast union wages, I'll be sitting pretty for a few months."

Ryan arches a brow. "I can always count on you to find the greener side of any assignment."

I laugh. "I guess I should bone up on a few key Russian phrases."

"It wouldn't hurt," Ryan replies. "In any event, those hired will have a government escort with them at all times, usually surreptitiously. All foreign media organizations are advised to rent their offices and employee housing through the UPDK, a real estate agency that is owned by the Russian government. They also provide translators, bodyguards, and office managers."

Jack frowns. "In other words, we'll be watched twenty-four-seven."

"Exactly."

"But, if Donna and I are out in the field, we can't do surveillance of Randall and his family," Jack points out.

"As you discovered with the screenwriter, Sebastian Gillingham, it's not unusual to pass secret messages via publicly distributed documents—newspapers, magazines, even a flyer, or a broadcast. Acme anticipates Hart Media will assign you to cities in which its reporters have dealings, knowingly or unknowingly, with foreign agents. If so, your bosses' instructions as to what you see and whom you see, and what and how you write or broadcast your news pieces, may be instrumental in the CIA making its case against Hart."

"Got it," I say.

I may sound nonchalant, but Russia and the U.S.'s new Cold War is chillier than ever. This assignment puts me deep behind enemy lines. For an American operative, going undercover in Moscow is akin to sticking one's head in a lion's mouth. You want to get out of there before the teeth clamp down.

Should Jack and I make credible hires, it will certainly make the mission easier with him at my side.

Ryan looks at his watch. "We've still got a lot to do. Arnie has worked up some simple disguises for you. When he's done, meet Emma in the studio, and we'll record the news items to round out your job submissions. Acme will plant them in Hart Media's in-house recruiter's call sheet for tomorrow. Your resumes are filled with glowing recommendations, so it may just work."

Seeing my worried grimace, Jack pats my hand. We realize that this assignment will take us away from the kids for a while.

Aunt Phyllis won't mind hanging with them now that she's found a hot yoga studio on our side of town.

Still, I'd worry less about our absence if Trisha could find a different set of school friends.

"...WHERE THE BALKANS, WHERE BOSNIAN...SORRY. I'LL PICK IT UP there...Where Croatian opposition parties have initiated a no-confidence vote in the deputy prime minister." Jack wipes away the sweat rolling down his forehead.

And no wonder. The sixty-eight-degree temperature inside Acme's studio does little to mitigate the warmth of Jack's heavy overcoat, gloves, and a scarf, let alone his tension over his eighth take of this one news item. His hair is now blond and he is wearing stark blue contacts behind glasses.

Abu stands behind the camera filming him in front of a green screen. He winces at Jack's flub then looks over at Emma, to see if she caught it too.

She cringes. "Do another take, Jack."

Jack frowns. "Give me a second or two, okay? I'm boiling under this getup."

"It's okay. You're supposed to look a little harried," Emma reminds him. "Remember, you're out in the field."

Still, she signals a stylist to flip on one of the fans that stand off-camera. Its breeze flutters the end of Jack's scarf.

I had it easier. Supposedly, Gwendolyn, ostensibly a British national, has most recently been stationed in some Middle-Eastern hotbeds—Afghanistan, Syria, and Iraq—where her all-purpose wardrobe included cool white cotton blouses worn over tan linen slacks, skirts, and the requisite headscarf.

Not that Gwendolyn looked pristine. The stylists made sure to smudge my clothes with dust. My face, neck, legs, and arms are tanned, but they were smart enough to leave the worry on my face. Truthfully, it comes from thinking about Trisha's angst, not the soundtrack of dropping bombs and gunfire from the war zone footage screening behind me.

Sure, I also flubbed a line or two. But by my eighth newscast, I had the patter down.

"This is only Jack's second attempt," I remind Dominic.

Dominic pouts. "That's not why he flubbed the line. Unlike me, or you, even affecting a posh accent, he's just not a natural in front of the camera. I'll never understand why our fearless leader didn't give me the on-air assignment instead."

Dominic glances forlornly at the security camera placed high in the corner of the room. Ryan is watching, and he knows it.

He lifts his wrist to gaze into a mirrored cufflink as if he'll find the answer there.

It didn't work for Snow White's Evil Queen. Why would it work for a mere mortal man whore?

I jerk his hand down to his side. "You're joking, right? I mean, come on already! You're a rabid whoremonger and an insatiable womanizer. When one looks up 'lounge lizard' in the dictionary, your photo is beside it."

Somehow, a tiny line breaks through the barrier of Botox etched permanently on Dominic's forehead. Looking panicked, he reaches for his phone to scroll through the Merriam Webster Dictionary app.

I've got to nip this obsession in the bud, and quickly. "Ryan knows what he's doing. You're a natural honeytrap! Shouldn't you embrace the whore within you? It's the role of a lifetime!"

His eyes open wide. "Why, you're right! It's time that I am true to myself and celebrate who I am!" Tugging at my new hairstyle—a wig, short-cropped and blond—he adds, "Those glasses are sexy, old girl. They make you look like a naughty teacher. This ash color becomes you. I take it, though, that your make-over didn't include matching the carpet to the drapes?"

I arch a brow. "Should I ask Jack to get back to you on that question?"

Dominic shakes his head adamantly. "Indeed, no! I've spent too much on my teeth as is." Just for a moment, his eyes darken with sadness. "Such a pity! You'll always be the one who got away, Mistress Stone Craig."

"*Ran* away," I correct him.

He shrugs. "Po-tay-to, po-*tah*-toe." This time when he looks at his cell phone, it's to open his Tinder app. "Time to share the wealth."

"And, I presume the seed," I reason.

"Indubitably! One mustn't disappoint the customers, eh?"

I leave him swiping right. And right again…and again…and again. Dominic lines up his dates one after the other like planes on final approach to LAX.

Now that Jack is done with his last newscast, I walk over to him. He greets me with a kiss. When he pulls back, he laughs. "I feel as if I'm making love to a strange woman."

I put my arms around him. In a posh British accent, I reply, "Then we must be properly introduced as soon as possible." I add in my normal voice, "But first things first. We should grab some stuff from home before we have to head for the airport."

He smiles. "Works for me. I can think of no better way to spend some of my frequent flyer points than in the Donna Craig Mile-High Club!"

I'd pretend to be shocked, but I feel exactly the same.

BY THE TIME JACK AND I MAKE IT HOME, IT'S AFTER MIDNIGHT. Aunt Phyllis' snores are bouncing off the guest room wall. Somehow the children are sleeping through it.

Our interview is at ten in the morning in Hart Media's head-quarters in Manhattan. One of Acme's private planes will be fueled up and ready to leave in less than three hours.

Jack shushes me. "The kids may not be awake, but we can still kiss them goodbye."

We do, one at a time.

When Jack opens Trisha's door, her eyes flutter, but otherwise she doesn't move.

Jeff doesn't open his eyes either, but my kiss garners a sigh and a smile before he flips over to his other side.

Finally, we peek in through Mary's door. She seems to be sleeping too, even as we graze her cheek with our lips.

But then her eyelids flutter open. Instinctively, she's about to throw her arms around my neck but my new hair mesmerizes her. "Ooooh! I love you both as blondes!"

Suddenly, I realize I'm still wearing my wig. "Oh! I'm just, you know, trying out a new look."

Mary sits up, hopefully. "Hey, can I dye my hair too?"

"No!" Jack and I say together.

Mary pouts. "Too bad. It's snatched!"

I throw up my hands. "There's that word again! Okay, tell me: What exactly does it mean?"

Mary guffaws. "The old-school definition would be cool, or awesome."

I sigh. "Ah. Got it."

Still, we get our hugs. When she pulls away, she's glassy-eyed. "Be careful," she warns us. She knows the dark side to our professional life.

Jack and I have a vow: we will always come home to them.

But when we're away, a piece of my heart goes missing until we do.

4

Blind Interview

When a journalist has an off-the-record conversation with a source, it's known as a "blind interview." In all cases, the source goes unnamed—that is, unattributed.

There are times when you also take blind interviews. For example, when a friend stops by with some juicy gossip. Or, whenever one of your kids tattles on another. Or when your husband's assistant spills the beans on where he really went for lunch, and with whom.

Neighborhood gossip can be taken with a grain of salt.

On the other hand, a confession by the naughty child absolves the tattler, and the punishment doled out is fair warning to both to do the right thing.

If you don't, Mommy will find out.

As for a husband's indiscretion? That's what a good divorce lawyer is for!

(Tip: Newspapers don't pay sources, but you can, so keep his assistant on your payroll too.)

THE BLACK GLASS SKYSCRAPER THAT HOUSES HART MEDIA PIERCES the sharp sapphire sky high above its neighboring buildings in Times Square.

Jack, Abu, and I will arrive within twenty minutes of each other and from different directions so street cameras can't detect a correlation. As far as anyone knows, until today Grant Larkin and Gwendolyn Durant will never have met. The same goes for Abu, who is using the alias "Arvin Rahbar."

Abu is called into his interview immediately, leaving Jack and me to cool our heels in the reception area.

I whisper, "Break a leg," as he walks by.

Apparently, we're not the only ones applying for jobs as field correspondents. As we scan the other applicants, Emma runs facial recognition on them then reels off the highlights of their dossiers.

"See the slight, long-haired brunette in the back, with those gorgeous cheekbones? Her name is Jeanette Conkling. She now works for Haaretz, an Israeli news service. She has both print and broadcast experience. And the guy beside her—Mister Tall, Blond, and Dimpled—is Luuk Jansen. He's a Dutch newspaper journalist with a long list of bylines, including Reuters and *The Financial Times*. He's certainly ready for his close-up!" She sighs appreciatively. "And the older, distinguished-looking gentleman is a former BBC talking head named Wendell Edwards. It looks as if his field experience is spotty. A posting in Munich, ten or so years ago for almost a year." She pauses then adds, "The woman to his right is Kimiko Satō. She works for the Japanese News Network. Besides Japanese, she lists her spoken and written languages as English, Korean, and German. She most recently worked in JNN's Seoul bureau. She's done solely broadcast, no print."

Jack and I absorb this news. Jack's smile is placid, but his poker tell is showing: he taps his right pinky against his thumb.

Like me, he realizes that making the cut may be more difficult than we thought.

A half-hour later, a door opens. Abu steps out. He is shaking the hand of a woman holding a clipboard. When he passes us, he nods slightly.

Well, at least one of us has been hired.

"You!" Clipboard Lady points to Jack. "And you!" She points to the Japanese correspondent. "Head up to the thirtieth floor. Our Newspaper Division Director, Vince Lawrence, is waiting to interview you."

Jack rises. Always the gentleman, he allows Kimiko to walk ahead of him.

"You and you." Clipboard Lady turns to Luuk and Jeanette. "Go to the fortieth floor. Ask for our Director of Television News, Rolf Mancuso."

They leap up.

Jeanette's four-inch heels clack as they head for the elevator banks.

She now points to Wendell and me. "I'll escort you to Valerie Blunt, Hart's Director of News Radio."

Wendell and I nod as we get to our feet.

When we follow her down the hall, Wendell keeps pace with me.

"I'm honored to meet you finally, Mr. Edwards," I say. "You're one of my idols."

He notes my accent. "Ah! You're a Brit too, eh?"

I nod. "From Manchester. But it's been awhile since I've been home. For the past year, I've been posted in Fallujah."

"Give over!" He looks me up and down as if seeing me for the first time.

49

I'm taken aback by his exclamation until I see his approving grin. "I say, I wonder if this look-see will take us through dinner?"

"I hope not," I exclaim. "But possibly through lunch."

He frowns at my response. He then starts to say something, but the Clipboard Lady interrupts us. "Ms. Durant, Ms. Blunt will see you first."

I shake Wendell's hand. "Again, a pleasure."

After taking a deep breath, I knock on the door.

Someone shouts, "Enter!" My first trial begins.

DESPITE JACK'S VOW TO RAVAGE ME AT THIRTY-SIX THOUSAND FEET in the air, we made the prudent decision to quiz each other on our bona fides until they were airtight.

Now that Valerie Blunt is scrutinizing my resume, I'm grateful that cooler heads (and one limp one) prevailed.

Her attempts to poke holes in my background is nothing but thorough. After noting that my birth certificate claims I'm from Manchester, she asks specific questions about my family there. (None, since my parents are deceased, and my only brother now lives in Australia.) Next, she questions me on my education (Barlow Hall Primary, in Chorlton-cum-Hardy). She then peruses my university transcripts from Corpus Christi College in Cambridge, in which I validate my Joint Honours degree in History and Politics by explaining my thesis topic: How Article 54 of the Rwandan Constitution restricts public speech to such an extent that it has effectively done away with any multi-party system.

Within five minutes Valerie has heard enough. She compliments me on my radio reports, going so far as to call one outstanding: a recent piece on Syrian genocide.

She was also taken with a piece on Hurricane Maria's damage to Puerto Rico. "What kind of field equipment do you use?"

"Either a Tascam HS-P83 8 Channel or a Zoom F8 Multi-Track. Worst case scenario, I've called in reports via my iPhone."

Valerie chuckles. "I hadn't previously heard of your employer, International Press Corporation."

"I've been with IPC for ten years now. It's based in Australia, but it feeds to larger organizations, and to news shows in countries that don't subscribe to behemoths like Hart Media."

"Should you get the job here, the move may be fortuitous," Valerie declares. "Hart Media is growing so quickly that IPC may soon be out of business." She lifts her glasses to look at IPC's mailing address. "Just curious: Do you think it may be open to a buy-out?"

I shrug. "I couldn't say."

Valerie glances skyward. "Well, Mr. Hart is on a buying spree. He wants to own the world. Or, at least the way it gets its news."

Ryan whispers in my earbud: "Too bad we didn't have the time to wait and see what he would have offered. It may have been the easiest way to infiltrate Hart Media."

Too late now.

After walking me out of her office, Valerie beckons Wendell to join her. Jack is now also sitting outside her door. He gives me a friendly nod. I guess we'll keep crossing paths as we're shuffled, along with the other correspondent candidates, from one interview to another.

When Clipboard Lady sees me, she barks, "Thirtieth Floor, newspaper division. Vince Lawrence is expecting you."

I tamp down the urge to blow Jack a good luck kiss as I walk away.

∼

VINCE'S TEST IS SIMPLE: AFTER READING A FEW FACTS, I'M directed to write a four-hundred-word article on a bomb blast that just rocked Fallujah. He points at the laptop on a small desk by the window.

He doesn't know that Lamar Crenshaw, the former DOD correspondent, is dictating my piece through my earbud. I assume Lamar did the same for Jack, who was just in here.

His efforts are impressive enough to get an admiring nod from Vince. "Not bad! And having read your resume, I assume you've actually visited al-Shohadaa."

I shrug. "A quick trip, but not fast enough. Sadly, I lost my translator."

Vince nods sympathetically. "For your protection, we have war-tested bodyguards on staff. Former Special Ops guys, now with a private military contractor."

Should either Jack or I make the cut, it's interesting to know we're to be shadowed.

"For my protection? Does that mean I'm a shoo-in?" I smile brightly.

Vince shrugs. "That's up to the Big Guy."

The Big Guy? Does that mean Randall Hart? I guess I'll soon find out.

Or not.

∼

"You've got quite a resume." Rolf Mancuso, Hart Media's Vice President of News, looks me up and down as if I'm a thoroughbred horse. "Six postings. Three in the Middle East, one in Africa, two in Eastern European countries, and all during political uprisings."

I can just imagine what he's thinking: *Is Gwendolyn Durant too good to be true?*

Rolf is thoughtful enough to ignore the blinking call buttons on his desk phone as well as the constant buzzing of his cell. Whenever harried reporters stick their heads in his door, he waves them away.

I'm not the only one who's getting such considerate treatment. Outside Rolf's door are three other candidates vying for a chance to be one of Hart's far-flung field reporters: Kimiko, Luuk, and Jack.

"Ms. Durant, it is certainly impressive how you conduct yourself, even when reporting from the middle of a siege."

He points to a video clip playing on the large monitor on a far wall. "Gwendolyn" is reporting as bombs fly overhead. They land on targets close enough to make me duck, but not so far away that viewers can't see the exploding targets light up behind me.

This is the first time I've seen the finished piece, and even I'm impressed with its production values. Although the volume is on mute, the tension in my face is palpable. Emma certainly gave me great direction. She should apply to the Directors Guild of America.

"Since you've already received a thumbs-up from Mr. Lawrence and Ms. Blunt, I'd like to offer you a position with Hart Media." He walks out from behind the desk to lean on it. "We have several openings right now, including some in our Moscow bureau. It's a small office that supports one cameraperson, whom we hired this morning. He's fluent in Russian.

You're one of the two reporters who will join him despite your lack of Russian. The other journalist speaks the lingo, so we feel we've got it covered."

Yes! Jack made the cut!

Through my earbud, Ryan whispers, "Congratulations!"

Rolf continues, "If you agree to sign on, we'll triple your salary. But you'd have to start immediately."

I nod. "As you know, I'm currently a stringer, so yes, I'm available."

He stands up, smiling. "Great. I'll have the paperwork sent in, along with your co-reporter."

He reaches for his phone. As he makes the request to his assistant, I stand and walk over to the monitor. 'Gwendolyn' stares back at me. The stylists made enough changes to my face —contacts, brows, and hairline—that I don't see me in her.

Maybe that's for the best.

A moment later the door opens behind us. Rolf's assistant comes in with my contract.

And Luuk.

Not Jack? Oh…no.

"Gwendolyn Durant, meet Luuk Jansen."

To hide my disappointment, I force a smile and hold out my hand. "A pleasure."

"No, it is all mine," he says as he takes my hand. He holds it much too long. Noting my discomfort, he chuckles before letting go.

Rolf looks up at me, but he's grimacing. "Ms. Durant, your field experience is second to none. But, since Moscow isn't exactly a war zone and Luuk is fluent in Russian, I'm assigning him the position of bureau chief."

Luuk's way of consoling me is to add, "I'm sure Moscow will seem tame after Fallujah."

I shrug nonchalantly. "It's just a different sort of war zone."

"You'll have plenty of time to get to know each other once you're in the air." Rolf glances down at his watch. "Your plane leaves in less than three hours. It's an eight-hour flight to Frankfurt. After a three-hour layover, you'll catch the three-hour flight to Moscow. Unfortunately, you'll have just one day to acclimate to the time change, and for that matter, the weather, before your first assignment. Russia is throwing a military parade. Its latest weapons technology will be on display."

"Having been shot at by some of Russia's Syrian-based artillery, it'll be interesting seeing it up close," I say.

Rolf shakes his head. "Sorry, but the Kremlin is only allowing one reporter and one cameraperson. And since questions will be allowed from the press, Luuk is the logical choice, since he speaks Russian fluently." He hands us two business-class tickets and pens to sign our contracts.

"Isn't the International Nuclear Disarmament Summit happening on the same day?" I ask.

Rolf grimaces. "It is indeed. Apparently, Mr. Putin doesn't feel the need to attend."

He isn't saying what everyone is thinking: Putin is thumbing his nose at the rest of the world.

Luuk glances down at his ticket. "Ah, Lufthansa! I'm a member of its Mile-High Club!"

"I think you mean its Miles and More Club," I say stiffly.

"Ja, of course, that is what I meant." Luuk winks at Rolf.

Oh, just great.

If Rolf thinks his weak snicker will soften my frown, he's sadly mistaken.

I pretend to glance over my contract. As I reach the last page, I pause before signing on the dotted line.

It's for the mission. Just do it.

I'm distracted enough by this turn of events that I start out by writing the letter D. But by adding a tail to it, I change it into an awkward G.

As we are walked out of Rolf's office, Jack looks up. I see a wariness in his eyes that questions why Luuk was asked to join us. When Luuk has his hand on the small of my back, Jack's eyes shift to mine.

I shake my head slightly then sweep my bangs from my eyes, as if the movement is one and the same. Jack knows me well enough to understand my signal: *Not what we'd hoped.*

But then I hear Rolf declare, "Kimiko and Grant, do you mind coming back in?"

Hmmm…

Luuk smiles down at me. "Would you care to join me for lunch?"

I smile. "Thank you, but no. Our flight is out of JFK. Truly, a gauntlet! All the more reason we should go back to our hotels and pack. I'll meet you at the gate."

I take off before he can say another word.

When I get to the hotel, Abu is already there. I knock on the door that connects his suite to Jack's and mine.

His look of commiseration tells me he already knows our dilemma.

"Jack went in after me. What's happening with him?" I ask.

"He's out now, and on his way here," Abu assures me. He hesitates before adding, "He got an assignment too."

Figures. "Where?"

Abu grimaces. "He wanted to tell you himself."

Interesting. Something tells me it won't be close enough for booty calls.

And with all the listening devices planted in the Moscow correspondents' private quarters there won't be much privacy there anyway.

I hope Jack comes out soon. As it is, we won't even have time for a quick kiss, let alone a quickie.

"So, um…I'll be based in London."

Jack springs this on me after his I-never-want-to-let-you-go goodbye kiss.

Okay, to be honest, a kiss wasn't the only thing involved. Let's just say that by the time his lips were done (except for some naughty talk) and his hands took over, I would have bought into anything he said.

But now it ain't happening.

I shove him off and sit up. "Let me get this straight. While I'm stationed across enemy lines trying to get a handle on how and why the Kremlin is pulling Hart's strings, you'll be having a jolly old time in London?"

"It's the assignment they offered," he reminds me.

"You…And Kimiko?"

He nods. "She's covered the Royals before, for JNN. Charles is quite taken with her, so it was a natural posting."

"I see. And what makes you a 'natural' posting? You're the one who speaks Russian, not me!" I get out of bed. "Well, you and Luuk, who, by the way, couldn't wait to tell me that he's a proud member of the Mile-High Club."

Jack guffaws. "Why am I not surprised?" He reaches for me, but I jump out of reach. "Well, you'll be happy to know Kimiko is the perfect lady."

"Trust me, I'm not jealous of *her*. However, I *am* jealous of her posting! She'll be curtseying in a designer gown while I'll be freezing my ass off in Moscow—if I'm allowed to get out at all, what with a bunch of GRU ops trailing my every step." The

Glavnoye Razvedyvatel'noye Upravleniye—Russia's intelligence agency—is notorious for its surveillance technique.

"Don't sell yourself short. You've proven quite capable of sneaking out of the stickiest situations."

"Thanks for that rousing display of confidence." I pout. "I'm surprised Ryan hasn't told you to abort your mission. What can you possibly do from London?"

"The posting may actually pay off," Jack insists.

"How, pray tell?"

"I'll be getting there in time for the International Nuclear Disarmament Summit." He smiles supremely. "And you'll be happy to hear that Hart News Corporation is televising it."

"Congratulations on such a plum assignment." I'm doing my best to sound as if I mean it, but from the look on his face I'm failing miserably. I just can't hide the listlessness in my voice. "I hope Hart Media feels it's worth the effort."

"There will be over a hundred nations in attendance," he replies.

"Sure, it's a great show of solidarity. But, Jack, the countries that actually have weapons of mass destruction don't attend."

"This time is different. For the first time, China, the U.S., France, Germany, and the U.K.—even North Korea—have committed to attend. I suppose this gives Kim Jung-Un a good reason to leave his gilded cage and play the diplomatic head-of-state instead of the petulant dictator."

This stops me cold. "Wow! So, U.S. Secretary of State, John Worthington, will be there?"

"Yes, and Lee too."

"That should be an interesting meeting of the minds!" I admit. "By the way, my first assignment is to cover Putin's upcoming military weapons parade. Supposedly, it's his excuse for not attending the summit."

I don't have to tell Jack that parade coverage has been

assigned to Luuk. I'm sure he'll find out from Ryan soon enough.

I slip on a pair of jeans. But when I untangle my bra from my blouse, Jack perks up. "Here, let me help you with that."

Instead, I throw it at him.

I've got others to take with me. And besides, it'll give him something to remember me by.

5

Happy Talk!

You know all those times when your local evening news anchors chatter away as if they're carrying on a meet-cute conversation, just between them? It's what news journalists call "Happy talk!"

And, for a good reason: Not only is this informal, light-hearted banter used as a "bumper" (that is, filler in between commercial breaks) it's also supposed to make you think that they're best buds.

"Happy talk" can also be a great communication tool for you and your significant other! By using it in public between arguments, even on the days you're ready to claw each other's eyes out, you'll give the perception of a happy couple. Just follow these three tips:

First, toss out a provocative question or statement that he can respond to quickly. (Note: anything using math, history, pop culture, or current events is a no-no, since it may highlight his ignorance. Just because he's an idiot doesn't mean people have to know it. Heck, you didn't figure it out until it was too late, right?)

Next, laugh as often as possible, as if what he says is clever, even though everyone watching knows, like you, that he's dull as paste.

Finally, call him by a few terms of endearment. (Sorry, no: "jerk," "two-timer," and "whoremonger" don't count.)

Abu's ticket puts him in coach, whereas Luuk and I are flying Business Class. (Yes, there is a pecking order in broadcast news.)

On the JFK-to-Frankfurt leg, we score side-by-side seats on the upper deck. Our little cubicles are roomier than steerage, but Luuk is still too close for comfort. I don't like how he's always looking for an excuse to touch me. Still, my goal is to tap into Hart's Russian contacts without raising any red flags. If I think it will help the mission, by all means, I'll play the coquette.

Unfortunately, due to the way Business Class is arranged two by two, like Noah's Ark, I'm not given much privacy to check messages or study the detailed map of the blocks that surround Hart Media's Moscow office. There is nothing I can do but tuck my carry-on in one of the storage lockers under my window and pray that Luuk dozes off sooner than later.

After one of the friendly flight attendants serves us a delicious meal of grilled halibut, Yukon Gold steamed potatoes, julienned vegetables, sponge cake, and a bottle of wine (a 2011 Taymente Malbec), Luuk has no one else to chat up, so tag, I'm it. "Tell me, Gwendolyn, what was your worst experience in the field?" When he turns to face me, his sharp blue eyes hit me full force, like tractor beams.

I pretend to think for a moment. Finally, I declare, "Watching my cameraman get blown to bits, right at my side. Truly horrific." I blink back alligator tears with a long sigh. "And yours? I'm sure there were some very tense moments while...Pardon, what kind of reportage did you do? Ah, yes, *Financial Times*! I can only imagine the drama at the close of the markets!"

Luuk laughs. "It is good to finally get a peek at your sense of humor. Seriously, I was worried that we were not to be… How do you say it in English? Ah yes! 'Bosom buddies!'" His eyes slip to my chest with a smile. "But you are right. Spilling hot coffee on my suit pants before an interview with the prime minister of France was nothing compared to your trauma." He lifts his index finger in the air as if taping an imaginary star on my side. "Here's to fate!" His grin fades when he asks solemnly. "But seriously, what is it like to face gunfire?"

"Scary," I confess. "I don't advise it."

"I will do my best to stay out of a gunman's range." In an attempt at sincerity he lowers his voice. "Unless that means leaving your side."

"I'm touched," I answer coolly.

His smile slips off his lips for a second, but he rights it quickly enough. "Do you currently have a significant other?"

I force a blush before answering with the response that is already part of my cover: "Yes. His name is Kunagwo Zwane. He's a doctor affiliated with the United Nations Refugee Agency."

Luuk rolls his eyes. "You are too good to be true."

"Why, thank you, Luuk! I shall take that as a compliment." Perhaps that's his way of saying I'm not his type. One can only hope.

"You are also quite beautiful, Gwendolyn." He leans in closer. "I'm sure that, eventually, you will get some airtime."

"I would imagine so. There are enough stories in Moscow to keep us both hopping."

"But as the bureau chief, I'll make all assignments. You write beautifully, so perhaps you will do mostly print stories, *ja*?" To make the point as to how I might earn the privilege, he puts his hand on top of mine.

I tilt my head as if seriously considering the possibility of his not-so-subtle offer.

Finally, I draw him closer with a crook of my finger. When our lips are just inches apart, I whisper, "And how about you, Luuk? Is there a Mrs. Jansen pining away for you back in Amsterdam?"

He laughs heartily. "Not at all. However, I'm sure a few ladies on *de Rosse Buurt* miss my patronage."

"The Red Light District? I don't doubt that."

His tone is pleasant enough, but his questions are annoying. And since I've already been through three interrogations today, I flex my seat into a bed and beg off with a yawn.

I AWAKEN SOME FIVE HOURS LATER TO FIND THAT I'M CURLED toward Luuk. Our knees are touching. When I pull away, he flips onto his other side.

Next time, I'll insist on First Class. With this guy, every inch counts.

No better time than now to check for text messages on my phone than while Luuk is asleep. When I turn to open the storage locker, I notice the strap of my carry-on sticks out from the locker door.

I glance over at Luuk. He snores gently.

Silently, I ease open the door. The clasp of my valise is shut, but that doesn't mean anything. When I open it, I find my cell phone in the left side pocket, right where I left it. However, the date and hour, set for Arabic Standard Time, crawls across the screen, which only happens when there is an attempt to unlock it: virtually impossible, what with all of Acme's security procedures needed.

I peek above the pod bays and notice that several are empty. Gently, I lift my carry-on from the locker and take it with me to the one farthest away.

ACME USES SCREEN-SHOT PROOF AND UNTRACEABLE CHAT software with an ongoing self-destruct program: think, Snap-Chat, but without all the goofy icons.

Except when Arnie uses it. Our team looks forward to the day he grows out of the need to embellish his texts with his homemade GIFs, most of which mash up footage of old *Three Stooges* comedy routines and Marvel superheroes.

As I suspected, they are already in touch with one another. It must be a relief to the rest of my team that I'm finally online because suddenly their messages pop in response to my answers:

RYAN: *In flight?*

JACK: *Affirmative.*

ABU: *Affirmative.*

ARNIE: *Yep, Boss. Happily ensconced in my new cubicle.* CHECK OUT MY TIMES SQUARE VIEW!

RYAN: *I assume you're doing more than looking out the window.*

ARNIE: *All good. Broke into Finance Dept.'s firewall. Will keep U posted.*

DONNA: *Sorry, Ryan, to be late to this party. Nodded off after Luuk's amiable but very persistent interrogation. Now that Sleeping Beauty is out cold, I'd like to request a full background check on him.*

JACK: *Why is that?*

DONNA: *I have a sneaking suspicion that, while I slept, he tried to Graykey my phone. If so, we need to find out why.*

EMMA: *On it.*

ABU: *Donna, brush pass your phone to me at baggage claim. When I get to my room, I'll check the secure enclave chip for any breaches.*

EMMA: *By the way, Donna and Abu, within an hour your Boeing Black cell phones and computers will have received government clearance on a CIA secure satellite that has yet to run into interference from Russia's COMSAT SIGINT. Abu, there is a tiny transmitter that fits into the USB port of any video camera gear assigned to you. Use it when you take footage, and it will instantaneously transmit to Acme's secure cloud.*

ABU: *Got it.*

EMMA: *Donna, I'll call as soon as I run a trace on Luuk. Wear your earbuds whenever possible.*

DONNA: *Will do, Emma. Hey, if a GRU spook sees me muttering to myself, so be it. And by the way, I loved how you littered 'Gwendolyn's' phone with such detail! If he has hacked it, at least it substantiates my legend. The emails to and from her editors and producers, and all those lovey-dovey fake emails and texts between Gwendolyn and Kunagwo had me blushing when I read them!*

EMMA: *Frankly, I enjoyed world-building for Gwen. She and Kunagwo are so great together, dontcha think? I guess I channeled the romance writer in me.*

JACK: *Gee, should I be jealous of this Kunagwo guy?*

DONNA: *I'll pass you the emails and let you decide.*

ARNIE: *Wait…Should I be jealous too?*

EMMA: *[SIGH] And now that we know that the "correspondents" are on their way to the Moscow and London bureaus, we'll assign a few Acme assets as cutouts within proximity of your buildings. They'll be helpful in coming up with evasive action plans and some surveillance detection routes. And we'll put a tail on Luuk too.*

DONNA: *Great idea. I don't think I'm compromised, but if my cover is blown, I want to protect Abu. Knowing someone has our backs is always appreciated.*

ABU <3 2u, Girl! Would <3 U even more if U could get me into Business Class.

DONNA: You're dreaming, dude.

ABU: Maybe. But, hey, it doesn't hurt to ask, right?

DONNA: Ryan, I assume our assets will recognize the GRU tails Luuk and I are sure to have.

RYAN: Depends on how many they put on you. If you're a significant enough threat, the GRU has been known to assign as many as a hundred agents to a single surveillance mission.

DONNA: I'll do my best to keep under the radar.

DOMINIC: BTW, Jack, congratulations on the plum assignment of the International Nuclear Disarmament Summit! Please give Princess Catherine my tender regards. [SIGH] She was always the one who got away.

DONNA: Really? Have you forgotten that you used that line on me just the other day?

DOMINIC: Please don't be jealous, Old Girl. As they say, "It's easy to fool the eye, but it's hard to fool the heart."

ARNIE: Boo-YAH!

EMMA: Really, Dominic? You're quoting Pacino in Scent of a Woman?

DONNA: Ignore him. Heaven knows I do.

RYAN: Now, now, children.

DONNA: You're right, Ryan. We need to stay focused. In fact, I've just had a fantastic idea. Since we know that Hart Media is televising the summit, why doesn't Dominic suggest to his bank that it, along with Hart Media, co-host a cocktail event for attendees? Acme assets planted as part of the staff can observe the Harts in the presence of suspected foreign agents. And Dominic can attend to keep an eye on the Harts—along with Jack, of course.

RYAN: Great idea, Donna.

DOMINIC: Agreed! Mrs. Stone, you are indeed brilliant! And you truly are the one who got away. XXOO

JACK: CRAIG. Her last name is CRAIG.

RYAN: Signing off.

DOMINIC: Ditto. A raven's job is never done.

EMMA: Dropping the mic. Donna, I'll have the recon on Luuk to you ASAP.

ABU: Turning in too. I've scored a row to myself so I can spread out.

DONNA: Goodnight, all.

I click off before Jack. If he wants to text further, the ball is now in his court.

JACK SCORES A THREE-POINTER BY TEXTING BACK WITHIN SECONDS:

JACK: What's up, Buttercup?

DONNA: Is that Japanese for "I'm sorry I'm not with you"?

JACK: If it were, could you forgive me?

DONNA: Speaking of Kimiko, how is she?

JACK: As reticent of me as I am of her. Should I be suspicious? I mean, you're trying to be close-lipped around Luuk because of your mission. Maybe she's got a hidden agenda too.

DONNA: Ask Emma to do some deep reconnaissance on her. In the meantime, until she gives Kimiko a clean bill of health, try being friendlier…but not too friendly.

JACK: Not to worry. I only have eyes for you. I miss you, Don.

DONNA: Good.

JACK: Hmm…That's it?

DONNA: Of course not. I miss you too! I love you so much that it hurts!

JACK: I wish I were there to kiss whatever aches and make it better.

DONNA: Then let's get this mission over and done.

JACK: On it. Now get some sleep. XXOO

I MOVE BACK TO MY ASSIGNED SEAT. LUUK HAS AWAKENED. HE grins up at me. "The lavatories are quite roomy on the 747-8's, *ja*?"

Instead of acknowledging, I reply, "I hope I didn't wake you when I slipped past."

"Not at all. I am...How do you say? Ah yes! A 'light sleep-er.'" He stands up so that I may pass to my seat but leans in close enough that our chests meet. "Perhaps you should have wakened me. I would have joined you."

The sudden urge to grab his nut sack and twist it until he squeals like a piggy is only appeased when he says, "You are right about the military parade and press conference. It is a huge story for Hart Media, and there are many angles to cover. Perhaps I can request an extra journalist's pass from Russia's Ministry of Foreign Affairs. The First Deputy Minister is an acquaintance."

"Thank you for using your influence," I purr. "It's nice that you have friends in high places."

In no time he's dozed off again.

When I wake, once again our knees are touching. I feign sleep until Luuk opens his eyes. When he does, he leaves his leg where it is. At the same time, he reaches over and grazes my breast with his fingertips.

The nerve of this guy!

The thought that I have to play along angers me. Well, it

won't be too long. I'm out as soon as I figure out if Russia's bank accounts are connected to those of Hart Media.

Which begs the question: Is that why Luuk was chosen as bureau chief?

If so, it justifies my staying close to him.

Already, I hate this mission.

6

Hard News

The factual coverage of serious and timely events is called "hard news."

A war, a pandemic, a political upheaval either at home or abroad, and an economic recession—all of these are given no-nonsense reportage and placement above-the-fold of any newspaper.

Every life has its hard news moments. Like, say, your husband loses his job; or your cousin is in an accident; or your sister learns she has cancer.

This is no time to (as you've just learned) "bury the lede." Instead, get the facts straight and put it out there for others who may provide pertinent insights that can bring about a more desired resolution.

Hopefully, your network won't just roll their eyes or click their tongues at your ill fortune. If so, they'll be proving that Ronald Reagan was right when he said, "Recession is when a neighbor loses his job. Depression is when you lose yours."

THE FLIGHT BETWEEN FRANKFURT INTERNATIONAL AND MOSCOW'S Sheremetyevo International Airport is much shorter: only three hours.

The customs line in the arrivals terminal seems just as long, especially after our fourteen-hour journey. Considering where we are and who we are (or, in my case, aren't) our passports clear us without any hassle.

By the time we make it to baggage claim, Abu is already there. We introduce ourselves and shake his hand. Abu then introduces us to the very tall, very bulky man who has just lowered a sign with the words HART INTERNATIONAL NEWS in large block letters.

"I am Yegor Povov, your producer," he proclaims. He then points to another man who is slighter, younger, and sporting an eye patch, who stands beside a baggage cart that holds our suitcases. "He is Nikolay Aristov. He is the bureau's office manager." After shaking hands all around, Yegor adds, "Your apartments are in the same building. We shall take you there now, as I imagine you are very tired after your trip."

"Perhaps after a quick stop at the offices first," Luuk counters. "We would like to go over the story leads left by the departing crew. We must also prepare our coverage plan for the military parade and the press conference tomorrow."

Yegor shrugs. "Your choice."

He leads us out of the airport door to a large passenger van waiting nearby.

Nikolay tosses a few rubles to the security guard who stands beside it: compensation, I imagine, for ignoring an obvious parking violation. He then opens the side panel for us before taking the driver's seat. Yegor sits shotgun.

Luuk holds out his hand to help me up into the van's first passenger bench. As I take it and hike myself into the vehicle, I feel a pat on my bum.

Son of a bitch.

Abu's coughing spell indicates he's caught it too.

The van swerves away from the curve and into the roadway leading out of Sheremetyevo International Airport.

Despite being early afternoon in Moscow, the sky is a charcoal hue. A frigid brown mist hangs over the city like a well-worn shawl. Even the snow, shoveled high on the sides of the roadway, looks dingy.

The driver's side mirror is extended far enough out that I can look into it. I anticipate at least one car will follow us to our destination. As my private road trip game, I see if I can spot which one is tailing us.

Half an hour later, we are at our destination: a five-story, mixed-use building on the three-lane boulevard known as Petrovka Ulitsa.

In the base of our building is a Bulgari Jewelers shop. Kitty-corner from us is the Bolshoi Theatre. This is undoubtedly a posh part of town.

A car did, in fact, follow us the whole way: a dark gray Lada Granta. I've never seen one before, but here they are as ubiquitous as puffy coats.

It passes us now as we exit the van. It seems as if Nikolay gives the driver a slight nod.

This doesn't surprise me.

The Kremlin is only a kilometer and half from us, less than a twenty-minute walk. Should I venture a stroll, I'm sure I'll be watched every step of the way.

HART MEDIA MOSCOW NEWS BUREAU IS WRITTEN across the office's sleek glass doors, which open onto a small reception alcove. It holds a modern couch and an ornate marble sideboard, where a fresh flower arrangement of oleanders sits.

A small galley kitchen is off to one side. Besides a microwave and small refrigerator, there is also a coffee machine on the counter.

Yegor hands us numbered key cards. "These should open the three apartments upstairs."

Nikolay and Yegor have separate offices. Luuk takes the only other empty room with a window and door, leaving Abu and me in the news pit, which consists of three desks surrounded by five-foot-high dividers: flimsy enough for every conversation to be heard.

The office mail has been placed on a small, round conference table. An envelope from the Ministry of Foreign Affairs' office is the only piece yet to be opened. Apparently, Nikolay has taken care of the rest of it, which is stacked in neat piles for Luuk's review.

Luuk eagerly takes the unopened envelope. Grabbing a letter opener, he rips it open and tosses its contents on the table. Besides press passes for Luuk, Yegor, and Abu, it also contains three identical manifests with information on the parade route, a full press itinerary, and publicity photos of the weaponry that will be on display. Luuk slips one into his valise and hands the other to Abu.

All eyes move to the whiteboard beside the table, where a few other interesting stories have been hastily scribbled in English:

Breaking/Investigative: Breakout of African Swine Fever at a privately-owned meat packing facility;

Business Feature: Russia's largest phone operator purchases stock in a retailer;

Politics: Overview of the opposition candidates in the upcoming presidential election.

LUUK GESTURES AT THE FIRST BULLET POINT. "THE PARADE TAKES precedence, of course," he declares. "But the ASF outbreak will also be of interest, I think."

"So would a comprehensive overview of Putin's political opposition," I point out. "There are only two opponents. You can reach out to the campaign of one, and I'll take the other."

Yegor, who has been taking notes, pipes up with a grunt, "I'll set up a meeting with the factory manager for Friday. By then he should have a good excuse as to why it is not the factory's fault but that of the farmers." He shrugs. "As for the opposition to our current president, I would not advise attempting a one-on-one interview—that is, if you wish to stay in the country. Perhaps covering a rally will get you the soundbites you need? And not to worry. We have enough gas masks to go around."

"Great to know," I retort.

"I'd like to see the camera equipment on hand and take a quick tour of the production bay," Abu says.

Yegor points to the cubicle at the far end of the room. "Follow me." The men head off in that direction.

I smile prettily at Luuk. "As you said, these other assignments must wait until we've covered the parade. Speaking of which, shouldn't you make that call to your friend in Foreign Affairs earlier than later?"

He nods. "I'll do so immediately."

He leaves for his office. But before he shuts the door, he leans out again. "When I get off the phone, why don't we grab a bite to eat before retiring?"

My nod is amiable enough. "Sure, okay." *Oh, hell. I am dead tired.*

I guess his favor earns me the role of his new bestie. But if he believes it means friends with benefits, he's got another think coming.

~

"*NA ZDOROVYE!*" LUUK EXCLAIMS.

While he toasts to my health, I should be toasting to the survival of his liver, considering the amount of vodka he's drinking along with our meal of borsch and beef tongue stroganoff. To lessen its effect on me, I make a point to take four sips of water for every gulp of vodka.

We found a cozy little restaurant just a kilometer away from the office. When Nikolay offered to drive us, I laughed. "Why even bother? Can't the man assigned to follow us protect us?"

He stared as if he didn't understand me. When Yegor translated for him, he snorted.

It must have been a good translation of my little joke.

Emma hasn't texted back with Luuk's dossier, which surprises me. Even before the appetizer he resumed his friendly inquisition:

How long have I been in the business? ("Eleven years. Hopefully, the next eleven or so will be well-spent with Hart Media.")

Did I enjoy Cambridge? ("Uni was aces, except for all the smug toffs...")

Do I miss England? ("It will always be home," I declare with just the right Queen-and-Country fervor in my voice.)

Luuk's last question comes with an interesting bit of information: "You know, they say this office is a stepping stone to the position of Hart Media Network's International news anchor in New York. If offered, would you take it?"

"Indeed! But that's putting the cart before the horse." I add coyly, "I assume you would, as well?"

"I wouldn't turn it down," he replies smugly.

"Then a toast to our mutual success." As I clink my glass against Luuk's, he brushes his fingers against mine.

We end our meal with Russian tea cakes and coffee, for me, anyway. Luuk sticks to vodka. By now, his English is sloppy, and some of his phrases are coming out in Dutch, so I giggle then demand he repeat them in English. I play the coquette because I want to stay on his good side—at least, until he hears back from his contact at the Foreign Ministry, which he insists will be no later than ten o'clock tomorrow.

"That's cutting it close," I remind him. "We have to be in the parade press stands by noon."

"He won't let me down." When he lays his hand on my arm, the implication is clear: Nor should you.

Ugh.

I stand up. "We should get some rest. It's been an exhausting day. Tomorrow promises to be even longer."

He takes the hint. However, after slipping two one-hundred-ruble notes under his glass, he whispers, "I've spotted our Russian escort. There is a back door by the lavatories. Leave from there now, and I'll do the same after I ask our waiter to pour our shadow a glass of vodka."

With a slight nod, I stroll casually to the back.

A few minutes later Luuk follows. He's laughing at his little trick.

I pretend to chuckle too, but only because I need to stay in his good graces until my mission is completed. I pray his little stunt doesn't get us kicked out of the country. Otherwise, I will have failed.

At that point, I'd have nothing to lose to make him pay. I'll start with breaking a few fingers. Maybe then he'll get the message that he should keep his hands to himself.

WE'VE STAYED OUT LATE ENOUGH THAT NIGHT HAS FALLEN, AND the streets are empty.

The back door leads into an alley. We turn right.

"Are you sure we're headed in the right direction?" I ask.

"*Ja!* Follow me," he insists. He's tipsy enough that he slips on a damp cobblestone.

I am not at all assured.

The drink has loosened his tongue to the point that he's humming something in Dutch. Now and then he belts out a lyric, albeit off-key.

My only consolation is that if he's drunk enough, he'll snooze off the moment his head hits the pillow.

In his bed, not mine.

We are a few blocks from our building when I hear footsteps. I turn to see two men approaching us. Both are large, block-headed, and broad-shouldered. They carry two-foot lengths of steel piping. It's too late and too cold for baseball, so I assume we're what they'll be swinging at.

Luuk, who is yodeling some ditty, seems oblivious to the impending danger. Oh, bother. This means I'll have to fend for him and myself.

The first thug uses his bat to shove Luuk against the wall. He growls something at Luuk, which I take to mean, "Your wallet or your life."

Before the second one can do the same to me, I kick him between the legs. As he doubles over, I grab his bat and hit him over the head with it.

When Thug Number One turns around to see what's happening, my sidekick throws him off balance and slams him into the wall.

Still, he hangs on to his steel pipe. When he comes at me and swings it, I block his strike. He pushes me off and strikes again, this time lower.

But I block that one too.

When he pulls back for a third strike, I take my bat with both hands and swing for the fences.

Or in this case, his head, cracking it with my bat.

He lands face down on the cobblestoned street.

Luuk stares at me. Suddenly he's stone cold sober. "You can certainly protect yourself."

"Yes, of course I can!" I retort. "I'm a woman who has traveled through some pretty savage places."

He nods, but his silence speaks volumes. I may have saved his life, but I've also spooked him.

I guess I don't have to worry about fighting him off after all.

Our apartment doors are next to each other. When we reach them, Luuk bows stiffly. "As you said, it has been quite a long day. Until tomorrow."

"Until tomorrow," I echo.

He waits until I close the door before entering his place.

I guess when you're a horndog, nothing kills the urge for romance quicker than watching your date bash in the heads of two guys who would have otherwise eaten your lunch.

By seven-thirty I enter the news bureau. I'm in a demure wool dress suit: a navy bateau-neck sheath with a matching jacket and low-heeled shoes.

On the way to my desk, I walk past the conference table to

peruse today's stack of mail. Nikolay has already sorted it. There is one envelope that Nikolay didn't dare open. It is stamped with the insignia of the Russia Ministry of Foreign Affairs and addressed to Luuk.

Thank goodness, my press pass has come!

Nikolay is already in his office. He holds a steaming ceramic cup and a small paper plate of something that looks like a pastry. Noting my glance, he points toward the kitchenette. "It is *tula pryanik*! You can eat too!" Once he's in his office, he closes the door. My guess: so that we can't see that he's monitoring the rest of us.

I don't need the unnecessary calories, but Nikolay's *pryanik* looks too good to pass up. As I pass the reception alcove to grab a cuppa, I notice that some of the oleander blossoms have fallen onto the table and floor. The mess is unseemly. Because I doubt the men will see it as their place to do anything about it, I pick them up and drop them in the kitchen's wastepaper basket.

ABU ARRIVES TWENTY MINUTES LATER. HE NODS FORMALLY BEFORE putting his satchel in the production bay. Noting my cup of coffee, he grabs one for himself.

He takes his time reviewing the manifest. I busy myself with a Russian dictionary, putting together a list of questions for the press conference.

Russian Times radio network plays on the television monitors mounted in the four corners of the room. The feed is closed-captioned in English.

Eight o'clock goes by without Luuk appearing, as do nine and ten o'clock.

It's now ten-thirty. Over the top of my cubicle, I finally see him.

I look down, pretending to review the government-sanctioned press photos that might work for our articles. Luuk doesn't go straight back to his office, so he must have stopped at the conference table to check the mail. Good, he'll see the press pass envelope.

A few minutes later he strolls past my desk without saying anything.

He has nothing in his hand but his valise.

I wait eight minutes before knocking on his door. "Come in," he barks. His tone is impatient.

Warily, I open the door and walk in. "Good morning. I guess the need for sleep finally caught up with you."

"Yes, I'm still fatigued. Is there coffee?"

I nod. "And pastries, if you care for one." I hesitate and add, "As for the press pass—"

"Ah yes!" He shrugs. "So sorry, but it never arrived."

"Oh." *Hmm.* "Perhaps you should call? We could pick it up on the way to the parade."

"In fact, Gwendolyn, I just tried my contact again. His assistant answered and informed me he is out. I asked again about the extra pass and emphasized the importance of it. She apologized profusely, but she was adamant they were not able to get one." He opens his hands as if to indicate that he doesn't hold the answer I seek. "You can start immediately on the tainted cow meat story, *ja?*"

No, you liar.

"And thank you for your offer to get me coffee."

"Yes, of course."

"Cream and sugar with it, please." He waves me away.

You son of a bitch.

THE COFFEE BEANS NEED TO BE GROUND. A PORTABLE GRINDER IS IN the cabinet, as are the coffee filters.

"Oh, bother!" I grumble as a filter drops to the floor.

I stoop to pick it up. As I drop it deep into the wastebasket, I palm some of the oleander petals.

Into the grinder they go, along with the beans.

I pluck a mug from the cabinet and add the cream and sugar as the coffee percolates. I also take two pryaniks and put them on a plate for Luuk.

When the coffee is ready, I pour it into the mug—all of it, because I made just enough for a single cup.

But before I leave the kitchen, I clean out the coffee pot and the grinder, dump the old grounds, and grind more beans for another fresh pot.

Now, I ask you: Am I a considerate co-worker, or what?

LUUK'S CRAMPS BEGIN A HALF HOUR LATER. WHEN HE LEAVES HIS office for the lavatory, his face is pale and sweaty.

I open my eyes wide when I see him. "Luuk, is everything alright?"

He starts to answer but then thinks better of it. Cupping his hand over his mouth, he stumbles through the news pit and out the front door.

A half an hour later he still hasn't returned. Yegor looks at the wall clock and frowns. "We must leave now for Red Square if we are to make the parade!"

"Shall I call Luuk?" I ask.

Yegor nods.

I pick up my company-issued cell phone and dial. (Not Luuk's phone, but Yegor doesn't have to know that.) "Luuk, it's time to leave…What…you're too ill to go? Oh! My poor dear man! Well, yes, of course, I'll go in your place! Do try to rest! I'll check in on you when we come back." I look up at Yegor. "He left his press pass and manifest in his valise. I should get it."

"Yes, please, and immediately! As it is, we will get caught in the parade traffic!"

I run to Luuk's office. Yes, in the valise on his desk is his press pass, along with mine.

I take both.

7

Two-Shot

Most often, a "two-shot" is the term for an interview in which the reporter and the guest are in the same shot, even when the camera is aimed behind the reporter's head. It also refers to any shot including two people; two anchors at a single news desk, for instance.

A relationship is always a two-shot. Solo selfies are cute, but don't you prefer the ones in which you're standing beside a loved one?

"OKAY, GWENDOLYN, WE ROLL VIDEO IN THREE, TWO..." ABU drops his raised fingers until he's down to one then points to me, and I begin:

"Russia's military pageantry is in full force today to a wildly cheering crowd as its state-of-the-art T-14 Armata battle tanks roll through Red Square. Considered the most sophisticated and technically advanced armored vehicle in the world, these tanks..."

I do a similar video piece when the Kurganets-25's promenade into view. These armored personnel carriers are considered the next generation of such vehicles.

All footage we shoot is also uploaded to Acme's secure data file, where Lamar can regurgitate these soundbites into print news stories that will appear on my computer. I'll then turn them in under Gwendolyn's byline.

I look at the pride on the faces around me. At the same time, I think of all these things the Russian people are coerced to do that restricts their freedom and perception of the outside world.

A dictatorship, even one masquerading as a democracy, works for the few, not the many. To keep the masses in their place, Russia uses these shows of strength to say: "Look at us! No one can dominate us!"

The subliminal message to its citizens: *No one is strong enough to save you from your dictator and his political cronies.*

There is just so much footage Abu can take of the passing battalions of goose-stepping soldiers. Thank goodness that, after ninety minutes, the *pièce de résistance* comes into view: rows of Topol-M nuclear missiles.

The blast of just one will incinerate tens of millions of victims. Terror comes in many forms.

Once again, I get in front of the remote camera and espouse the details of yet another chess piece in the sensitive war games between Russia and the democracies it despises.

After the parade, press members will be shuttled into a large exhibition hall known as the Moscow Manege, right off the parade route, where it promises a different kind of show: a movie showcasing weapons prototypes. It is being billed as "a glimpse of Russia's military future."

I'm sure it ain't pretty; more like pretty frightening.

~

LIKE THE OTHER REPORTERS, YEGOR, ABU, AND I ARE ESCORTED TO seats that match the numbers on our manifests. Luuk's chair is conspicuously empty.

The Russian president's head appears on a giant floor-to-ceiling screen. "He could be Big Brother in the novel *1984*," Emma whispers through my earbud. Through the transmitter on Abu's camera, she sees and hears it too.

For the next two hours, Putin harrumphs about his nation's growing weapons arsenal. A surreal film, created with computer-generated imagery, supports his bellicose claims. It features a small-scale nuclear-armed cruise missile that can travel at unlimited ranges and outwit antimissile systems.

"It is invincible!" he exclaims.

In the next animation, a hypersonic cruise missile is launched from a jet. If, as claimed, it moves at blinding speeds, it should easily evade any interceptor rockets sent to chase it.

"It sounds like a video game in the making," Abu says to me.

Another toy is a nuclear-powered submarine torpedo. Its awesome sauce is its supposed unlimited range. Once it's in the water, it can travel forever.

Or until it hits its intended target.

In the film's finale, a Hypervelocity Glide vehicle is launched into space, only to fly back down into earth's atmosphere at such a high speed that it outwits the United States' defense systems.

In the video, it detonates right over Hilldale. It's Putin's joke on POTUS: He knows Lee loves the few times a year that he can visit what the media calls the "Western White House."

As far as what Putin has to say about Russia's lagging economy, his one quasi-mea culpa is a vow to cut poverty in half and increase the average Russian's life expectancy rates to those similar to Japan's.

"It might help if he doesn't put his country in the middle of a nuclear war," I mutter to Abu.

Abu frowns. "He just said that Russia is spending three hundred and sixty million dollars on all these toys in the coming decade and a half. Could you imagine if he put it toward growing his economy instead? Russia covers eleven percent of the Earth's land mass. Twice as large as Canada! And yet, its economy is just half of that of the state of California."

He's right. A society is only as strong as its economy.

NATO nations have a reason to be skittish. This goes double for the United States, which would rather unite the world through innovation and commerce than fear and treachery.

Finally, Putin gives credit to his youthful team of tech scientists from the Russian Federal Nuclear Center, the entity that is overseeing its weaponry innovations. "Russia's military brains have made America's response obsolete," he declares.

With that, he cedes the microphone to the project's head scientist, Timur Orlov.

WE'VE BEEN TOLD THAT SHOULD WE BE CALLED ON, WE ARE TO state the name of our organization first. We will only be allowed one question.

Practically every person in the room raises their hands, including me. A stern-looking woman who seems to be in her twenties walks up and down the aisle. She holds a clipboard and taps the reporters who will be lucky enough to get airtime before they hustle the scientist off the stage.

Luuk wrote his interview question in his manifest. It is thought-provoking, so I'll stick with it:

How long do you feel it will take China and the United States to catch up with the technology you've shown here?

I'm about to think I won't be called upon when Ms. Clipboard taps me on the shoulder.

Abu may be manning the camera, but since I have to ask the question in Russian, he whispers the translation into my earbud, which I repeat in the microphone verbatim.

Timur Orlov stares at me. I guess he's trying to come up with an answer that won't get him in trouble with his superiors. Finally, he states, "*U nas byla roskosh' nachal'nogo starta. No chto boleye vazhno, nashe intellektual'noye prevoskhodstvo ne imeyet sebe ravnykh.*"

I listen as Abu recites the translation: "We have had the luxury of a head start. But more importantly, our intellectual superiority is second to none."

I nod, thank him, and sit down.

As he walks off, I realize I was Orlov's last question. It may piss Luuk off, but I'll score brownie points with Rolf.

Getting out of the auditorium with the other reporters is akin to a scrimmage. As the crowd maneuvers into their coats before grabbing their gear and rushing out the doors, someone bumps into me: It's Ms. Clipboard. Without saying a word, she slips something into my hand: a thumb drive. When our eyes meet, hers reflect her fear.

She's wondering if she's doing the right thing. I slide it into a hidden pocket in my coat then I blink to assure her that she is.

Well, this is certainly an interesting turn of events. I can't wait to see what's on it.

When we get back to the office, Abu goes into the editing

bay. He will download the digital footage into the editing system. But since it has already been transmitted to Acme ComInt, within an hour, television and radio news packages will have been created and uploaded to his computer.

I too have work to do. I must download the two news articles that Acme has already put together based on the parade and press conference.

They are excellent in their tone. Saber-rattling isn't needed. The pieces lay out the facts without editorializing on the ferocity of Putin's hawkish stance.

After downloading them, I take another twenty minutes to look busy with the chore of "writing" them. I then transmit it to Yegor for distribution to Hart Media. I wait a moment for him to email back:

In receipt of your articles. Will transmit now.

Now for the real work: open the thumb drive, analyze it, and transmit it to Acme—something I can't do on my company-issued computer.

I stop by Nikolay's office. "The time lag has caught up with me. I think I'll go upstairs and take a nap."

He gives a nonchalant shrug. We both know he'll be watching me anyway.

I take the elevator up to my apartment floor. As it rises, I take off my heels. Nikolay will think it's because my feet hurt. In truth, it's because I want to slip by Luuk's door as quietly as possible.

WHEN I GET INTO MY APARTMENT, I TURN ON THE RADIO, standard operating procedure to deter prying ears and inquiring minds.

The place is nice enough: a large studio with a fully stocked galley kitchen and large modern bathroom with a tub, a separate double shower stall, and a double-sink with a marble bathroom counter. It also has a toilet and a bidet.

Before heading to the bathroom, I pass my closet to grab a robe. I place my computer under it.

By leaving the bathroom door open, the view of the toilet, shower, and tub are concealed from the vanity, affording me some privacy in case the GRU installed a two-way mirror. I suspect the light fixture over the vanity holds a mic.

It's possible that Nikolay searched my things while I was out, including my computer. Its memory holds just the litter planted by Emma: the fake email correspondence with my old bosses or my boyfriend; photos of Gwendolyn while on her various journeys; and a substantial number of electronic travel receipts.

What they don't know is that I'll bypass the building's Wi-Fi signal by accessing the CIA's secure SATCOM connection when I'm ready to upload the content from the thumb drive.

As I do so, I'm shocked at what I see: diagrams of the small-scale nuclear-armed cruise missile that was showcased at the press conference.

Through my earbud, I connect with Ryan. "Intercepted something of interest. Check the cloud soon."

"Will do," he replies.

I slide the thumb drive into one of the computer's USB ports. While it's uploading into Acme's secure cloud, I change into my robe.

I'd love to tear off my wig, but I can't since I'm moving from room to room as if going on with my usual routine. The only place it comes off is in the shower, where prying eyes can't see me.

God, I can't wait to be Me again.

Just as the intel upload is completed, I hear the click of my door. Quickly, I take out the thumb drive and hide it in the closest thing I can find: one of my discarded heels. I tuck it into the toe of the shoe then toss it into the closet. I'm about to throw the other heel in there, but it's too late.

Luuk stands in the doorway.

～

HE STILL LOOKS PALE, BUT HE'S FORCED HIMSELF TO STAND RAMROD straight. He shuts the door. In a few strides, he is next to me. Before I know it he's shoved me into the shower stall, slamming me up against a wall.

As the frosted shower door clangs shut, he presses himself against me. His hand moves to my throat.

I don't know if Nikolay can see us in here. If so, he might assume this was a pre-arranged tryst. I wonder what he'll think if Luuk strangles me to death? I guess it won't matter if Luuk is GRU anyway.

"Where is it?" Luuk growls in my ear.

"Where is what?" I ask. I'm shocked at how calm I sound.

"You were given something that belongs to me."

"I don't know what you're talking about," I hiss.

He slaps me across the face. Instinctively, I raise my knee, but when I try to put it between his knees, he grabs it and lifts it high so that I'm standing only on one foot. Before I can shove him away, he takes my head and bashes it against the wall. I'm still too stunned to fight him as he twists the wrist of my free hand behind my back. I groan from the pain. To make matters worse, he leans into me, pressing my folded leg against my backside until I'm flat against the wall.

"Tell me where it is," he hisses in my ear, "or I will kill you now."

Like hell, you will.

It's not like I can defend myself with the only thing within reach, which happens to be a loofah. But then I remember that my free hand is still holding my stiletto heel.

I stab him in the neck with it.

He backs away, dazed.

One good stab deserves another. I'm about to hit him again when Emma frantically hisses in my ear: "Donna, don't kill him! Luuk is on our side! He's an operative with the Dutch intelligence agency, AIVD—the *Algemene Inlichtingen- en Veiligheidsdiens!*"

Now she tells me!

Luuk's hand goes to his neck. Yes, there is some blood, but thankfully it's only a flesh wound. Now that he sees I've missed the carotid artery, he charges at me instead.

"Our contact there suggests using the code: *"De winterregens stoppen niet in maart!"* Emma screams.

As he pushes me up against the wall, I say it out as best as I can, *"De…de winter-raygens…stoppen nite in maht!"*

Luuk freezes. Warily he whispers, "Who the hell are you?"

"U.S. covert ops." I gasp. "Acme. I'm a CIA contractor."

He relaxes and lets go of me. In fact, he's smiling even as he rubs his wound. "Acme, eh? Well then, you must know Dominic! How is the old boy?"

"I PRESUME YOU WON'T MIND SHARING THE INTEL WITH US," I SAY as I pour Luuk another glass of bathtub gin.

Actually, it's vodka, stolen from the office liquor cabinet. If we don't need a drink, I don't know who does.

Because the bathroom door is still open, it blocks any view of us from the vanity mirror. We're sitting on the edge of the tub. We aren't undressed, but the water is running, and I've turned up my iTunes mix of Barry White love songs to tune out audio surveillance.

Every now and again we let loose with a few sighs, slaps, grunts, and some heavy moaning in the hope that our voyeurs' imaginations are running wild.

Luuk chuckles at my question. "In any event, it's too late now, since it's already been transmitted." He then groans loudly and exclaims, "*Ach*! Gwendolyn! I...love it when you do that!"

I try my damnedest not to burst out laughing. When I get control of myself, I whisper, "Last night, when we were attacked by those thugs, were you just going to let them beat us up?"

He shakes his head. "They too are AIVD operatives. It was a test." He grins. "By the way, you failed miserably. No frozen fear or girly squeals from you! Poor fellows! The way you roughed them up put me on alert."

"Which is why you hid the extra press pass," I reason. I then shout, ecstatically, "*Yes! Yes! Yes!*"

Luuk shows his kudos for my performance by throwing me a kiss. "A question: How did you make me ill?"

I shrug. "Oleander petals in your coffee."

He frowns. "It could have been fatal."

"Sure, had I used more," I admit. "Next time, think like a woman and don't ask a stranger to get you a drink."

He stifles a laugh then follows up with some loud naughty talk.

I answer with a few choice words of my own.

"Were you sent here for the same intel?" he asks.

"No. Acme is investigating Hart Media. We feel it may be laundering money for..." I point in the direction of the vanity mirror.

He gets it. "I'll do what I can to help. What specifically are you looking for?"

"That's just it. We don't know. Perhaps it's using the bureau's reporters as unwitting couriers, or for that matter, our two babysitters, wittingly." I let go with a passionate moan.

As Luuk slaps the water to indicate we're in the throes of aquatic ecstasy, he whispers, "*Ja*, this is possible."

"Who was your inside contact?"

"The lead scientist who was onstage. His wife is also on the team. She made the brush pass to you. Next, I must arrange their exfiltration. Needless to say, she was surprised that 'Luuk Jansen' was a woman." He raises a brow. "No matter. My superiors don't mind sharing the intel with your country. Sometimes the stench from our discretionary bankers is quite foul and needs airing out." His smile fades. "Speaking of which, a scandal has broken in the States regarding your president."

I freeze when I hear that.

He motions for me to groan in unison with his slaps. As I accommodate, he adds, "It seems that one of the companies in his blind trust has been linked to an offshore account being laundered by one of our banks. It was a client of Wagner Klein."

Ouch! That will garner some bad publicity for Lee. It couldn't have happened at a worse time. He's about to start campaigning for re-election.

The other party's candidates will be sure to jump all over that. And since it has control of both the House and Senate, it's sure to be quite a sideshow.

"Who broke the story?" I whisper between loud sex yelps.

"Believe it or not, it was one of Hart Media's other new hires: Jeanette Conkling. She'd been given the position of special correspondent, reporting from Berlin. She got the tip from a Wagner Klein employee and followed it from there."

He yodels ecstatically in unison with my moans. We've reached "climax."

With a sigh, Luuk slaps the bathwater one last time.

"Interesting," I reply. "I'll read Hart Media's take on it the moment we, er, get out of the tub."

Luuk lifts a foot out of the water. "I'm feeling a bit water-logged anyway. Still, I appreciate that you are willing to help burnish my cover as a drunk and heartless lothario—not that you'll be doing it for much longer."

I frown. "Oh no? Why is that?"

"I got an email from Rolf. You're being transferred stateside. Hart Media is putting a lot of manpower behind this story about your president. Rolf says it has legs."

"Why didn't they ask for you?"

"They did, but I was adamant that I wanted to head up the Moscow bureau. It's the best way for me to serve my country. Besides, I don't think my accent would go over too well on American talk radio."

"The position is with Hart Radio Network?"

Luuk nods.

I'm surprised, but I'm also pleased. On radio no one will recognize my face.

The transfer means I'll be going back to the States. And working at headquarters will make it easier to snoop around the Hart family's corporate lair.

"In any regard, Rolf is happy that you're willing to go. He was impressed with your coverage of the parade and on getting in a question for the scientist." He grins. "I'm glad you asked one I'd written. Otherwise, our countries wouldn't have this intel."

Nodding silently, I rise.

Of course, Hart Media wants to stick it to Lee. He's

following the money. They want to bring him down before it leads to Hart Media, and for that matter the Quorum.

I'm dressed only in a towel when I walk Luuk out. For any viewing audience, we linger in the doorway wrapped in a stage kiss.

At that moment, Abu passes. A raised brow is his way of showing that he can't wait to hear what I did with my spare time.

He waits until Luuk closes his apartment door before declaring, "It was a pleasure knowing you, Gwendolyn. By the way, I just got word that I'm being transferred stateside. Hart Media wants me to work in the D.C. bureau. I guess the U.S. election season is already heating up, among other things."

I nod so that he knows I catch his drift.

"The video pieces are live, and so is your print piece. You should check it out."

I don't like the sound of concern I hear in his voice.

Quickly I access the piece via the secure SatCom Internet signal. After opening the final draft of my story, I pull up the version that was distributed through the Hart Media Network.

I see why he was perplexed. A few paragraphs have been added to the very end of the piece:

Lawmakers have been publicly expressing their concerns that President Lee Chiffray's reluctance to ramp up the United States' nuclear arsenal may have something to do with the recent revelation that a company held in the president's supposedly blind trust was siphoning funds into Trident Union Bank. Located in the Dutch Antilles, it is one of the offshore accounts managed by Wagner Klein.

The German law firm also set up accounts in Trident Union Bank for several Russian oligarchs as well as Russia's president, Mr. Putin.

This coincidence has already come to the attention of the U.S. Justice Department. Today, Attorney General Timothy Gardiner appointed Blake Reginald Reynolds to serve as special counsel in such a probe.

In this capacity, Mr. Reynolds will oversee an investigation based on three criteria:

1: Any links and/or coordination between the terrorist organization known as the Quorum, foreign governments, other terrorist organizations, and individuals associated with the administration of President Lee Chiffray;

2: Any matters that arose or may arise directly from the investigation; and

3: Any federal crimes committed in the course of, and with intent, to interfere with the Special Counsel's investigation, such as perjury, obstruction of justice, destruction of evidence, and intimidation of witnesses.

BLAKE REYNOLDS?

Oh...*no.*

I've crossed swords with Blake on a couple of occasions, specifically in regard to Carl's prosecution. Both times Blake was under the impression that I aided and abetted Carl and the Quorum.

I've got to catch the next plane out.

8

Remote

When video footage is shot live from somewhere other than the studio, a satellite truck transmits the image.

For example, news stations will use this setup when a hurricane is approaching. At that point, a reporter dons a yellow slicker along with a rain hat and boots and stands on a remote pier in pouring rain and, say, a seventy mile-an-hour wind doing its best to toss him into the churning white-capped waters below.

The point of this sort of news piece is to show viewers that they've already blown the opportunity to grab any remaining candy bars and boxes of sugared cereal from the local convenience store's shelves before the lights go out.

"Remote" is also how we feel when we are far away from our loved ones. No amount of texting or calling can replace holding a hand, a genuine hug, or a sweet kiss —

Especially when the lights go out.

ABU AND I LEFT MOSCOW FOR FRANKFURT WITHOUT INCIDENT.

Nikolay drove us to the airport. During the ride, his eyes were as much on me through the rearview mirror as they were on the road. I guess he enjoyed my performance with Luuk.

Will he play the recording over and over again on lonely nights? Who knows?

Yikes! Maybe I should ask Emma to search online for it in a couple of days, just in case he posts it on the Internet as audio porn.

AFTER HAVING LANDED IN FRANKFURT, ABU AND I HAVE A FEW hours before our departures, so we sit together in the Lufthansa VIP Passenger lounge before catching our flights, me to New York; Abu, to Washington D.C.

We take turns reaching out to Ryan by text, but all we get back is a one-word reply:

INDISPOSED.

The lounge has television sets perched high in every corner. All of them are tuned to Hart International News. It is indeed the network of choice throughout the world.

It's hilarious to watch Blond Jack, a.k.a. Grant Larkin, doing voice-over commentary for the World Nuclear Proliferation Summit, especially since Lee is currently speaking about all the reasons the nations of the world should be disarming as opposed to ramping up their nuclear missiles.

Now the camera cuts to the empty chair that was to be occupied by the Russian president. It drives home the point that he had better things to do, like basking in the world's dismay of his show-of-force parade.

One of the Hart Media cameras cuts to Kim Jung-Un. He scowls. Obviously, he isn't getting the message.

Jack shares his camera time with Kimiko, who has lined up interviews with various heads of state. Her English has a British lilt to it.

After Lee's speech, she snagged a one-on-one interview with Kim. But because they've called the last boarding for my flight, I can't stay to listen. But from the look on Kim's face, he's undoubtedly flattered by her demeanor toward him.

Let's hope he sees the benefit in joining other world leaders in negotiating deterrents to war as opposed to instigating them.

I SCORE A BUSINESS SEAT. THE POD NEXT TO IT IS EMPTY. I WAIT until the flight attendants lower the lights so that passengers will nod off. Not me. I've got a few West Coast calls to make.

Sadly, Jack will still be at the private cocktail reception thrown jointly by Hart Media and Dominic's banking employer, so my first call goes to the children and Aunt Phyllis because I miss them so darned much.

Mary squeals when she hears my voice. She puts her cell phone on speaker, so the rest of the family can listen in as well.

Unfortunately, this also allows them to talk all at once until I say, "Please! Please! One at a time!"

"Okay, then Trisha will go first," Aunt Phyllis declares.

"Mom, guess what?"

"I give up, sweetie."

Exasperated, Jeff sputters, "Just go ahead and tell her!"

"Madison—you know, the most popular girl in the class— she told everyone that I'm her BFF!"

"Ah." I do my best to sound enthusiastic when I'm anything but. I know better than to have a heart-to-heart about her friendship when we're not face-to-face. "You really like her, don't you?"

"Well...yeah...of course!" Why is there such hesitation in her voice? "I mean, our teacher, Ms. Sawyer, calls her 'an acquired taste,' so...I guess she means it as a joke."

"I see." Yikes! Trouble...

"Hey, Mom, can I quit soccer?"

Trisha's request comes out of the blue. "What? Why would you do something like that? Coach Middleton says you're one of the best forwards she's ever had the honor to coach!"

"I just think practice and the games take up too many of my afternoons."

"Oh, I don't know, Trisha. It's a great form of exercise, and you love your teammates. Best of all, you're a natural athlete in the sport! I'd hate to think that you'd leave the team then regret it later. Besides, other than homework, what would you do with all those free afternoons?"

"Well..." Trisha takes a deep breath. "I'd hang with Madison and the rest of her girls."

"'Her girls?'" *Hmm.* Not a good sign. "And what do they do with their afternoons?"

Trisha goes radio silent. Finally, she mumbles, "Stuff."

"Ah, I see. Listen, sweetie, I think you should stay on the team for now. It's an important enough move to put some serious thought behind it. Dad and I get home this weekend. We'll discuss it then."

"Oh...kay." By Trisha's tone, I can tell she's disappointed with my request.

Well, too bad.

I hear Jeff yelp, "Hey! Why did you hit me?"

Trisha shouts back, "Because I hate it when you say, 'I told you so!'" I hear her stomp up the stairs.

I put the phone on mute for just a second so that my family can't hear me curse.

"Mary, you're up to bat!" Aunt Phyllis declares.

"Why her?" Jeff huffs.

"Ladies first, young man," my aunt replies primly.

"Mom, guess what?" Mary's excitement raises her voice an octave higher.

"If you're not quitting something, I'm sure I'll be pleased with it, so go for it."

"I scored the fashion interview of the year for *The Signal*!" Mary is practically squealing in my ear.

For a second, I have to take my earbud out. When I put it back in, I ask, "Inside voice, please! Okay, now who? Kendall Jenner?"

"No, no! *Way* bigger!"

"Okay...um...Emma Watson? ScarJo? J Law?"

"Even better! *The First Lady*!"

"Oh...great." *Gag.*

"You don't sound excited for me." By Mary's tone, I can tell she's disappointed.

"Well...we've had such an uneven acquaintance with Mrs. Chiffray."

That's putting it mildly.

When Jack and I were planning our wedding, Babette attempted to highjack it to use it as a publicity ploy to show that she was in touch with us common folk. She then had the nerve to declare herself my maid-of-honor although I'd already promised Mary that she'd serve in that capacity.

When Mary heard about it, she was heartbroken.

Instead, I gave Babette the heave-ho. No way could I let the mission, or Babette, ruin the most memorable day of my life.

"Why the change of heart regarding the First Lady?" I ask.

Mary chuckles deviously. "You can't guess? I'll give you a

big hint. What impact do you think it'll have on my college admissions?"

Point taken.

"Especially, now that President Chiffray is being investigated," Jeff explains. "If Mary asks the right question, we may get a scoop! Hey, we may even win a Pulitzer! It would be a first for a high school newspaper!"

"I think you're getting ahead of yourself," I counter. "The investigation has just begun. And the president has a fund manager who handles the blind trust for him. He or she will be the first person called by the special counsel."

"It's a woman," Jeff replies. "And she's disappeared."

Ouch.

"Well, we'll see how the story unfolds," I say nonchalantly. Time to change the subject. "How are other things going?"

"We lost our basketball game." Jeff sounds dismayed.

"Not my fault!" Aunt Phyllis retorts. "As the official team mom, I've done everything I can to keep the morale up since their Number One scorer—*COUGH! JEFF!*—has taken to skipping a few practices. You're missing out, kiddo! Your teammates certainly enjoy those *Maxim* magazines I bring them!"

I roll my eyes at the thought. But what really worries me is Jeff's absence. "What gives, Jeff?"

"Mom, the news biz is twenty-four-seven!"

"But your newspaper goes out only once a week!"

"Not anymore. I got Mr. Franklin to agree to our expansion. To create more content, we need more staff. The good news is everyone wants to write for the new improved *Hilldale High School Signal*. The bad news is that half of them don't know a complete sentence from a dangling participle."

"You need to hire an editor or two so that you can have some downtime," I point out.

"I'm on it. In fact, I've got a couple of candidates applying tomorrow. The one who does the best copy editing gets the job and the title of Copy Director. It's one way I can sweeten the deal."

Titles instead of money. Yep, it's the newest form of "compensation."

"Gotta run, Mom. I've still got three articles to clean up."

I chuckle. "You're excused. Now, Aunt Phyllis, how are you?"

"Tired, but gorgeous! That hot yoga certainly melts away the pounds! I no longer fit into any of my clothes, which is why I'm so happy I found the hidden door in your walk-in closet! You know, the one with all those role-play costumes and the stuff that looks like you stole it off a porn set—"

"Aunt Phyllis! *Oh my God!* Are the kids still standing there?"

Silence. "No, of course not."

Thank goodness. "Why are you rummaging in my closet anyway?"

"Like I said: my clothes practically hang on me!"

"I permit you to purchase some new clothes, on me. It's my way of saying thank you for being there while Jack and I are out of town. Mary has an emergency credit card. You can put it on that."

"Okay, if you insist." Aunt Phyllis sighs. "Hand it over, girly! The mall stays open until nine!"

"Wait! I thought you said the kids weren't in the room!"

Phyllis, Mary, and Jeff are laughing so loudly that all I can do is hang up.

I could throttle my aunt, but then I'd have to figure out where to bury her body.

I ASSUME EMMA IS ALSO TIED UP IN WHATEVER IS KEEPING RYAN

from calling me back. And, although it's late in London, I've texted Jack a couple of times, but he hasn't responded.

When I'm halfway over the Atlantic, I finally get a call from Emma.

"Hell of a day," she grunts.

To lighten her mood, I chuckle then say, "Give, Queenie."

"Seriously, words cannot describe it! You'll have to see for yourself. I left a video in your Acme secure cloud folder. Afterward, feel free to call back. Of course, by then Jack should be around to talk too." She clicks off.

I pull out my computer, access the cloud, and open my folder. As promised, a video has been uploaded. I open it.

The footage intercuts action seen through Jack and Dominic's lenses as well as the security cameras in and around The Royal Albert Hall in London.

It starts with Jack, in a tux, running up the hall's steps. Three guards try to stop him, but when he shows his security pass, they wave him into the lobby.

A string quintet plays in the center of the auditorium floor. Jack looks up toward the second-story gallery that circles above the seats. There, the crowd for the cocktail reception is thick and lively.

He takes the circular staircase two steps at a time. Emma has coded the video so whenever he passes a dignitary or celebrity their names appear over their heads.

Of course, Lee is there too, as is Babette, who looks stunning in a form-fitting Tom Ford chain-strap bustier gown with a front slit.

When Jack strides past her, her pout turns into a simper. She thrusts out her breasts, straining the deep V of her dress.

Lee follows his wife's gaze. Finding the object of her interest, he frowns in annoyance.

Apparently, she doesn't recognize Jack. Thank goodness, Lee doesn't either.

At the pace he's moving, it's apparent that he doesn't want to stop and say hello. The way his eyes scan the room gallery, I can tell he's looking for someone. Who, I wonder?

Finally, he sees Dominic, who seems enthralled with Randall Hart's daughter, Charlotte. My guess: It has nothing to do with what she's saying to him but the fact that she's tall enough that his eyes are level with this exceptionally endowed woman's deep-plunging, sequined gown.

To break her spell over him, Jack waves his hand in front of Dominic's face. "Ah, there you are, Mr. Fleming! If you have a moment, I'd like to interview you about your bank's generous sponsorship of the nuclear disarmament summit."

Charlotte stares at Jack. "You're new with Hart Media, aren't you?"

Jack nods genially.

She extends her hand. "I was impressed with the way you handled your interviews with the various dignitaries," she coos.

Modestly, Jack smiles as he takes it. "Thank you. It's an honor and a privilege working at Hart Media."

She meets his attempt to let go of her hand with reluctance.

Dominic frowns. "It's Mr. Larkin, isn't it? Yes, then, let's get this over with." He forces a smile for Charlotte. "If you'll excuse me, Ms. Hart."

When her gaze turns to him, it moves from head to toe before meeting his eyes. She preens as she declares, "I look forward to taking you up on your offer for further, er, discussions, regarding the bank's private services."

As they walk off, she turns to look over the balcony and into the auditorium, where the quintet has begun playing a soulful sonata.

Dominic follows Jack, who strides to an alcove a few yards away. Seeing that it's empty, they walk in. "I'm looking for the other Hart Media correspondent, Kimiko Satō. Have you seen her?" Jack's tone is urgent.

"You mean the sylph-like, silken-haired goddess who came in on your arm wearing a pearl beaded vee-neck deep cowl-back Naeem Khan gown with a side slit?"

Jack does a double take. Exasperated, he replies, "Seriously, Dominic, no man should know that much about women's couture."

"You're wrong, Jack." He honors my husband with a knowing smile. "It's the best way to bond with them."

"Yeah, I guess…if you plan to borrow their clothes."

Dominic's back stiffens.

Jack ignores his scowl. "Look, I don't have time for your dating tips. Where is she?"

"Sadly, out of view." Dominic shrugs. "Albeit the last time I saw her, she was regaling North Korea's Supreme Leader with her knowledge of Italian cuisine, especially that of Tuscany, which seems to be his favorite region. At least, that's where his personal chef hails from." He points across the gallery to a small conference room that is being watched by two beefy bodyguards with earbuds.

"Let's go. When we pass the guards, keep them busy while I get her away from Kim."

Dominic grumbles but does as he's told.

As Jack and Dominic walk by, casually, Jack glances into the alcove. "Ah, Kimiko, there you are!"

Kimiko has Kim Jung-Un enthralled with whatever she is saying. A white-jacketed waiter has just handed them tall champagne flutes.

Seeing Jack, her smile disappears, and her eyes deaden. Still,

Jack holds his smile. "Ah! The Supreme Leader is here as well. Sir, it is truly an honor to meet you finally!"

He begins to walk over, but one of the guards blocks his entry. Hesitantly, Kim nods his acquiescence and Jack and Dominic are allowed to enter—proof positive that flattery will get you an all-access pass.

But then, as Dominic gets within a few feet of Kimiko, Jack trips him.

And he stumbles onto the waiter, who spills the tray of wine on her.

The commotion sends the guards rushing in. They hustle North Korea's skittish dictator out of the room.

Angrily, Kimiko turns to Dominic. "You fool!"

"It was just an accident, Kimiko. Why are you so upset?"

The waiter, now frowning, backs away toward the door. But he doesn't get far because Jack punches him in his gut. When he keels over, Jack pounds a sharp elbow into the back of his neck. The man goes down like a sack of potatoes.

Kimiko is running out of the room, but Dominic blocks her.

Until she punches him in the throat.

He may have fallen to the floor gasping, but Jack is up quickly and on her heels. He makes it to the door before she gets there and slams it shut. Realizing that she's trapped, Kimiko reaches into one of her long sleeves and pulls out a karambit. The curved blade of the stiletto must be made of Kydex to have passed through the metal detector without notice. But, the way in which it slices off the corner of Jack's open tuxedo jacket, it demonstrates its steely sharpness.

I gasp loudly enough that I get shushed by a flight attendant.

Jack grabs the fallen waiter's tray then uses it as a shield as he dodges, dekes, and ducks Kimiko's onslaught of slashes.

Step by step he closes in on her. Noting this, she bends low and runs at him.

But he wallops her on the head with the tray.

She falls to the floor, stunned.

Dominic staggers to his feet. "Brilliant footwork, old boy! But how did you know that she was an assassin?"

"She was so cold to me that I asked Emma to do a facial recognition scan," Jack explains. "It turns out Kimiko is an operative with Japan's Defense Intelligence Headquarters. I was late to the party because I asked Arnie to do a remote hack of her computer. Her coded kill order was in there. It took a while for Emma to decipher it."

"Interesting! But can't say that we can blame our Japanese allies. They must find Dictator Kim's missile stash a bit unsettling, eh?"

Jack jerks Kimiko to her feet. She tries to pull away but can't because he keeps a firm grip on her. Glaring from Dominic to Jack, she hisses, "Kim is a madman! Sadly, *Heiwa-boke*—the faith we Japanese hold so dearly in our peace constitution—is a luxury we can no longer afford."

"If you and your friend here had succeeded in poisoning Kim, the nuclear disarmament summit would have been deemed a farce. Worse yet, it would have disgraced every country in attendance, including Japan. You're getting off easy, Kimiko. As it is, the CIA has already back-channeled the Japanese Ministry of Defense its willingness to keep the assassination attempt a secret among friends: Japan, the U.S, and of course, our host country. I'm sorry, but you're going home."

By now, two British MI6 agents—one female, one male, both in formal dress—have joined them. The female places handcuffs on Kimiko. The other agent cuffs her accomplice and hustles him to his feet. Still, Kimiko holds her head high as she and her pal are escorted out of the room.

Dominic shakes his head sadly. "I give you credit. I would have never caught on!"

"Why do you say that?" Jack asks.

Dominic grins. "She would have never given *me* the cold shoulder! Unlike you, I'm utterly charming."

One thing about Dominic: you can always count on him for comic relief.

"You're quite a hero." My voice is husky because I'm tired.

And, yes, I'll admit it, lustful too.

"All in a day's work." Even through the phone, I hear the desire in Jack's voice. "I have to admire Kimiko. She went to quite some lengths to take care of the biggest threat to her country."

"So, what are your thoughts? Was the conference a bust?"

"You know the game. Despite the joint effort to play nice, everyone wants to hold onto their toys. With Putin not only skipping it but putting on such a big dog-and-pony show, the other countries now feel the need to ante up." Jack sighs. "And despite POTUS's efforts to tone down the rhetoric, our Congress is more hawkish than ever. It won't let Lee stand in its way, either. Word has it that Vice President Edmonton is leading the charge."

I shiver at the name. My one meet-and-greet with our country's charismatic vice president left me wondering about the depth of his allegiance to Lee. I guess this answers my question: barely skin deep.

Lee had better watch his back.

"I heard about Jeanette's scoop. I thought the timing was interesting."

"Me too," Jack concedes. "But hey, it proves Hart Media

made a great investment in her and put her in the right city to prove it. Speaking of home runs, congratulations on snagging some vital intel that will help level the playing field."

"It was more of an interception," I admit. "The project's lead scientist and his wife wanted out bad enough to contact Dutch Intelligence. Luuk must now arrange the exfiltration op."

"Yeah, about Luuk. I guess you warmed him up finally."

I snort. "Not before we tried to kill each other."

"I'm glad that both you and I have lived to see another day." Jack's voice has lost its playful lilt.

To bring it back, I proclaim, "Did you hear that I got a transfer? Manhattan, here I come!"

"I may be joining you across the pond," Jack declares.

My heart leaps in my chest. "What do you mean by that?"

"The boss lady and I are talking tomorrow. Charlotte wants to transfer me to the New York News Bureau as a special correspondent. I told her she'd have to make it worth my while."

"From the way she was eyeing you, like a juicy prime rib, I'm sure she'll be happy to take you up on your offer."

"Don't bet on it. Dominic is with her right now, in the townhouse she shares with her latest victim—I mean, fiancé—the Russian tech oligarch, Mikhail Gorev. He's out of town. In fact, I'm heading over there."

"For what, a threesome?"

He laughs. "Only in Charlotte's dreams! I'm party-crashing. Not that she'll be aware of it. While Dominic is keeping her busy in the bedroom, I'll be cracking Mikhail's office safe. Apparently, it's where he keeps the deeds of all his properties around the world. Some are set up in the names of dummy corporations owned by Putin and some other government officials."

"You may be starting the next Russian revolution, Mr. Craig!"

"We can only hope. In any event, tomorrow morning, Charlotte and I are negotiating my new compensation package."

"Sweet! Benefits, but not 'friends with benefits,' I hope?"

"Now, now, Mrs. Craig! Reign in your little green-eyed monster. Remember, Dominic is the raven on this mission. I've got my hands full just following the money. So yeah, if all goes well—and I don't see why it won't—I'll be jetting back to New York tomorrow," he pauses, "on Charlotte's private plane."

"That should be cozy," I purr.

"Not as cozy as, say, a bathtub."

I feel my cheeks reddening. "Oh...so you do know about Luuk and my, er, surveillance diversion tactics!"

"I'll say. And I was impressed, in fact, *too* impressed with its realism," Jack grouses. "Alas, I don't think my acting is in the same league as your bathtub antics with Luuk. Still, maybe I should give Charlotte a broad hint that I'm open to a 'friends with benefits' package."

"Not funny, Mr. Craig! If you were here, you'd realize that by my pout."

"If I were there, my dear Mrs. Craig, I'd know all the ways to turn that frown upside down...including some slap-and-tickle tub games that would curl your toes."

"Perception is nothing like reality. Seal the New York deal, and I'll let you prove it to me tomorrow evening."

I sign off to his appreciative chuckle.

9

Shock Jock

Talk radio shows can cover a variety of topics: culture, news, sports, or political commentary.

The most popular talk show hosts are known as "shock jocks." They are also the most provocative.

They derive their success by pontificating fear-mongering insults that pass as a point of view on a recent event. Doing so riles up the audience, who then pick up their phones and call the host to give their two cents, filling the airtime between commercial breaks.

In most cases, their comments echo the host's.

Or do his mimic theirs?

Does it matter?

Most comments are not derived from fact; it is just personal opinion.

These shows aren't about promoting political discourse. It's about ratings.

Make no mistake. That is not news. That's entertainment.

"SO, YOU'RE SUPPOSED TO BE THE BIMBO." LARRY ZORN, ROTUND and red-bearded with a face made for radio, gives me the once-over. He hosts Hart Radio Network's *Hot Topics with Larry*, which is the number-one syndicated radio talk show in the country.

"Pardon?" The disdain dripping from my voice has the opposite effect than I'd hoped. He's practically drooling.

"Did they tell you what you're doing here?"

"I've no clue at all," I confess.

"It's to sit there and look pretty." He points to the chair next to his. Both are facing extendable microphones.

"I doubt it. This is radio. Hart Media will want me to say something."

"Okay, sure, you can say something—as long as it compliments whatever I said first."

"Must I always wait for your lead?"

"Would you prefer to be the dom in this relationship?" Larry leers at the thought.

I sigh. "Considering the frequency in which you toss out such vulgar innuendos, how have you avoided getting tossed out of this job?"

"I've got too much on the boss man, Harold Hart." He winks conspiratorially. "More than likely, it's the reason you're here in my evil lair: as a peace offering. He's always had a great eye for...talent."

That's interesting.

"Well, if you're as naughty as you like to think you are, I suppose you spell that, 'p-i-e-c-e.'"

He chortles at that.

"If you've got gossip to dish about our fearless leader, after the show I'll let you take me out for happy hour." I flutter my lashes.

Not that he notices. He's too busy scrutinizing my white

blouse for any nip slip. Failing to do so, he finally replies, "Honeybun, every hour is happy hour."

To make his point, he lifts his coffee mug to my nose.

I reel back at the smell of whiskey.

"You're perfect, Gwenny baby, except for one thing: Can you lose the posh British accent? You sound as if you've got a stick up your ass."

"Imagine how much more cultured you'd sound if we found one wide enough to fit in yours," I counter.

"I'm in love," Larry crows.

"Does that mean I'm hired?" I coo.

"Does a wild bear shit in the woods?"

"Not if he's got a stick up his ass," I remind him. "Now, who's today's guest?"

As it turns out, Larry's guest is Vice President Bradley Edmonton, who is making the rounds to encourage listeners to, in his own words, "Rally around the president's agenda for a safe and secure America."

No surprise that he's willing to ingratiate himself to the talk show host. After all, it was Larry who coined Edmonton's famous nickname: "Washington's silver-haired, silver-tongued fox."

All three adjectives fit, especially the one that likens him to the critter known to rob henhouses. His recent backbiting comments about the president are evidence of that.

When introduced to "Gwendolyn," Edmonton's stark blue eyes bore into me like tractor beams. I hold his gaze while declaring, "A pleasure, sir."

"All mine, I'm sure," he responds. "Have we met before?"

I shake my head. "The honor would not be one I'd easily

forget. Alas, my previous postings were never stateside," I add with a demure smile. "And I doubt our paths have crossed in Syria, Africa, or Afghanistan."

His eyes narrow. "I see. You're brave to put yourself in the line of fire."

"You are too." I nod toward Larry, who is berating a production assistant about the task of keeping his coffee mug filled at all times.

Edmonton laughs uproariously.

Just then the producer motions for us to take our places around the studio's half-moon conference table.

Edmond's interview is twenty minutes. Let's see how long it takes for him to sell out Lee.

LARRY STARTS WITH: "OKAY BEFORE I INTRODUCE OUR VERY SPECIAL guest, I'd like to invite our listeners to welcome my very smart —and just to assure you guys listening that she's worth all the grief she's sure to dish out—'veddy, veddy' beautiful new sidekick, Gwendolyn Durant!"

"Thank you, Larry, for making me feel right at home," I purr.

"Yeah, well, wait until the requests for nude fan pics come pouring in," he says.

"I'm duly warned," I reply dryly. "We'll send out yours instead."

"Touché." Larry snorts. "Now, with no further ado, I'd like to introduce our guest, Vice President Bradley Edmonton! Welcome to your home away from home, Veep!"

To prove the remark rolls off his back, Edmonton replies, "Oh, I wouldn't exactly call it that. More like a comfortable hangout with an old pal."

"I'll drink to that!" Larry takes a swig from his mug.

Edmonton rolls his eyes. I guess he's in on the joke.

Larry's first question to him is a softball: "On a scale of one to ten, how would you rate our Commander in Chief's performance at the recent nuclear disarmament summit?"

"As close to a ten as anyone can get," Edmonton pronounces firmly. "President Chiffray is quite aware of the chicken-and-egg game the Russian president is playing with the world, and he isn't going to fall into that trap. The Chinese and North Koreans feel the same way, as do our NATO allies."

"So, the takeaway you have for the American people is that everyone smoked POTUS's peace pipe?"

Edmonton pauses. "Well, it's gotten…a positive response."

"From whom?" Larry prods. "Kim Jung-Un was anything but all smiles."

I jump in. "He's new to the process. But he wouldn't have been there in the first place if he didn't want to play with the A-Team, wouldn't you say, Mr. Vice President?"

Edmonton eyes me warily as he leans back in his chair. "I think the president did his best to chip away at the frost, yes." He sighs as if burdened with what he must say next. "Of course, it would have helped if Russia's president had made an appearance."

Larry snickers. "Maybe he was afraid of being subpoenaed by Special Counsel Reynolds."

Edmonton laughs uneasily. "I don't need to vouch for our president's integrity."

"So, you're saying this is a witch hunt?" I ask.

Edmonton's pause is so long that if I were listening, I'd think the network had lost its transmission. "The term 'witch hunt' implies that this is partisan-based chicanery. Our country has a Constitution built on a series of checks and balances. If our current Commander-in-Chief has nothing to hide, why wouldn't he cooperate with the Special Counsel?"

Current Commander-in-Chief? Wow. Talk about subliminal suggestion.

"Which President Chiffray is doing," I point out.

Edmonton shrugs before bluntly adding, "He has no other recourse."

That's Edmonton's way of saying that Congress isn't playing games, and neither is he.

Even Larry feels the tension. "Gee, you guys! The way you're going at it, why don't you get a room?" He thinks for a moment, then adds, "Hey now, there's a thought! Why not ask her out on a date? I mean, she's a real looker, right? Hey, I'd date her myself, but I'm already paying alimony to three ex-wives!"

Our glares are now aimed at him, but he's too busy slinging blarney to notice it.

Finally, our silence speaks volumes. "Yeah, okay, I get it!" Larry raises his hands in surrender. "It's a 'swipe left' for both of you, right? That's alright. I shouldn't be playing Cupid anyhow. I'm much too fat to wear a diaper!"

Not according to your last wife's People *magazine interview,* I want to say. Instead, I grant him a tight smile.

Thank goodness the music announcing the show's commercial break comes on. It's probably the only way to stop Larry's constant flow of bullshit.

"We want to thank Vice President Edmonton for stopping by and setting us straight on the fact that both parties get along, at least, as it pertains to any witch hunt that may be going on with our president. And now, we're going to take a commercial break. But stay tuned because our guest is Congressman Chris P. Bacon. Hey, Gwendolyn, what do you think I'm going to ask him first?"

"*Hmmm*, let me guess. Perhaps how he got elected with a name like that?"

"Ha! Yeah, that sounds like something I'd do...but, um...*no*."

"Okay then, maybe you'll ask if he's offended by pork barrel legislation?"

"Seriously, Gwendolyn, if you keep this up, they'll make you the star of this show...*Damn it!* Is that what this is all about? *But my contract isn't up for another three years!*"

THE SHOW ENDS AFTER A THIRD GUEST. AFTERWARD, I'M OUT OF there in a flash. I've got too big a headache to make good on my offer to let Larry treat me to a happy hour drink. And besides, as he pointed out to me, he's happy all day long.

I've yet to hear from Jack. I guess that means "negotiations" are going well. Just how well? I'm almost afraid to ask.

By the time I'm in the elevator, I've decided to go back to my hotel room, call the kids, and order in room service. (If I have to do this talk radio gig for much longer, it'll drive me to a liquid diet similar to Larry's.) But, suddenly, my Acme cell phone buzzes with a text:

ARNIE: *Welcome to the Big Apple! Hey, let me buy you dinner! Found a great little hole-in-the-wall Vietnamese joint a few blocks away, so no prying eyes (broad hint).*
DONNA: *I AM SO THERE.*

ARNIE'S RIGHT: THE PHO IS EXCELLENT, AND THE PLACE IS TOO

downscale to attract Hart Media's movers and shakers. Between slurps of noodles and broth, Arnie whispers, "So, I think I'm on to some kind of money trail."

As I tear up a basil leaf, I whisper back, "Don't keep me in suspense."

He looks over his shoulder. Satisfied the other two patrons are too busy texting, eating, or yapping on their phones, he nods. "One of Hart Media's biggest advertisers is a firm known as Get Outta Here."

"What does it do?"

"From what I can tell, not very much of anything."

"What I meant is, what does it advertise?"

"Travel deals. It's supposed to be a travel agency. The ads run in Hart Media's newspapers. It also buys radio and TV spots. And the company always pays top dollar: no bundles, no deals, no breaks whatsoever."

"Why would this be a red flag?"

"Well, for one thing, the address for the company is a P.O. box."

"Yeah, that does sound fishy."

A noisy party of college students take the table beside us. They're chatting up a storm so Arnie fairly shouts, "Also, I had ComInt do SigInt analyses on both its print and radio ads and *BINGO!*"

I shush him. "What does that mean?"

"Emma's team came up with correlations between the ads' tour dates and locations and power grid failures."

"Seriously?" I drop my chopsticks and lean back in my chair. "Is it happening just in the U.S.?"

"Nope. All over the world. Mostly NATO countries, but a few less developed democracies too."

"So, whoever's hacking the grids is running tests."

Arnie nods vigorously.

"Can you tell how long Hart Media has had this account?"

"Several years. It's been a real cash cow."

I give him a thumbs-up. "Great job, Arnie. Dinner is on me!"

"Yeah, I hear you just got a raise *and* you're working with one of my idols, Larry Zorn!"

I roll my eyes. "You're kidding, right?"

"Heck no! He's a hoot! Hey, can you get me his autograph?"

I sigh. "Yeah, I guess."

But if that oaf offers to sign a boob or something, I'll break his fingers.

I'VE JUST JUMPED OUT OF THE SHOWER WHEN I NOTICE THERE'S A new video file in my Acme folder. Emma has uploaded it with a message: "ACTION JACK!"

Okay, I'm at a loss here…

I open it on my iPad. Apparently, Emma thought I'd be interested in some of Jack's security lens footage.

Um, no…wait: Is he making love to Charlotte?

She's apparently on top and in the throes of ecstasy.

"Darling, if I'm hurting you, let me know."

Why that–

Wait, that's Dominic's voice. *Yuck!*

Emma's voiceover is a whisper: "Sorry, Donna! Uploaded the wrong lens footage! Between the street cams, the house cams, Dominic's and Jack's lenses…So many intercuts, so little time, right?"

The correct footage shows Jack walking casually through a street that boasts some of the poshest row houses in London: on Cambridge Terrace, adjacent to Outer Circle, on the southeast side of Regent's Park. At some point, Jack ducks into an alley and toward the back gate of one particular townhome, where he disarms the silent security alarm before picking the back-door lock.

Then he stealthily moves into a large hallway. He puts on a portable pair of night vision goggles, which help him find his way through the stately four-story mansion without tripping over the gilt furnishings in its large, well-appointed rooms. However, the one he seeks must be on a different floor. He skips the elevator, choosing the staircase instead. He ends up on the third floor, inside a home office. From the masculine appointments, it must be that of Charlotte's fiancé, Mikhail Gorev.

To Jack's obvious relief and mine, the grunts and groans of our mission mate are coming from the floor immediately above him.

It takes only a minute for Jack to find what he's looking for. The safe is behind an authentic-looking Van Gogh, hung above an intricately carved sideboard.

The painting slides to one side on bolted casters, revealing a safe.

Opening it is a delicate and time-consuming process, but the reward is worth it. Dominic's intel was right. The safe holds property deeds.

One by one, Jack takes photos of each deed with the camera in his night vision goggles. He has just completed the task when he hears the front door open.

Yikes.

The love tussle going on in the master bedroom has quieted down. Apparently, Dominic and Charlotte are onto the fact that the master of the house is home.

Men's voices are heard, coming from downstairs. They're speaking in Russian.

Emma has given Jack the same feed I'm now seeing, from the house security camera: Mikhail is talking to his chauffeur and his bodyguard. His employees nod, walk off the front stoop, and drive off.

Slowly and silently, Jack puts the documents back in the safe and shuts it. At the same time, Mikhail is taking the elevator—

To his third-floor office.

Jack has just made it to the door. But hearing the elevator, he pauses.

Until he turns his head toward the door's near-soundless hiss, indicating that it's opening.

Jack ducks behind the door.

Mikhail saunters to his office. He flips a wall switch, which illuminates the desk and the sideboard with gentle lighting. He walks over to his desk. The top is devoid of papers, file folders, or any other clutter.

Jack peeks out from behind the door, watching.

Mikhail doesn't sit down. Instead, his eyes scan the room. Finally, his gaze stops at the Van Gogh.

What about it catches his attention? It seems to have slid back into its proper place.

Or maybe not, because he walks over to it.

Jack notices this too. He watches as Mikhail stands before it, just staring. Finally, Mikhail reaches out—

For one of the crystal decanters displayed on a silver tray atop the sideboard. He pours some of the liquid into a glass, turns around, and flops down on the large leather chesterfield.

Slowly, he sips his drink.

The minutes tick away in the silent house.

Until Charlotte lets loose with an orgiastic moan. Apparently, she and Dominic assumed the noises heard earlier weren't Mikhail's homecoming after all.

Mikhail sits up stiffly. His eyes move skyward as if he can see through the ornate ceiling above his head.

"*Eta shlyukha snova v etom!*" he growls.

Emma translates the Russian declaration: "That whore is at it again!"

Since Jack speaks the language, he knows what comes next, and why. As suspected, Mikhail leaps off the chesterfield. Just in time, Jack slips back behind the door, and not a second too soon because Mikhail walks back over to the desk and pulls out a gun.

He starts for the door.

As he passes the door, Jack steps out from behind it. His arm goes around Mikhail's neck, putting him in a rear-naked choke, bracing his other arm on Mikhail's shoulder to tighten the headlock. Mikhail, now suffocating, fights for his life. But Jack refuses to let go. Instead, he lifts his captor off his feet with all his might.

Finally, Mikhail blacks out.

Jack doesn't let him go. Instead, with his supporting hand, he presses Mikhail's nostrils. Instinctively, the unconscious man's body fights for air, but his raspy whimpers die in his throat.

It is over in less than three minutes.

Jack drags Mikhail's lifeless body back to the chesterfield and puts it in a sitting position. He then places the glass in Mikhail's hand.

The gun goes back in the desk drawer.

Jack's last act is to open the safe and pull out the property deeds. He tucks the folded documents into a pouch pocket in the back of his jacket before locking the safe again.

He leaves the same way he came in.

Jack's ride, a black Lincoln town car, is parked several blocks away, on Albany Street. He sits in it for a moment before texting Dominic:

Sir, the car you requested will be at the designated location in five minutes.

A few minutes later, Jack gets a text back:

Righto! Thanks!

Right on time, Jack swings in front of Mikhail and Charlotte's townhome.

Dominic saunters out and hops into the back seat.

"Drive, Jeeves."

Dominic is oblivious to Jack's angry silence. Instead, he babbles on about his studly performance.

Only when they reach Westminster does Jack stop the car and inform Dominic that, at any moment, he'll receive a call from Charlotte and that she'll be in hysterics, having just discovered the body of her dead fiancé in his study.

"My lord! The rumor is true! She _is_ a black widow!" Dominic shudders at the thought. "Ah well, I guess she'll need a shoulder to cry on as we cross the pond." He shrugs. "I don't mind hopping a lift back to the States on her Lear, but she'll be disappointed if she expects a proposal."

Jack, as though gobsmacked, stares at him in disbelief.

The next thing I know, he's laughing so hard that his hand hits the horn.

"Get control of yourself, old boy," Dominic scolds him. "The term is 'covert,' not 'overt!'"

Jack is right. Dominic is undeniably oblivious.

I guess that's what makes him such a good honeytrap.

SOMEONE IS IN MY ROOM.

I open my eyes. I keep still.

I can tell it's the middle of the night, but a sliver of streetlight slips through a slat in the blind.

The intruder is moving very slowly from the doorway toward me.

I inch my hand between the mattress and box spring, where I keep my Sig Sauer P229.

When I have it in my hand, like lightning, I roll off the side of the bed. Crouching, with two hands, I aim it at the intruder. "Stop right there."

He has his back to me. Slowly, he raises his arms. Then Jack says, "I know I'm late, but that's no reason to shoot me."

He's got a point.

I flick on the bedside light.

He flops down on the bed.

I drop beside him.

"Welcome back," I offer.

"Hey, you almost blew my head off! I think you can do better than that." He rolls over to kiss me.

Yet another good point.

And I know just how to make it up to him.

THE SUN IS RISING. WE SHOULD TRY TO SLEEP FOR THE FEW HOURS that are left before we have to head back to Hart Media, but we've still got some catching up to do.

Verbally, anyway.

"How was your 'negotiation'?" I ask.

"I got what I wanted. I'm here with you."

I poke his arm. "Don't leave me hanging! As every good reporter knows, we're told to ask, who, what, where, when, why, and most importantly, how much?"

He laughs. "I like how you paraphrase. Okay, the details: who is *moi*, as we already know. What is *Good Morning Hartland!*—"

"Wow! The mothership of morning shows!" I doff an imaginary hat to him. "So, you'll be joining the two 'Queen Bees of Morning TV'! What are their names again? Oh yes, Lolita Jamison and Beverly Manville. So, you'll be on the celebrated 'jungle red couch,' chatting up stars who are pitching their latest movies?"

Jack looks skyward. "Something like that. But so I'm not completely stripped of my dignity, I'll also be doing the news breaks."

I snicker. "Does that include weather?" I raise my hands, palms open, as if shoving storm fronts around a green screen.

Jack smacks me with a pillow until I'm laughing so hard that I beg him to stop.

"The answer to your question is no. That happens to be Lolita's function. And since it's the only thing they trust her to do onset by herself, I couldn't possibly ask the producers to take it away from her."

Again, I convulse with giggles. When I finally get ahold of myself, I reply, "That is very kind of you, Mr. Craig—I mean Larkin." I snuggle next to him until we fit like two spoons in a drawer. "Listen, I'm just happy that we're in the same town!"

"I'm happy we're in the same *bed*."

He spends the next half hour proving it.

By five-thirty, it's off to work he goes.

10

Stagger Through

A full rehearsal of a news show is known as a "stagger through."

Here are a few reasons why this name is spot on:

First, the term is a misnomer. It's more like a read-through, or the time to work out needed camera shots, cutaways to previously recorded footage, and on-air patter.

Also, because there isn't enough time for a real rehearsal, news broadcasters keep cheat sheets on their desks and use teleprompters. The cameras' close-ups are one way to keep TV viewers from seeing these little cheats.

Finally, even if an anchor or host is smart enough to think on her feet, invariably she will stutter, or say something stupid or silly, just like the rest of us.

Except that millions of viewers or listeners caught it.

Hopefully, it won't be something that makes viewers spew their coffee. Otherwise, the anchor's next stagger through will take place at her local unemployment office, just like the rest of us who have put our foot in our mouths while at work.

≈

"Yo, Lady Gwendolyn! Here's today's cheat sheet." Larry slaps a cue card in front of me.

"Pardon?"

He taps the card with his index finger. "Cheat sheet...you know, today's party line." Placing two fingers vertically above his upper lip, he clicks his heels together.

I glare at him. "Larry, darling, one can always count on you to make your point in the most distasteful way possible."

Still, my eyes scan the card:

1: (Suspiciously:) The big question is, what did the president know about his offshore accounts, and when did he know it?

2: The president claims his blind trust is handled by a funds manager named Helen Drake. But suddenly she's disappeared. You can understand why this seems suspicious to the American public.

3: (Shocked:) If, in fact, he's colluding with the Russians...well, then Congress must, and should, impeach him.

4: (Indignantly:) How is it possible that he's sullied the office of the presidency in that way? It's...unfathomable!

I frown. "Are you seriously telling me that the producers want us to slip this kind of opinionated blather into our conversation?"

"Of course! We're on talk radio, remember? We're here to stir the pot! Stuff like this gets the listeners hot and bothered. It keeps them tuned in, which ups our ratings, which brings in more ad dollars, which pays us our salaries, and allows me to pay off my alimonies AND drive a Ferrari! *Capisce?*" He shakes his head, awed. "Where are you from again?"

"The news bureau," I remind him. "There, the goal is to report *facts.*"

"Oh...yeah." He shrugs. "Well, chickie-baby, talk radio is *entertainment.* So, which would you prefer, odds or evens?"

I shake my head uncertainly. "Odds, I guess."

"Hey, me too!" He closes in with a leer. "Wanna arm wrestle for them?"

I arch a brow. "Larry, considering your lack of staying power in general"—my eyes drop below his belt and the large belly that balloons over it—"do you really want to be beaten, on-air, and by a woman?"

"Only with a cat-o-nine-tails, babe."

I drop my head, ashamed for him. "Okay, so, who's our first guest today?"

"It's a really big get! POTUS's National Security Council liaison, Todd Courtland."

Yikes. Todd and I go way back. I don't know if he's always crushed on me, or just wanted to set me up for a fall.

For that matter, I also go back and forth on whether he crushes on Babette and wants to set up Lee for a fall.

Gee, relationships are so complicated.

I get into Gwendolyn mode and pray that, between the accent, the glasses, the colored contact lenses, and wig, he won't recognize me.

As it turns out, the chance of Todd recognizing me isn't a problem. He can't come to the studio and is doing the interview by phone.

Larry and our producer are pissed off about it, but I am tremendously relieved. It's easier to be Gwendolyn if he's not staring at me while trying to figure out if he knows me. Or, worse yet, blows my cover.

Larry leaps right in with his take on one of the cheat sheet soundbites:

"So, Todd, answer the question of the hour without the usual namby-pamby doublespeak and whitewash. What did the president know about his offshore accounts, and when did he know it?"

Todd chuckles warily. "Hello to you too, Larry—and, if yesterday's show is any indication, your better half, Gwendolyn."

"My pleasure," I say with proper British elocution.

"*Sheesh!* You've got her practically curtseying!" Larry crows. "But that doesn't get you a pass from answering the question that's on everyone's lips right now."

"Fair enough," Todd replies blithely. "The president released a statement early this morning, which simply states that he left his blind trust in the hands of a funds manager who came highly recommended by a close advisor. Also, he is fully cooperating with the Special Counsel's investigation on the one asset in which funds were, without his knowledge, put into an offshore account. If there has been co-mingling of these funds with any foreign power or political actor, he has no knowledge of it."

Larry nudges me to say something.

"Mr. Courtland, certainly you can understand why the American public might find the matter somewhat dismaying—"

"'*Dismaying*'?" Larry hisses. "What is this, a garden party?"

I pinch him to shut him up. "And to make matters worse, the one person who should be questioned in the matter, the fund's manager, Helen Drake, is nowhere to be found. Truly…disconcerting."

I feel like a traitor playing along with this ratings hound.

"As it is for the president," Todd assures us. "Again, he is cooperating fully with the investigation. In the meantime, he is carrying on the business of his administration, including negotiating with other nations for a slowdown in the production of even more nuclear weapons."

"Gotcha," Larry retorts. "Except for Russia, which is ramping up. So, if we slow down, they win, *thanks to President Chiffray*. What part of this *doesn't* smell like a payoff? And if it is, why shouldn't the Senate try him for high crimes and misdemeanors?"

"Larry, you're jumping the gun, guy! The investigation will demonstrate who, if anyone, is guilty." Todd sounds exasperated. "We are a country of laws; a country that believes in a person's innocence until proven guilty. We're not going to try President Chiffray in the court of public opinion!"

Larry lifts my hand to slap me high five.

He then sticks my middle finger in his mouth.

At that point, I slap his face—something I realize I should have restrained from because he seemed to like it.

That does it.

As the producer cues the bumper music for the commercial break, I grab the mic. "Thank you, Mr. Courtland, for putting things in perspective for our listeners. Like you, they believe in this great country of ours. And thus far, our president hasn't done anything to sully his high office. In fact, the thought of him doing so would be…Well, it would be unimaginable."

As the commercial runs—for Get Outta Here, of all things—Larry exclaims: "What the…have you lost your mind?"

I smile benignly. I'd rather think I've found my voice.

THE LISTENER PHONE LINES ARE RINGING NONSTOP.

According to the producers, ninety percent of them feel like me: Lee has been a great president and a good man. So, he made a mistake. Let the investigation play out. If he was negligent in choosing the wrong person to run his business, he'll take his lumps. Most politicians don't get more than a slap on the wrist.

For the hour's other two interviews, Larry is as pale as a ghost and sticks to the cheat sheet. He's somewhat relieved that I'm doing this too.

At the end of the show, he looks exhausted.

"What's with you?" I ask.

"I told you already: we have a job to do," Larry growls. "Look, if you're going to make a habit of going off-script, maybe you're not right for this gig—"

He stops when he sees someone over my shoulder. I turn to see who it is.

Our producer motions to us. "Harold wants to see you. *Both* of you."

"Damn it," Larry grumbles. The way his shoulders drop, you'd think he was going to the electric chair.

I follow him down the hall and into the elevator.

LIKE THAT OF HIS SISTER AND FATHER, HAROLD'S EXECUTIVE OFFICE is on the top floor of the seventy-seven-story Hart Media Corporation Building. From this height, it towers over the other Times Square buildings and has a bird's eye view of Central Park to the north.

The phalanx of assistants outside Harold's office is all of a kind: buxom and bored. When we enter, they look me up and down. One of the women picks up the phone to inform Harold that we're here.

I take their stares head-on.

Not to worry, ladies. I wouldn't be you for a million dollars.

But then, I realize if I get canned here and now, I'll either have to infiltrate Hart Media again or be taken off the mission altogether.

So groveling may be in order.

From the way Larry is sweating, he must be thinking the same thing.

The assistant on the phone with Harold nods us through.

As we walk toward the door, Larry mutters, "Lady Gwen, this time let me do the talking."

I nod, but there are no guarantees. Whatever Larry has on Harold, it's every man—or, in my case, woman—for herself.

HAROLD STANDS MIDWAY IN HIS FOOTBALL-FIELD-SIZED OFFICE. HE stoops over the golf club he holds with both hands. Silently, Larry and I wait while Harold lines up the shot on the golf simulator's putting green. Suddenly he slices—

Hitting Larry in the gut.

Larry doubles over in pain. He gasps. "What the hell?"

"What happened on your show?" Harold scowls from Larry to me, and back again. "Why the hell did you ignore the cheat sheet?"

Larry glances over at me.

He's doing his best not to sell me out, and I appreciate that, so I speak up. "I'm sorry, Mr. Hart. I misread the phrases on the card."

Harold's eyes move to me. A cruel smile breaks on his lips. "You're the new sidekick, right?"

I nod.

He takes a few steps closer. Too close.

Still, I hold my ground.

Larry's plaintive whine interrupts our staring match. "The audience ate it up! They like her. And actually, they liked what she said."

"Yeah, I know," Harold retorts dryly. "Even Hart Media's newspapers picked it up!" He points to the cover of the company's flagship newspaper, *The New York Examiner*. The headline screams:

'Hot Topics with Larry' News Commentator Empathizes with Chiffray's Woes

"At least the paper had the right spin on it," Larry points out. "'Woes' works."

"Yeah, well, that's because the editors took it *from the cheat sheet!*" Harold barks. "And you, Mrs....or is it Ms.?"

"Ms. Durant," I answer. "Gwendolyn."

"Do you?"

"Do I what?" I squelch the urge to back away.

His eyes lock onto mine. "Do you sympathize with the president?"

Play it cool.

"I...I feel, as most Americans do, that one is innocent until proven guilty."

"Huh." He chews on that for a moment. Finally, he retakes his place on the simulated putting green. "You're a waste of Hart Media's time and money—"

Oh, hell! Here it comes. I'm getting fired.

"—by being tied to Larry's show," Harold continues. "Anyone can shoot the breeze with this blowhard."

"Hey...Wait!" Larry whines. "I resemble that remark!"

Harold shuts him up with a chip shot that sends Larry ducking.

Now that Larry has gotten the message, Harold continues: "As I was saying, you're much too valuable an asset to be heard and, frankly, not seen." His lips lift into a leer. "How would you like to be Hart Television News' newest White House correspondent?"

"The...White House?" I'm so shocked that I almost lose my accent.

He nods. "Larry, get lost. Gwendolyn and I need to go over terms."

"But she gives great patter! We were developing a rhythm and we've got sexual tension! It's obvious in our voices!"

Harold jerks his thumb toward the door. "There's a whole office of sexually tense talking-head wannabes out there!" he shouts. "Choose one, for Christ sakes! Only this time, make sure the next one keeps to the cheat sheet! And don't marry her! I'm tired of paying off your alimonies!"

Larry frowns. Still, he takes the hint and scurries out the door. His one act of defiance is to slam it behind him.

Harold rolls his eyes. Then he plops down on the couch and pats the seat beside him. "Gwendolyn, what say you and I come to an understanding?"

WHEN I SIT DOWN, IT'S FAR ENOUGH AWAY THAT ANY manspreading would be too obvious a ploy.

Not to be deterred by my reticence, Harold sidles closer. "I think this position will be right up your alley. Considering all that is currently going down in Washington, we need someone who will treat it as a war zone; as if reporting the decline and fall of the Third Reich. You know, when Hitler cowered in the bunker."

"You're comparing Lee Chiffray to Hitler? Isn't that a bit melodramatic?"

"Not if I say so. *And I do.* The press corps are bloodhounds, and they're all over Chiffray's trail. He's already cracking under the strain."

"Who says he is?"

Harold's eyes narrow. "I just did."

"Will it be on tomorrow's network-wide cheat sheet?"

"What if I say yes?"

"Ironically, I'd believe you," I retort dryly.

"Ha, ha! You're a very clever girl. Too clever, I hope, to turn down the position. It comes with a six-million-dollar-per-year salary and a five-year contract. Additionally, your compensation package will also include a chauffeur-driven town car and an expense account for entertaining, and an allowance for clothing and a personal trainer. As for a residence, you'll be given a key to a penthouse a few blocks away. It's owned by the corporation."

"That's...very generous!" Cha-*CHING*! Gee, maybe I'm in the wrong business after all. "I gather that the position entails reporting on the administration's daily press briefings?"

"For six mil a year, I'll expect a bit more than that." He smirks as he moves in closer still. "Your job is to get into the bunker with the president and report back."

I inch back from him. "You're really going to stick with that Hitler theme, aren't you?"

"Hey, who knows? If Reynolds rattles him enough, he might actually put a gun to his head! Now, wouldn't that be a scoop for Hart Media!" He closes his eyes as though the thought makes him practically giddy. When he opens them again, he scrutinizes me. "Have you ever met Lee Chiffray?"

"No," I say firmly. "Our paths never crossed in any of the war zones I covered."

Harold shrugs. "Good, then you're fresh meat. And you're right up Chiffray's alley. He likes icy blondes. Just look at the cold mannequin he married!"

"As for 'being right up his alley,' if we're to talk at all, it won't be one-on-one, and certainly not over candlelight and champagne." I try to keep a straight face as I add, "And besides, the Chiffrays are happily married."

Harold chortles at what he thinks is my naivety. "Don't be so sure. In fact, the disappearance of this Helen Drake person may be proof of it."

"Pray tell," I murmur.

"Rumor has it she wasn't just his financial manager. She was also his mistress."

"Did you hear this rumor, or did you start it?"

"I think we've just established the fact that neither matters." He chuckles. "And here's another reason it shouldn't matter to you. There's a bonus in it. Half a year's salary, for the run of your contract—*if you get the scoop that proves the rumor is right.*"

"You mean, the rumor you just made up?"

He sighs exasperatedly. "Another definition for a rumor is a yet-to-be-proven truth."

"I'll take your word for it," I say coolly. "Mr. Hart, I still don't know how I'm supposed to wheedle my way into the president's confidence. Most White House correspondents never get any further than the press fence as he crosses the White House lawn toward Marine One, or to shout out a question in the oval with a scrum of other reporters. If he's lying low, what makes you think he'll take an interview with me?"

"That may be the easiest part of all," Harold counters. "After Todd Courtland's interview with you and Larry, he called me. He says that the Administration was heartened by the listener response to your platitudinous pandering—so much so that the president is open to a no-holds-barred interview with Hart Media. The president feels it will clear the air about...Let's see, how did Todd put it? Oh yeah! 'This sad misunderstanding of the president's role in his blind trust.'"

"Did Mr. Courtland suggest that I conduct the interview?"

"No. It came from the big man himself."

Darn it! Did Lee listen in and recognize my voice?

"Well, if the president asked for me, I guess I should."

Harold guffaws. "Not him! I meant the CEO of Hart Media: Randall Hart."

"Oh...your father!"

Although he can't guess the source of my blatant relief, he frowns, as if it's an affront to him. "Nepotism isn't the only reason I'm the boss of several thousand employees, *including you, Gwendolyn.*"

"No, of course not! I didn't mean to imply—"

He stops me by putting his tongue in my mouth.

I'm too shocked to react.

Then again, considering that my first instinct is to chomp down on it, maybe it's for the best.

He pulls back with a smug smirk. He liked having caught me off guard. "Let's not keep the old man waiting."

He points to a double interior door. "Ladies first."

It doesn't surprise me when I feel him nudging me forward with a hand on my bum.

RANDALL HART IS TALL BUT STOOPED ENOUGH TO NOW LEAN ON A cane. His shoulders are no longer broad enough to fill out his elegant bespoke suit. His eyes sink into the sagging flesh beneath them, like an aging Halloween mask. The sharp cheekbones that once anchored a full, florid face now protrude from his sunken skin.

Interesting. I guess the photo of Randall used in the company's investment prospectus was digitally enhanced to make him look as virile as he once was.

Ignoring Harold, he squints through his glasses at me.

"You did the reporting from the Russian parade."

"Yes, sir. I'm Gwendolyn Durant."

"It was a good piece of journalism." He sighs. "It's why I agree with Harold that you take the White House beat."

I have to ask: "Why me?"

A slim grin breaks his lips. "Are you looking a gift horse in the mouth?"

"Not at all. I'm just wondering why others who have been with the network longer weren't considered."

He bends to glare at a sheet of paper on his desk. "Your background is perfect. Foreign correspondent, broadcast, and print. War zones, political unrest, deep investigative pieces. Let's make one thing clear. This assignment shouldn't be a puff piece or a hit piece. A comprehensive investigation is warranted. And you have the on-air presence to weave our president's sad, complicated tale into a cohesive tapestry: one that the world wants to hear. One it *should* hear."

My eyes go from Randall to Harold and back again. "Even if the president is innocent?"

When he smiles, he resembles a cadaver. "Especially if he's innocent."

"Then yes, I'll do my best to report the facts, wherever the investigation leads."

More so, to stall until Acme untangles the financial threads that bind the Hart Media Network to Russia.

"One last thing, Ms. Durant. Has my son propositioned you in any way?"

The color drains from Harold's face.

I hesitate, wondering how I should answer him.

"Your silence speaks volumes." Randall's cane smacks Harold in the face.

His son yelps and holds his cheek, which is already reddening.

"Ms. Durant, you'll report only to me. I won't let our network be dragged through the mud because my egotistical son has no self-control." He shudders at the thought. "My secretary has your new contract. Take it home with you. Today is Friday. Take the weekend to go over it with your attorney. The offer is good until noon on Sunday. Should you sign it, tell your legal counsel to email a signed PDF version to me." He hands me a business card with his private email. "Report to our D.C. news bureau on Monday morning."

I nod goodbye and leave.

Harold faces away from me.

Are these men in league on the mission to destroy Lee?

It sounds as if they're at cross purposes.

I'll know one way or another if Harold reaches out to me.

11

Puff Piece

The journalistic definition of a "puff piece" is a feature article that is excessively complimentary about a person, an event, or a product.

You hear puff pieces all the time, and not just on TV.

For example, when your husband is teased by his work buddies about some cute co-worker who makes it a point to bring him his coffee every morning. However, Hubby insists on laughing it off, but at the same time, he opines on this adorably sweet act of kindness.

Well now, there's a puff piece for you.

Solution: Send him into work with a thermos of his favorite brew!

Should Cute Co-Worker figure out another way to wile her way into his heart, send her something too: perhaps a cute coffee mug laced with something that will have her thinking twice about her morning caffeine and his.

JACK'S HOTEL ROOM CONNECTS TO MINE, ALLOWING US TO ENTER and leave separately.

He's not at the hotel when I get there. I yank off my wig. It'll stay off until Monday when I'm due at the Hart Television Network's Washington D.C. Bureau.

As I hoped, Emma has already uploaded Jack's first day at *Good Morning Hartland* and intercut it with actual footage from his first appearance on the show.

The footage starts with Jack's initial meeting with his producer, Suzanne Pettigrew.

As he shakes the hand of this aging Bronx babe, Jack apologizes for being a few minutes late. "Your building security was a lot tougher to get through than I anticipated."

"Hey, at least you didn't ditch on us! I thought maybe you'd believed the rumors. Ha, ha!" She takes a good look at him. Then, in a rapid-fire patter, she exclaims, "My Lord, Grant Larkin! You are even more handsome in person than you are on TV! Be still, my heart!"

She walks him onto the set, where the other hosts, Lolita Jamison and Beverly Manville, have taken up separate corners of the set's sizable serpentine couch.

Beverly, the older of the two, has been with the network for almost thirty years. Other than her attire and hairstyles, her looks don't seem to have changed that much. It may have something to do with the amount of makeup troweled onto her face.

I recognize Lolita as a former Miss Wyoming in some recent pageant. She is stunning: a natural auburn beauty. If only she'd keep her mouth shut! Metaphorically speaking, she makes a habit of sticking her five-inch Manolo in it. If she isn't spouting some backhanded compliment to a guest of the show, she's espousing her air-headed take on a current event. Twitter lights up with her Lolita-isms on an almost daily basis. I guess it's one of the reasons the producers keep her on.

The women's make-up and hair stylists flutter about them, but they ignore each other, choosing to click away on their cell phones instead. "Oh, my GAWD," Lolita squeals. "I've surpassed Taylor Swift in Twitter followers!"

Beverly doesn't look up, but her collagen-filled lips drop into a pout. "Knock off the fake squeal, Lo. Everyone knows you use a Twitter farm."

Lolita's hair stylist gasps.

Her client's lip quivers at the insult. "Why, you old hag! You're just jealous because your core-demo audience hasn't figured out how to use Twitter—"

Hastily, Suzanne bellows, "*Yoo-hoo, ladies!* Look who I have with me! It's your *new co-host!*"

The women's bickering pauses as they turn to face their producer and scrutinize Jack. They must like what they see because suddenly they're all smiles.

Beverly gets to Jack first, but only because she shoved away her makeup person to do so. "You're our new man candy, eh?" she purrs. "Welcome to our humble little show."

"You have nothing to be humble about." He leans in, searing her with his now baby-blues. "Your ratings are twice that of the closest morning show. Beverly, I'm sure a lot of that has to do with the way you seduce the audience." He takes her hand as he looks soulfully into her eyes.

She practically preens at the comment. "Ah yes, well, intimacy is something I excel at." She winks broadly.

"Yeah, when it comes to intimacy, our Bevvy has had many, many years of practice," Lolita butts in. "You could say that a lot of our audience has grown up with Bev! Some of them have even grown *old* with her."

Before Beverly can slap Lolita's simpering smile, Suzanne swats away her hand. "Watch the nails, darling! Mustn't smudge the manicure!"

How many of these catfights must she break up on any given morning? No wonder a little vein pops on her forehead.

"Sadly, my gorgeous morning team, we don't have time for a stagger through of the show before our guest arrives. So, go ahead and take your places on the couch. Grant, you're in the middle," Suzanne says.

"New meat for our manwich," Beverly drawls. "*Yummy!*"

Jack strides to the couch with the women on his heels.

Lolita sits on his right. Okay, make that practically in Jack's lap. Not to be outdone, Beverly lays a hand on his wrist, then leans in. Her breasts bulge through the V of her low-cut blouse.

When one of the production assistants attempts to attach Jack's lapel mic, Lolita snatches it out of the guy's hand. "Here, let me do that." She grins.

Hmm. I've been around enough mics to know that pinching Jack's nipple between her fingers is no way to test the sound level.

Suzanne gives the production assistants a wave, indicating that they are free to let today's studio audience take their seats. After they've settled in, she mouths into the talent and crew members' earpieces: "Okay, cue music…and…"

Suzanne points to Lolita.

Lolita squeals brightly, "Good morning, Hartland!"

"Yes, good morning *Hart*land." Beverly's tone oozes sensuality. "We're here *every* morning to make *your* morning!" She winks at the camera. "With that in mind, let me introduce you to a man who, like me, you'll enjoy waking up with *every* morning: Grant Larkin."

The camera moves in on Jack, who rewards it with a broad grin. "It's great to be sharing the couch with you, Beverly."

Lolita giggles. "Imagine if it were a bed instead."

Not phased by her coquettishness, Jack chuckles. "Interesting proposition. But fair warning: I'd easily take both of you in a pillow fight."

"Promises, promises," Beverly says. "Hey, maybe today's

very special guest would like to join us in that!" Reluctantly, she pulls herself away from him in order to face the camera. "First Lady Babette Chiffray is here to discuss Peace Meal, her new initiative to encourage Americans to share a dinner with a stranger."

Yikes! *Babette is there?*

Will seeing Jack a second time jog her memory as to who he truly is? Considering all the times she's attempted to pick him up, I would think so.

Jack must be thinking the same thing because just for a second his smile falters.

"We've just met Grant this morning," Lolita points out. "Does he count as a stranger?" She licks her lips as she makes eye contact with him. "I'm free for dinner, by the way."

Despite Lolita's silly remark, the strength of Beverly's latest Botox injection holds on her forehead. However, the edges of her mouth push it into a grimace. "Now, now, Lolita! No need to appear so *desperate!* He'll find out soon enough why you suffer through so many lonely nights."

Lolita's cheeks pink up. Hotly, she retorts, "I do not! Why, *I* have a *boyfriend!*"

Beverly rolls her eyes. "Then why hasn't anyone met him?"

"He sure is a lucky guy," Jack says to the camera through gritted teeth. "After this commercial break, we'll welcome the First Lady of the United States: *Babette Chiffray.* So, stay tuned."

"Cut!" Suzanne shouts. She walks over to the couch. "Look, ladies, it's the new guy's first day. What do you say we cut him some slack? You know, forego the catfights for a week or so. No?"

She loses their attention to the beehive of activity now surrounding her on-air talent as their glam squads descend in full force.

Suzanne sighs mightily as she walks over to Jack. Shaking her head, she declares, "Well, I tried."

"Just out of curiosity, what happened to the last guy who had this gig?" Jack asks.

"He retired to a farm in the country."

Jack squints. "Really? You're using that old canard?"

Suzanne snickers. "You know, my kids never bought that line about our Airedale either!" She hands him one of the infamous blue cards.

"This isn't on the monitor crawl, but I promised the First Lady you'd say this, which brings up an important point. *The one thing you can never screw up, New Guy, is anything written on a blue card.*" She taps her finger on a phrase with a star beside it. "In this case, after the First Lady lays down some patter on her cause, you'll respond by saying, 'We should all make a new friend now then. It should be a worldwide effort! So, folks, write down the number at the bottom of the screen. Then call to see how you can get involved.'"

"Got it," Jack assures her.

If Jack reads it, he'll be signaling a covert op command.

Unfortunately, since this footage is from several hours ago, it's already too late for me to stop him.

Instead, I pace the room.

Where in the hell is he now?

I SEND JACK A TEXT. WHILE I WAIT FOR HIM TO RESPOND, I WATCH the rest of the show.

After the commercial break, the camera sweeps through the cheering waving audience before settling on Beverly, who proclaims, "Our guest today is a fashion icon, an inspiration to women all over the world—and lately, the calm eye of the gathering storm around the White House."

Lolita's sad nod is a subliminal message to the viewing audience: *We should be worried about our president.*

Okay, yeah, fashion icon I'll give Babette. But "worldwide inspiration" and "calm eye in the storm?" Hardly!

Hell, she has *been* the storm since the first day she and her first husband, Jonah Breck, stepped into Hilldale. I live to get enough evidence to prove that she inherited his seat in the Quorum.

"She is now the country's Humanitarian-in-Chief, too," Beverly continues. "Without further ado, let's welcome my idol and I'm sure yours, too! *Babette Chiffray!*"

Oh, gag me. Babette's entry is made to a jazzy riff that puts a burlesque spin on *Hail to the Chief.*

In hindsight, maybe it is appropriate.

She waves at the studio audience. Then, making eye contact with the camera, she blows a kiss.

Who was *that* for, I wonder.

Babette then shakes hands with Beverly and air-kisses Lolita, who is thrilled at the gesture and squeals with glee. When Babette turns to 'Grant,' her eyes drink him in before she holds out her hand to him.

Jack takes it, only to find himself being pulled in for a kiss.

Oh hell. Babette must recognize him.

When, finally, she pulls away, she pretends to fan herself. "Wow! Maybe this is how I should spend *every* morning! You lucky ladies!"

Beverly preens at the compliment. Lolita practically faints.

To Jack's credit, at most he looks bemused. He points to the couch and says calmly, "After you, First Lady."

"Please, call me Babette," she purrs as she pulls him down with her.

As the morning's grand inquisitor, Beverly takes her place on the other side of Babette. She's a smart cookie: one of the three studio cameras will keep them in a two-shot, whereas a second camera draws back to take in everyone on the couch. The third camera is also a two-shot: of Babette and Jack.

She is still holding his hand.

The nerve of her!

Beverly gushes even more compliments before segueing to the topic of Babette's charity. "How did you come up with the idea?"

Babette's smile fades. "As First Lady, I eat alone on many nights. You know, my husband is very busy with…well, with affairs…"

She pauses so long that Beverly's eyes open wide. Instinctively the host leans closer to her guest—

"…of *state*," Babette says as she wipes away a crocodile tear.

Dissing Lee on national television about an imaginary affair? That takes some nerve, considering her own lineup of lovers—including the father of her toddler son.

"I hear ya, sister!" Lolita's strangled gasp has Camera Three swinging her way for a close-up. Realizing this, Lolita puts her hands on her cheeks, like a silent screen actress in distress.

Oh, brother…

Camera Two, the wide shot, catches Babette patting Jack's hand as if she hopes to find her solace there.

With his next statement, he sorely disappoints: "I'm sure, Babette, your country appreciates the sacrifices you've made for it. Consider the strain on the president too! Every moment away from you must break his heart."

Babette's woe-is-me gaze turns to daggers as she stares up

at 'Grant.' Apparently, I'm not the only one who hears the irony in Jack's voice.

To prod Babette back to her mission, Beverly says, "So, tell us how this cause works. Is it like the dating site 'It's Just Lunch,' where you're set up on a blind date, only he may not be much of a looker?"

Babette sniffs. "In the first place, it may not be a 'he.' Secondly, there is no matchmaking because your dinner companion is randomly assigned."

"Oh..." Lolita seems disappointed. "You mean you can't swipe left if the person leaves you cold?"

"You haven't met yet," Babette counters. "You know nothing about this person! *You are meeting because you're lonely.*"

Lolita snickers. "I'm not that lonely!"

Beverly leans in toward Babette and 'Grant.' "Ha! Give her a decade. That over-inflated silicon job won't stay perky forever."

Suzanne hisses in Jack's earpiece: "Only twenty seconds until the commercial break and FLOTUS flies the coop! Go to the cheat sheet banter!"

Oh, hell, here it comes...

Jack nods slightly. "Mrs. Chiffray, how many Peace Meals have you gone on thus far? Five? Ten? More?"

Babette sits there, stunned. Finally, she stutters, "Why, *er...* none. I mean, not *yet.*"

"None?" Grant frowns. "Oh...well...*Hmm.*" He shrugs. "Still, you've done your country a great service by at least heading up such a *wonderful* cause. In fact, I'm willing to give it a go!" He turns to Beverly. "What do you say, Beverly? Will you do it too?"

Clearly appalled, she frowns. Finally, she croaks, "Yeah, okay, what the heck."

Jack's head turns to Lolita. "How about you, Lolita? Think

about the joy you'll get from impressing someone who's never met you!"

Lolita brightens at the thought. "Okay...sure, Grant!...Wait! Does this mean you're asking me out on a date?"

The cause's telephone number is now flashing below them on the screen. As the break music rises, Suzanne shouts, "Cut!"

The cameras on the set go dark. Babette's mood does too. Leaping up from the couch, she jabs her finger at Jack. "How dare you put me on the spot like that!"

Jack feigns surprise. "I'm sorry, Mrs. Chiffray! It was supposed to be a softball question. I'd thought you'd hit it out of the park."

She growls, "Suzanne, what the hell? He was supposed to plug my charity, not make me look like a fool!"

"Frankly, Mrs. Chiffray, I think we did you a service by sprinkling it with a little star power." Jack points to Beverly and Lolita.

Incensed, Babette stalks off the stage. Immediately, she is enveloped by her usual posse—Narcissa Belmont and Chantal Desmarais—who hustle her out of the studio.

Exasperated, Suzanne whips around to Jack. "Why the hell didn't you follow the cheat sheet?"

He lays his hand on her shoulder. "You're a great producer. You know as well as me that we did her a favor."

Suzanne's anger wavers under Jack's piercing gaze.

Clueless about the tension around her, Lolita leans into Jack. "So, were you serious about that date?"

Emma's footage goes dark.

FOUR O'CLOCK ROLLS AROUND, AND STILL NO JACK. *GRRRR.* SO, I text him:

DONNA: *Packed for the both of us. Wheels up at 1940, but if you hurry, we can catch an earlier flight. Where the hell are you?*

JACK: *Sorry! Cohosts kidnapped me to an early happy hour. It's their "initiation ritual"—drinks at the Marriott Times Square View Lounge.*

DONNA: *Well, la-dee-dah. Let me guess what's on the menu: A MANWICH. And what's for dessert?*

JACK: *Probably airline peanuts. I promise I'll be out of here by 1800. Scout's honor. xoxo*

I REFUSE TO SIT AROUND AND TWIDDLE MY THUMBS. MY NEXT TEXT is to Arnie:

DONNA: *Buy U a drink?*

ARNIE: *I thought you'd never ask! Reunion Sur Bar? Fish tacos! Slurpee tropical drinks! Meet me there, like 1700? I'm catching a flight home for the weekend. Gotta be at the airport by 1940.*

DONNA: *OMG! You're on our flight! Okay, see you there.*

THE PLACE IS PACKED, BUT ARNIE HAS SECURED TWO SEATS AT the bar.

He's sipping on something called a Coco-Loco, but I wave down the bartender for the specialty drink known as the Mermaid (a frozen mojito) and a couple of fish tacos.

By the time Arnie is halfway through his platter of three beef short rib tacos and a side of "Tot-Chos" (tater tots smothered in nacho toppings), it dawns on me that Acme may know more about the Special Counsel's investigation of Lee's trust than it realizes.

Nonchalantly, I ask, "Hey Arnie, when you scanned Wagner Klein's database, did you come across any of Lee Chiffray's companies?"

Arnie stops slurping on his drink straw and shakes his head. "I wouldn't know. I mean, doesn't he own, like, a million of them?"

"You're right. There are a lot of them. Hey, can you do me a favor and run a cross-reference?"

Arnie furrows his brow as he drags yet another tater tot into the small lake of guacamole, chili, and jack cheese that takes up a good bit of real estate on his platter. "Can you give me a specific company name?"

"That's the problem. The Special Counsel may not have subpoenaed the one in question, so it isn't public record as of yet. But because Global World Industries is registered with the SEC, you grab its public filing or stock report and cross-reference all of its companies with the Wagner Klein database."

Arnie nods. "Sure, no problem. Here's hoping I find it quickly! Emma needs me home. She isn't doing so well at single parenting."

I nod. "Yeah, I hear you. It's a hard task to be on call, twenty-four-seven."

Arnie guffaws. "In Emma's case, it's the opposite! Nicky is enjoying preschool so much that he whines when she arrives to take him home! She's beginning the think she's the worst mother in the world!" His face softens. "God...I love that woman."

I pat his hand. "She's one lucky lady."

Arnie blushes. "And Jack is one lucky guy." He frowns. "Where is he, anyway?"

"Getting 'initiated' by his cohosts, Beverly and Lolita—whatever that means."

Arnie's eyes open wide, but he says nothing.

Oh no.

Calmly, I ask, "You know something, don't you?"

Arnie shakes his head firmly.

With my left hand, I slap his palm flat on the table. Naturally, his fingers are spread out. With my right one, I take my steak knife in my fist and stab it between his index and middle finger. "Your call. Should I try this blindfolded?"

"No! Of course not!"

"So then, tell me what you know about the Queen Bees' initiation party." I jerk the knife out of the table and place it back on my napkin.

He gulps. "Every interoffice email goes into Hart Media's secure cloud." He sighs. "And because I'm searching it for correspondence related to Wagner Klein and the Dutch Bank, I'm perusing everything, including the Queen Bees' correspondence to each other. Their little ritual includes drinking games."

I shrug. "Jack can hold his liquor."

"Not if he's been roofied!"

My heart falls into my gut. "Why would they do that?"

"So they can...You know, they take the guys to bed. Then they take turns putting him in compromising positions." He pauses, then exhales. "And they take photos. The man's face—or a more randy part of him—is always in the picture, but the women wear disguises or pose in such a way that they never show their faces."

I shake my head, incredulously: "I still don't get it!"

"It's a power trip, I guess. The moment they have the goods on the dude, he's their bitch. They can run all over him, on-air and off. They get first dibs on perks, like all those free tickets to glitzy events that come to the network. Also, they can coerce him to into giving up the best assignments. If he complains about it, they may release the photos to the press, and there goes his career."

"Arnie, if something like that happens to Jack..." I'm so angry that I'm shaking.

"Don't worry, Donna. I always have Jack's back. If they take any photos of him, they'll be gone—*poof!*" He waves his hand like a magician.

I nod, but that doesn't make me feel any better about how his night might end up. I text him a warning:

Your co-workers are fiends! Get outta there. NOW.

I hope he gets it in time.

In any case, if I'm to take Jack at his word that we'll make the flight, I should leave.

I tap Arnie on the shoulder. "I'm heading back to our hotel. But you've still got a few moments, so the next drink's on me." I order Arnie a mango-raspberry frozen margarita like the one he's been eyeing from across the bar.

Arnie asks, "How about the taco you haven't touched?"

"Sure. Consider it payment in advance." I give him a kiss on the cheek, then I'm off.

I RUSH INTO MY HOTEL ROOM—

And find Jack standing there.

He wears a towel around his midriff. He's wiping his head with another. From the streaks on it, I can tell his hair is now brown again, if only for the weekend.

"Oh, you're back! So...soon?" I rush into his arms. "You got my text?"

"As it turns out, I didn't see it until I walked out of the Marriott." He chuckles. "That text of yours—you must be psychic!"

"At least I'm not *psycho*, like your cohosts!"

Jack sighs. "So, you saw the news?"

I shake my head.

"So...how did you know what they were up to?"

"I met Arnie for happy hour. Apparently, he's seen photos from the Queen Bees' previous 'initiations.' He says it's not a pretty sight, especially for their victims. So, what happened there?"

Jack snorts. "The Marriott's lounge has more mirrors than a French whorehouse. I caught Beverly giving Lolita the high sign about something. After Beverly waltzed off to the little girl's room, Lolita slipped a mickey into my drink. But as she fielded a call, I switched it with hers. First, I poured half of it in Beverly's glass too." He grins. "They fell asleep in each other's arms. By the time they woke up, I'd taken off. From what I can tell on social media, they got into a slugfest over Lolita's supposed screw-up. Some fan took a video of it, and it went viral."

"My God!" I gasp. "Talk about bad publicity for the show!"

"On the other hand, the other networks are ecstatic. They're running the video on their news shows. But don't expect to see it in any Hart Media newspapers or newscasts."

"Jack, how did you know the cheat sheet contained a covert message?"

"Emma clued me in. She said you'd bumped up against the same issue with Larry." He shrugs. "Charlotte has already called me to apologize for the Queen Bees' behavior on the network's behalf. But by what she said, Beverly and Lolita's public brawl may have been just the excuse she needed to break their contracts. Hopefully, she'll find cohosts who get along, at least while we're on the air." His smile widens. "The best news is that I may get a few days off next week while Suzanne retools the show."

"Speaking of good news, I got a promotion today."

Jack's jaw drops. "What? You're leaving Larry? That must have broken his heart. He seemed to enjoy being your whipping boy!"

"That may be the case, but Randall Hart himself asked me if I'd transfer to the D.C. bureau...as"—I brace myself for Jack's reaction—"the new White House correspondent. Ryan likes the idea. He thinks it may bring about a break in the case."

Jack's smile fades. He can't shake his frustration over my friendship with Lee. Finally, he grunts, "I guess congratulations are in order."

"Jack, I know you're not happy about it—"

"You're right. I'm not. But I'm sure that Lee will be tickled pink."

He leaves my room for his, closing the door behind him.

It's going to be a long flight home.

12

Open-Ended Question

To encourage a source to give a lengthier answer to a question, a reporter will hit the source with an open-ended question. This is one way to avoid "yes" or "no" answers that don't really tell the full story.

To keep your life from resembling a charades game, you should try the technique too!

For example, if you want to find out if your teenage daughter is dating the wrong kind of boy, ask her, "Why does your boyfriend have to report to his parole officer?"

And you can ask this question the next time you eat out in a new restaurant: "Excuse me, can you point out the dishes that brought you to the attention of the city health inspector?"

And this classic gem may also prove revelatory: "When was the last time you beat your wife?"

Remember: the best questions receive the best answers.

"MOM! MOM! WHAT DO YOU THINK? IS THIS OKAY FOR MY

interview with Babette?" Mary stands at the top of the stairwell. She's wearing a new dress. It's quite retro in style: formfitting to just above the knee in canary yellow, with black piping around its three-quarter sleeves and bateau neck, which also sports a bow on one side. Her hair is tamed into a French twist. She wears large glasses.

Realizing that she's stunned me, she heads down the steps on her black kitten-heel shoes. "Well, how do I look?"

"Very sophisticated. By the way, why the glasses?"

"Because they'll make me look smarter."

"You *are* smarter. If you'd work harder in school, you'd have the grades to prove it. But yes, you look perfect. The glasses are a cliché. Where did you get them, anyway?"

Mary snickers. "In your costume closet."

"Really, Mary?" I throw my hands up in the air. "First Aunt Phyllis, and now you? *Agh!* Okay, I'm putting a lock on that door!"

We're interrupted by the doorbell.

I'm still in my pajamas. The flight was late and bumpy. By the time Jack and I made it home, it was midnight on the West Coast. "It's ten o'clock on a Saturday! Who could that be?"

"I told you. I'm interviewing Babette Chiffray today!"

"Wait! You mean, you're doing the interview *here*?" I look down at my flannel pajama pants and a T-shirt that was a birthday gift from the children. It proclaims:

**I'M A
DROP THE F-BOMB
KIND OF MOM**

I SPUTTER, "WHY AREN'T YOU DOING IT AT LION'S LAIR?"

Mary nods. "Babette thought it would be a good change of place for her to come to our house. And since Janie is with her, I knew Trisha would love to show off her room, so I said yes."

I run to the living room window.

Yep, there's Babette. She holds Janie's hand. Her daughter is all smiles. And, as always, her Secret Service detail is tagging along.

The bell rings again.

"I'll get it!" Jeff races out of the living room. He's dressed in khakis, a button-down shirt, and a tie that he must have taken from Jack's closet because it is much too long for him.

"Why is he dressed up too?" I ask.

"He's my camera man," Mary explains. She nudges me into the living room. Mary's iPhone is set up on a tripod that faces one of our twin sofas.

Jeff flings open the front door before I have a chance to duck out of sight. Immediately, three Secret Service agents stride in. I recognize one of them—Lurch Muldoon, who heads the First Family's security team. He comes over to shake my hand. Noting my tee-shirt, he smothers a grin, but he manages a straight face when he exclaims, "Mrs. Craig, always a pleasure!"

I blush. "Same here, Mr. Muldoon. But, as you can see, I wasn't expecting company. Of course, Janie and Babette are always welcome—as are you."

What do you say to a man who once saved your life, and on your wedding day no less? Lurch will always be welcome in my home.

"May we search the premises?" he asks.

"By all means."

He motions to the other men to spread out.

As one of the agents starts upstairs, Lurch asks, "Is Mr. Craig in?"

I shake my head. "He's jogging." As I predicted, Jack barely talked on the flight home. When I woke up this morning, he'd already left the house. The note he left on my bedside table had one word on it:

Jogging. —J

BY NOW, HE COULD HAVE RUN TO MALIBU AND BACK, BUT LURCH doesn't need to know that.

Nor does Babette, who, having gotten Lurch's okay to enter, strolls in with Jeff.

She is dressed in a blush-toned short-sleeved scalloped sheath, studded with tiny stones. Her hair falls softly around her shoulders. As always, her makeup is impeccable, unlike me, who was too tired to wash my face last night after we arrived.

Awed by Babette's elegance, Mary's smile wavers. Still, she straightens her shoulders as she makes her way to Babette's side. "Hello, Mrs. Chiffray. So good to see you again." She reaches out to shake the First Lady's hand—

But suddenly, a scream rings out from upstairs: from Trisha, who is now bounding down the stairwell.

Janie screams too as she runs toward her—

And joyously, they hug each other at the foot of the steps.

A third scream comes from Aunt Phyllis, who bounds into the foyer from the great room. A damp sheen covers her leotard-clad body. Her yoga mat is rolled tightly. Suspicious of Lurch, she raises it like a bat.

Drawn by their cries, the two roving agents also come running in: one from upstairs and the other from the kitchen.

Despite the anxious scowls on their faces they lower their raised guns when they see what the ruckus is all about.

They face off with Aunt Phyllis when Lurch shouts, "Agents! It's only Mrs. Craig's aunt! *Weapons down!*"

I look left to right and pray...

Slowly, the men drop their weapons.

Aunt Phyllis' eyes open wide. "That was one hell of a workout! Gee, my heart is racing!"

Babette shakes her head in annoyance. "Janie, see what you caused? Quit acting like a hoodlum!"

"So sorry, Mummy!" She lowers her head, duly chastened.

But then Trisha nudges her and they run out toward the kitchen, Lassie and Rin Tin Tin bounding at their heels. Finally, Trisha gets to show her friend the backyard playhouse: a perfect place for them to plot and scheme what to do in the few precious hours they have together.

One of the agents sighs, but nonetheless follows them out.

Just then, I notice that Jeff has caught the whole thing on his iPhone. I motion him to put it away. Reluctantly, he slips it back into his pocket. Still, something tells me it's going to end up on the *Hilldale Signal*'s online edition on Monday.

Suddenly, Babette notices me. Eyeing my attire, she sniffs. "Gee, Donna, had I known it was a slumber party, I would have dressed down." She looks around. "Speaking of dreamy, is Jack around?"

Bluntly, I reply, "He's out on a jog."

Nope, I'm not surprised she asked. I just hope it isn't to taunt him about his double life as *Good Morning Hartland*'s man candy.

Babette gives a disappointed sigh. Still, she leans in for the perfunctory air kiss.

Reluctantly, I accommodate her. *Oh well, when in Rome, or something like that.*

But when Aunt Phyllis moves our way for her version of a group hug, Babette holds out her hand to stop her. "This is a *Valentino*, Mrs. Lindholm! So please, let's forego your usual bear hug."

Phyllis takes the request with a grain of salt and a middle finger salute. I'm able to smack it away before Babette sees it, or one of her trigger-happy agents blows it away. My unflappable aunt sticks her wireless buds back into her ears as she heads back into the great room.

Thank goodness Mary has already ushered Babette into the living room.

MARY STARTS OFF POLITELY. "IT'S AN HONOR TO INTERVIEW YOU, Mrs. Chiffray, especially in light of all your accomplishments since entering the White House."

Babette rewards Mary with a glowing smile. "Thank you, Mary. It's very kind of you to acknowledge them."

"In fact, I know our viewers would like to hear what you feel your greatest accomplishment has been thus far."

Babette pouts as she thinks through the question. "Why... motherhood, of course." Babette lifts her head proudly. "Raising a happy and healthy child in this great country of ours is an honor and a privilege!"

"I've no doubt," Mary insists. "But, considering the esteem and power that comes with your position, surely there is one *public* accomplishment that makes you *especially* proud?"

"Yes..." Babette's eyes narrow. "Certainly you've heard about my new cause: Peace Meal."

"I think it's wonderful," Mary exclaims promptly.

Babette preens at the compliment.

"In fact, this brings up my next question. Would you be open to sharing a Peace Meal with someone today?"

"What...me?" Babette's head jerks back, as if someone has just slapped her. "No!...I mean...I've got such a busy schedule and all—"

"But, when I set up this interview with your aide, Ms. Desmarais, she told me the day was wide open...Oh, except for your mani-pedi and physical training session. So, we called over to the Hilldale Senior Living facility to see if one of the residents might be free for dinner. There were so many who have relatives living too far away, or who have no family at all. We had to pull a name at random."

Appalled, Babette's eyes open wide. "That won't work for me!"

"But...it's your signature movement," Mary points out. "And since, as it was just reported, you've yet to experience it yourself, don't you want to?"

I have to hold my breath to keep from snorting out loud.

Babette's face turns bright red. No doubt the memory of "Grant's" gotcha moment still haunts her. Babette's eyes narrow as she scrutinizes Mary, but my daughter's wide-eyed innocence muzzles her as she clearly contemplates the best way to get out of this dilemma. When Babette finally answers, her tone is not just firm; it's menacing: "I'm sorry, Mary, but you're mistaken. In fact, Janie and I have arranged to take a tour with the principal of the local elementary school."

Mary is so excited by this bombshell that she sits straight up. *"You're moving back to Hilldale?"*

Babette drops her head before nodding. "Yes. I don't think we'll be in Washington much longer," she says ominously. "At least, Janie and I will be living here."

Oh, brother...

Mary's mouth drops open. Her head whips around to the camera, where she mouths one word: DIVORCE!

And yet, she is so touched by Babette's theatrics that she takes the woman's hand. "But President Chiffray is cooperating with the Special Counsel! He's innocent...I mean, right?"

Tears glisten in Babette's eyes. "I...I hope so. You see, the asset in question...well, he told me he'd sold it! So it shouldn't have been in the portfolio to begin with!" She lowers her head to hide a deep sob.

Which company? Say the name so I can verify this...

"Cut!" Mary exclaims.

NO! NOT YET!

Wild-eyed, Jeff looks up from the iPhone's viewfinder. Apparently he agrees with me because adamantly, he shakes his head.

"I said *CUT!*" Mary insists. She moves closer to Babette to shield her face from the camera.

Jeff grumbles but does what he's told.

A wisp of a smile rises on Babette's lips.

When she looks up, the tears have miraculously vanished.

Mary doesn't notice because she's too busy wiping away tears of her own.

LURCH KNOWS BABETTE WELL ENOUGH TO HAVE THE AGENT watching Janie bring her to her mother as quickly as possible.

When the girls appear, there is a frown on Janie's face. "Must we leave so soon?"

"Now, now Janie," Babette says firmly, "Don't you remember? We have an interview with the principal of your old school, Hilldale Elementary. You remember Miss Darling, don't you dear?"

Hearing this, Trisha is jubilant. "We might be in school together again?" She hugs her friend. "Janie, that's awesome! I can show you around and introduce you to everyone! Hey, you said you play soccer at your D.C. school, right? I play too! I'm a forward. We're on a winning streak! Wait until you meet Coach Middleton! She works us hard, but we adore her. You will too!"

My heart sings to hear Trisha's pride in her soccer accomplishments. Anything that gets her off Madison's posse works for me.

Janie's eyes light up. "I can't wait! I'm a midfielder, but sometimes my coach puts me at goalkeeper...but"—she turns to her mother—"Mummy, I thought the interview is on *Monday?*"

"You're mistaken," Babette replies darkly. "I didn't want everyone gawking at us, so I made the interview for today. The *tour* is on Monday."

Liar. She wants to bluff her way out of Mary's Peace Meal photo opp.

There's one way to prove it, I tap Babette's shoulder, "If you're looking for privacy, the Monday tour defeats the purpose, doesn't it? Why don't you call Ms. Darling and suggest that it wait until Monday for both?"

Janie takes her mother's hand. "Please, Mummy?"

"I...well..." Babette glares at me, knowing she's been caught. "Let me call Chantal to see what she can do." With as much dignity as she can muster, she moves into the dining room.

After a conversation (with herself, I'm sure) she's back. "Chantal is making the arrangements." She sighs. "Perhaps it's for the best, since it would have been tight to get back in time to meet with the realtor."

Mary gawks at her. "You're selling *Lion's Lair?*"

"I'm considering it," Babette replies airily. "It's much too large for just...Janie and me."

She'll be asking for a divorce?

Jeff slaps his forehead. I guess he's frustrated that he doesn't have that on video too.

That's okay. He doesn't know it but we've got security cams in every room. I'm sure he'll be ecstatic to receive the missed moments from an anonymous source.

"Since you've got such a busy afternoon, can Janie hang with me?" Trisha is practically pleading.

Janie begs, "Please, Mummy?"

"Well, Peter Bing *can* take all afternoon." Babette smiles at the thought. "So, I guess it's okay." She turns to Lurch and nods. In turn, he points to one of the agents: *Tag, you're it.*

The guy rolls his eyes.

At that moment, Jack strides up the front porch and opens the door.

The agents' hands slide to their weapons, but with a shake of his head, Lurch warns them off.

Jack smiles down at her. "So sorry I almost missed your visit."

Jack's tee-shirt is soaked from his run. Otherwise, I'm sure Babette would have insisted on a bear hug to rival Aunt Phyllis's usual greeting. Instead Babette leans in for a kiss. "My, I'm so glad I caught you before I took off!"

If we weren't in front of the kids and a Secret Service detail of three, I'm sure Jack would have passed on accommodating her.

Or maybe he's not so sorry, considering the way his lips graze her cheek.

Is this his way of punishing me for getting the White House correspondent position? He should know better! I'm only doing it because it's part of the mission.

Then again, Jack could argue that he's now taking advantage of an opportunity to engage with a possible Quorum operative.

She's certainly taking advantage of *him.*

And he is *definitely* not arguing about it.

"Well, I *do* have a few more minutes." As if she's caught some naughty boy with his hand in the candy jar, Babette wags a finger at him. "In fact there is something I must discuss with you—*in private.*"

She nods toward the dining room.

Oh no...here it comes! She's going to blow his Good Morning Hartland cover.

Try as I might, I can't overhear what they're saying, mainly due to the chatter going on around me. While Jeff and Mary are reviewing their video footage and discussing post-production considerations, Trisha rhapsodizes on and on of all the wonderful things her school has to offer. "And wait until you meet my posse! Madison is totally cool!"

I throw up my hands. With all the *chatter, chatter, chatter,* covert surveillance is a moot point—

Or maybe not. I've just remembered that we have a security camera in the dining room! It's hidden in the eye of the portrait hanging over the fireplace.

At that moment, Babette and Jack reappear in the foyer. He's just said something that makes her gush, "Why, I think that is a marvelous idea!"

I don't like the cunning wink she gives him.

He responds with a naughty grin.

This time, when Babette goes in for a kiss, it's right on Jack's lips.

Afterward, she looks around to make sure I caught it. Seeing my stunned stare, she sweeps out the door with a triumphant smile.

I blink away the urge to cry. I don't know if he's doing it for the mission, or because he's angry at me about my new assignment. In any regard, Babette now knows she's succeeded at hurting me.

As Lurch follows her out, he nods his farewell. He frowns because he's embarrassed for me.

Jack is walking to the stairwell as if he doesn't have a care in the world.

Angrily, I follow when my cell phone pings. Jack's does too. Simultaneously, we stare down at it:

Ryan. The message:

Meeting. NOW.

Darn it.

I follow Jack upstairs.

He uses our shower.

I use the one that Mary shares with Trisha.

Afterward, we drive to work together. In silence.

Except for Ryan, Jack and I are the last ones to enter Acme's conference room. We circle the room for chairs on the opposite sides of the round conference room table.

Emma is tapping away at her computer. So is Arnie, but it's harder for him because Nicky sits in his lap. He's so excited about having his daddy at home. Whenever Arnie leans in to type over him, Nicky squeals with delight.

From what I can tell, Abu is editing video footage. I'm sure he's prepping it for some story he's already been assigned by Hart's D.C. news bureau. It'll be great to have him covering my back there.

As I pass Dominic, I look over his shoulder and see that he's texting. I take a closer peek, and sputter, "My goodness! You're sending someone pornographic GIFs?"

Miffed, he draws back to block my view. "Pardon? It's not pornographic if the sender and the recipient are the video's subjects!"

I snatch the phone out of his hand. He's right. It's Dominic and Charlotte. Their position isn't just compromising. It's exhausting.

I toss the phone back to him. "Yeah, okay, keep telling yourself that."

"Well, well! Someone is in *quite* the mood," he grouses.

That does it. I'm not sitting next to him. And since the only other chair is next to Jack, I elect to stand instead.

Ryan strides into the room. As he lowers himself into the seat next to Dominic, he declares, "It's great to have you folks back in the country, and on this coast. As everyone knows, a lot has happened since we were last together, so let's play catch-up." He nods at me. "First, I want to congratulate Donna on the interception of the Russian military arms intel."

I blush at my team's applause. Even Jack slaps his hands together, albeit tepidly.

"And Jack's suspicions about the Japanese operative, Kimiko Satō, saved the World Nuclear Proliferation Summit from turning into a disaster."

As I clap along with the others, Jack glances over at me. "Donna's run-in with Luuk gave me the idea," he admits.

I nod. Still, he'll have to do better than that before we kiss and make up—like, say, *tell me what the hell Babette said to him.*

"Which brings me to the extermination of Charlotte Hart's fiancé, Mikhail Gorev. Jack did a credible job of making it look like a heart attack. However, with all the unfortunate mishaps befalling Russian nationals on U.K. soil, any coroner assigned to the body is going to be looking for suspicious causes, especially if the expat was a friend of the Kremlin. With this in mind, I took the liberty of alerting the Cousins that the kill was ours. They in turn have assured me that the coroner's report will reflect death by natural causes. This should be a relief to his fiancée." Ryan turns to Dominic. "Speaking of which, how is your target?"

"As anticipated, we are a definite item." Dominic frowns. "Not anticipated, however, is her voracious libido! To put it bluntly, the woman is insatiable!" Perplexed, he slams his cell phone onto the conference room table. "Needless to say, I have infiltrated the target."

A video now appears on Dominic's phone screen. Charlotte can be heard chattering away in the universal language of naughty talk.

In unison, we tilt our heads toward it…

Ewww!

Arnie covers Nicky's ears, while Emma puts her hands over his eyes. The toddler giggles at this new game.

Abu stares down at Dominic's phone. "I'll say you have!"

Wearily, Ryan closes his eyes. "Put. That. Away. *NOW*."

Dominic clicks off and tosses the phone into his jacket. Then, without missing a beat, he adds, "On the plus side, Charlotte has proven to be very open to discussing Hart's business practices."

"She seems open to *a lot* of things," Jack replies.

Ryan pierces him with small, angry eyes. Assured that Jack is duly chastened, he looks at Dominic again. "Has she mentioned Wagner Klein?"

"Not with any concern or at any length other than to bemoan the fact that Hart Media didn't break the story first," Dominic assures him. "However, she was very happy that the Conkling woman got the scoop about POTUS's standing as one of its clients. She says it makes for many great leads for her reporters to follow."

On that note, I raise my hand. "By now, I guess everyone knows that as of Monday 'Gwendolyn' is being transferred to Hart's D.C. news bureau. My new title is White House Correspondent."

My teammates nod then glance over at Jack, whose face is as stony as a poker pro's.

I lift my new employment contract out of my valise and hand it to Ryan. "I've already signed it, but as my 'attorney,' please follow Randall's protocol and email a PDF to his office before noon Eastern Time tomorrow."

"Will do," Ryan agrees. "Abu says it's a hotbed of activity, and that the cheat sheets are handed out to all reporters and anchors. He does his best to collect them and passes them forward to Emma and her team. But since the news bureau is Hart's largest, he'll welcome the help."

"Amen," Abu declares.

"By the way, the Hart Media cheat sheets you've been passing forward have gone a long way toward helping the ComInt team in its encryption analysis, so keep them coming," Emma says.

"Arnie also has another promising bit of news. A breakthrough, sort of." Ryan nods to Arnie.

The happy father hands the toddler to Emma. Or attempts to, anyway. Nicky whines and wiggles to get back in Arnie's arms. Emma is embarrassed. Still, she holds the child firmly. When she hands him his favorite teddy bear, he calms down.

Arnie sighs with relief. "Okay, sorry about that, folks." The harried daddy takes a deep breath. "As everyone knows, I've hacked Hart Media's corporate database. I'm hunting down anything that leads to a money trail into Wagner Klein or Trident Union Bank that launders its clients' offshore funds. It's a massive endeavor. All banking intel is encrypted out the wazoo! However, I have noticed one anomaly. If it's what I think it is, we'll have nailed Hart directly to the top players in the Kremlin, and I'll be dancin' in the end zone like Deion Sanders—"

Ryan buries his head in his hands. "Anything else of importance?"

Arnie thinks for a moment. "Oh yeah! Hey, Donna, as you requested, I went through the whole Wagner Klein database and found nothing related to any of the companies in the GWI portfolio. I also searched under Lee's name and Babette's."

I frown. "But that can't be! The Special Counsel must have found *something*."

Arnie shakes his head. "Whatever it is, I don't see it."

"Maybe it was planted there after the fact," I insist. "Or maybe it really is just a witch hunt!"

"We'll find out soon enough," Ryan promises. "The subpoenas will start rolling out."

Poor Lee! And that rat, Babette, is jumping ship…

Speaking of whom: what the hell did she say to Jack?

I look sharply at him—

Only to find him staring back at me.

I temper the urge to stick out my tongue at him.

Nope, I've got another way of getting it out of him. Casually, I announce, "We had a visit from Babette this morning."

This time, all heads swivel to me.

"She agreed to sit down to an interview with Mary and Jeff for their school newspaper."

"Well, now, *there's* classic spycraft for you," Emma says admiringly.

"She did drop some interesting soundbites. She and Janie are moving back to Hilldale, without Lee, if what she says is to be believed."

Emma snickers, "So much for 'til death do us part!"

"She said she may have to sell Lion's Lair, and that she's putting Janie into public school."

Abu rubs his thumb and forefinger, as if playing a tiny violin.

"She's priming the pump for her departure," Ryan says softly.

Ryan too is thinking: *Poor Lee.*

The bomb is ticking in slow motion, giving her enough time to move away from the debris field.

The one she created. We all know that.

Even Jack no longer buys into her pity party.

Or does he?

In the most innocent voice I can summon, I ask, "Jack, when she had you alone, what did she say?"

Jack's eyes meet mine. Nonchalantly, he replies, "Ryan agrees with me that for now we should keep it on a need-to-know basis only."

How dare he! I need to know. NOW.

Our eyes never waver—

Until he blinks first.

But he also gets the last laugh.

I spend Sunday in the laundry room.

It's the one place I know Jack avoids at all cost.

On the other hand, I don't mind all the pre-treating and pre-soaking needed for the precarious mountain of athletic pants and shorts and tee-shirts and jeans on top of the dryer.

Load after load is moved from washer to dryer. I pull out the ironing board because the kids deserve a real treat: creases in their jeans.

To salvage the elasticity of my delicates, I put them in a special mesh drawstring bag, which I then toss in with the cold-water wash.

Then the folding begins. Nice squares of warm fragrant clothes are sorted by owner and placed into baskets that will be left at the bottom of a bed.

Everyone's things, but Jack's.

He left early this morning again.

The way I see it, he has tomorrow off anyway. He can do his own laundry.

Had he not removed the dining room security footage while I showered yesterday, I might have reconsidered.

Until he comes clean with his little secret, his laundry is on a need-to-do-it-yourself basis.

JACK WALKS INTO THE HOUSE JUST A HALF HOUR BEFORE ABU IS DUE to swing by so we can head out to the airport.

"Don't bother seeing me off," I sniff.

"Fine, if that's the way you want it," he retorts.

I don't. But my pride won't let me say it out loud.

Instead, I jibe cruelly, "Hey, since Babette is taking Air Force One straight from Hilldale to New York on Tuesday, maybe 'Grant' can hitch a ride with her. Isn't it a hoot that she didn't recognize you on *Good Morning Hartland*? I guess that's the advantage of having her look no higher than your crotch."

Jack takes the bait. "You should talk! I'll give you three-to-one odds that Lee doesn't recognize you either *since he never looks beyond your breasts!*"

Furious, I toss my suitcase to the floor. "I'm not just some bimbo to him, *and you know it!*"

Jack frowns. "You're right. You're not. You're his ideal woman: beautiful, strong, and you always have his back."

"Why shouldn't I have his back? *It's my job!* He is the President of the United States!"

"Be honest, Donna. If it wasn't your job and he wasn't the leader of the free world"—Jack puts air quotes around the moniker—"you'd still feel that way about him! Go ahead. Admit it."

I stutter, "That's what friends are for, isn't it?"

"*Friends*? No! That's what *spouses* are for!"

Outside in the driveway, a horn toots. Abu is here.

I pick up my suitcase again and start for the door.

By the time I open it, Jack hasn't said a word.

Not even "goodbye."

On the way to the airport, Abu keeps up a cheery monologue because he knows I'm too morose to answer back.

It's all I can do to keep from crying.

13

Tease

It's to a news show's benefit to hold your attention between commercial breaks. The strength of its ratings depends on it!

To do so, the newscaster will provide a short but tantalizing description of what you'll see, should you stick around. This is called a "tease."

You've often played the tease, so you know how it works. Only, in your case, the words may have been naughtier. Perhaps even X-rated. Shall we say, "For Mature Audiences"?

If he didn't hang in there, it's his loss. I mean, let's face it: there is nothing in your fridge as yummy as you!

"AH, HERE SHE IS NOW: OUR NEW WHITE HOUSE CORRESPONDENT, the very gracious Gwendolyn Durant!" Wendell Edwards, the former BBC news anchor, waves me over from across Hart News Tower's very crowded newsroom pit.

On the flight over, I reviewed Acme's intel on my D.C. co-workers, including Wendell's dossier. It pleases me that the company was smart enough to put such a distinguished journalist on its prime time anchor desk.

I was also not surprised to learn that, like me, Jeanette Conkling's reportage earned her a transfer to the Washington Bureau.

In fact, when she hears Wendell call out my name, she looks up and scans the newsroom until we lock eyes. When I smile, she rises and walks over with Wendell.

Other than a bullet to the head, in my line of business the best offense is a compliment. I hold out my hand to her. "Ms. Conkling? I remember seeing you on our initial interviews. Bravo on breaking the story about the president's travails."

Politely, she says, "Your Moscow piece was a great bit of reportage, too."

I shrug. "It wasn't a historical investigative scoop, like yours! It was only what the Kremlin wanted us to see, and to believe, about its capabilities."

Her eyes widen. "You doubt Putin's scientists can create the technology?"

"His slideshow was impressive enough. But let's face it: the latest Marvel Comics movie has better CGI graphics," I counter. "It's in the math. Russia spent seventy billion last year on its military. That is only eleven percent of the United States' defense budget. Putin will need more money to pull it off, and his economy doesn't come close to supporting that level of funding, especially with the way he and his ministers siphon from the till."

"His little show certainly ruffled NATO's feathers," Jeanette points out. "Berlin is a very tense city right now."

"As it should be. With its latest shenanigans, we should all be alert. But democracy dies in darkness," I reply.

Wendell chuckles. "Not so loud, old girl! Bandying about the competition's motto may topple you from this lofty perch."

His arm sweeps toward the window, toward the shorter building of Hart's biggest competitor, the *Washington Post*, across from us on K Street.

The White House can also be seen easily from the fiftieth floor of the Hart News Tower.

Wendell follows my gaze. "Imposing, isn't it?"

"Yes," I declare.

"Good luck tomorrow," Jeanette says as she heads back to her cubicle. "Perhaps Chiffray will say something so astounding that you'll be renowned for the 'get of the year.'"

Not funny. "You mean, like admitting he knew about the account?"

Jeanette nods. "Anything is possible. And we both know that everyone has something to hide. Otherwise, what would we write about?"

At that moment, a woman taps me on my shoulder. "Gwendolyn, I'm Polly Bernard. I'm your producer."

We shake hands.

"I'm sure, like me, you want to prep for the interview. To start with, we'll also be accompanied by three camera people. Security has already cleared us for entry." She hands me a manifest stamped with the White House's official seal. "Just be sure to bring your Hart Media photo I.D. and your driver's license."

I glance through the manifest, which includes the names, company photos, cell phone numbers and occupations of our party. One of the camera persons is a woman. I'm relieved to see that 'Arvin Rahbar' is included among the names of the two men.

Thank goodness Abu will be there too! Should Lee suddenly shout out my real name and the interview blows up in my face, he'll know how to doctor the footage before Hart Media shows me the door.

"The interview with the president is scheduled for three o'clock tomorrow," Polly continues. "Talk about a great lead-in to the evening news!" She looks at Wendell. "And we've already lined up expert legal commentary to join you on the regular news broadcast."

"Brilliant!" Wendell proclaims.

"Although it's to be aired live, it will be transmitted by a remote feed because the President's people insist that it take place in the Oval Office," Polly adds. "The Administration requests that it does not exceed forty-five minutes, so do arrive promptly."

"The president's people have also agreed that no subject is out of bounds," Wendell adds. "With that in mind, perhaps we should go over the questions your producers and Mr. Hart himself have chosen."

My heart sinks as Wendell holds up one of Hart Media's infamous cheat sheets.

The last thing Lee needs is to be used as a conduit for relaying covert messages to terrorists or unfriendly country's agents.

This broadcast will be watched by tens of millions of Americans. Afterward, they will parse every word that came out of Lee's mouth.

Blake Reynolds and his prosecutorial team will be doing the same thing.

For Blake, Lee's head is the target and I'll have pulled the trigger if, even unwittingly, Lee makes a statement on national television that incriminates him.

I'd hate to have that on my conscience.

POLLY THOROUGHLY UNDERSTANDS MY DESIRE TO TAKE THE

afternoon off to move a few things into my new digs and get to bed early.

Harold's penthouse is well-appointed but the style is stark. It's not a home; it's a rich person's flophouse.

The number of condom wrappers on the bedside table in the master bedroom bears this out.

If I had any doubts, the dildos kept in the lower vanity drawer of a second bedroom confirms it.

I've made up my mind to sleep in the third bedroom, despite its two twin beds.

But before I do, I call home.

"IT'S GONE VIRAL!" MARY SQUEALS. "THE SCHOOL'S YOUTUBE account has over two hundred thousand hits in just one day! And over a million on Facebook, half a million on Twitter, and a quarter-mil on Instagram!"

"Oh…Congratulations, honey." *Poor Lee.*

Jeff comes on the line, having grabbed the phone from his sister. "Mom, Mary promised to mention the name of the boutique where she got her dress for the interview, but she forgot. I'm glad, because that would be crass. Now the owner wants us to tack on a commercial. I say no, but Mary says we have to do something. What do you think?"

I think my head is going to explode, but I know that's not the answer he wants to hear. So instead, I say, "Type in the name of the shop with a credit line for the dress."

"Yeah…okay, that'll work," Jeff concedes.

I ask, "Hey, is Trisha around?"

I hear Jeff clomp upstairs with the phone. He muffles it while he knocks on his younger sister's door. Finally, I hear Trisha whisper, "Hello, Mom."

Something isn't right.

"I miss you, sweetheart," I say softly.

Her response is a sob.

My heart sinks. "Honey, what happened?"

It takes Trisha a moment to speak again. "Madison stole Janie from me."

I think that one through. "What do you mean?"

"Today, when Janie came for her tour, I introduced them. Madison was really nice to her, but at the same time she was really mean to *me*. then the other girls started being mean to me too! And when Janie saw how they were, she played along."

"Janie was mean to you too?"

"She had to be. Or they wouldn't accept her."

"I see." I then tell her what she already knows, but what she needs to hear again if she's to believe in it: "Friends aren't mean to each other."

"Then I guess…Janie isn't my friend." Her cries are muffled. She must have covered the phone with her hand so I can't hear her crying.

"It's time to make new friends, honey."

"I…I can't."

"Why not?"

"Because most of them are too afraid to speak to me! They think I'm a snob."

This surprises me. "How did they get that impression?"

"Because I *was* a snob…when Madison liked me." Trisha sighs. "Madison was only nice to me because she wanted to get close to Janie for whenever she showed up in Hilldale. She and her girls couldn't care less about me."

"If what you say is true, it's their loss, not yours," I declare. "Trisha, you're smart. You're beautiful. And you're fun to be around! Of course people like you."

"Mom, every parent says that to their kid. And every kid

finds out the hard way that it's B.S." Trisha is crying very hard now. "I know you mean well, but this is my life right now! *And I'm not even in middle school yet!*"

She hangs up.

I curl up into a ball and throw the covers over my head.

Every now then, a parent wishes she could take the place of her child; to share her years of learned adult wisdom with the young soul who will find out soon enough about heartbreak.

But no, we can't pass knowledge forward. All we can do is be there to hug them when they need it most.

Trisha needs me now, and I am a continent away.

I am such a bad mommy.

WHEN THE HART NEWS INTERVIEW TEAM ARRIVES AT THE OVAL Office, Lee's assistant, Eve, welcomes Polly, Abu, and the other two camera people with handshakes before turning to me. "And this must be Ms. Durant..." She squints as she tries to place me. Finally, she shrugs off the notion that I'm anything more than a familiar face from her television set. "I've allotted fifteen extra minutes for setting up prior to the president joining you."

"Thank you for being so considerate," I say primly.

"Please follow me."

She leads us into the oval office. "Ms. Durant, let me suggest that you and the president take the armchairs flanking the fireplace."

It's a sound recommendation. A portrait of George Washington hangs over the fireplace. Honesty and integrity is the subliminal message.

One camera will catch me in close-up while another will be

trained solely on Lee. The third will pull out to get the two-shot.

Knowing Abu, he's figured out a way to feed all three cameras to Acme's secure cloud.

Polly chooses the left chair for me. After I'm mic'd by the camera woman, the other cameraman places lights aimed at the empty chair and me. It takes some finagling before he achieves a warm skin tone.

While Polly touches up my makeup, I notice that Lee is standing just within my peripheral vision. I feel my lip quiver. Polly notices it too and pauses, lip brush in hand. "Did I press down too hard?" she asks.

"No..I...Everything is fine." I thank her, but then I wave her off to stand and greet our Commander-in-Chief.

When ours eyes meet, he smiles. "Gwendolyn, pleased to finally meet you."

"Thank you, Mr. President, but the pleasure is all mine." I'm shocked that my accent doesn't waver in his presence.

After we shake hands, Eve calls in the official White House photographer to take pictures. Not only is there a group picture, Lee is gracious enough to take photos with Polly and the rest of the crew.

When it's my turn for a picture alone with him, he moves in close enough for me to feel his breath on my cheek. Even as he inches toward me, he manages to keep his hand on the small of my back.

"You're not smiling," he murmurs.

He's right, so I force my lips into a slight grin.

After the last camera click, he adds, "Don't worry. I don't bite."

I laugh out loud at that.

Then Polly hands me the note cards.

Oh hell.

THE OPENING REMARKS ON THE CHEAT SHEET ARE GENTLE enough. "Thank you, Mr. President, for allowing me to sit down with you here in the Oval Office for an honest and open conversation. Doing so allows the American people to assess for themselves if the Justice Department's appointment of a Special Counsel is warranted, or if it's politically motivated."

I speak the words slowly, all the while wondering which word or phrase is a call-to-arms for some foreign agent, either abroad or on American soil.

Lee leans forward in his chair. He makes sure that he's got my full attention then says, "Gwendolyn, I have nothing to hide. Ask away."

I believe that Lee will tell me the truth.

Will the viewing audience believe it too?

Even if he does, nothing will stop Blake Reynolds from doing his civic duty for which he pledged under oath.

Lee would want it that way.

I, too, must do what is best for our country. It's why I make the decision to flip over the cards with Hart's handpicked questions and raise honest concerns that need truthful answers.

"SIR, THERE IS A LOT OF CONTROVERSY ABOUT A FUND HELD IN your blind trust. Can you state, unequivocally, that the trust is blind to you?"

"Yes," Lee says without hesitation.

"Have you any knowledge of any offshore bank accounts held in your name, or by any of your companies?"

"No," he states firmly.

"Mr. President, where is the financial manager who handled your frozen assets?"

"I have no idea."

"What can you tell us about Helen Drake?"

"Nothing at all."

Noting the shocked look on my face, he adds, "Ms. Drake came with the highest recommendation of...of a close, personal friend. I assumed the references I was shown were real; that she was beyond reproach." Lee frowns, as if annoyed with himself for his own stupidity.

"You never met Ms. Drake?"

"No. We corresponded only by email, and only up until the day of my inauguration."

"The Special Counsel has yet to issue subpoenas to those who handle your business affairs. If such an account comes to light, how will you explain it?"

Lee leans back in his chair. He opens his hands wide. "Gwendolyn, I can't explain something that I have had no knowledge of. That is the essence—the *purpose* —of a blind trust."

"Did you sign the documents that opened the account?"

"No. At least not that I'm aware of."

"And if your signature is on such documents?"

Lee shakes his head. Grinning, he retorts, "Then, Gwendolyn, I guess I, or someone, will have a lot of explaining to do."

Sad but true.

Eve gives the high sign that our time is up.

I close out the interview by saying, "Mr. President, thank

you for taking the time to clarify this subject for the American public."

"You're welcome, Gwendolyn. It is my honor and privilege to do so. I am their servant and yours."

I let the pause sit until Polly calls, "Cut! We're off the air."

For a moment, the stress of my situation exhausts me. For a few seconds I close my eyes.

When I open them again, I see Lee watching, concerned.

I smile wanly and rise. "I think you did well."

He grins. "So did you—*Donna*."

Oh...shit.

Lee stands up and walks over to the crew, who are packing up the network's gear. Calling each of them by their names, he says goodbye and walks out of the room.

Polly's phone buzzes with feedback from Twitter and Facebook, where the network has been live-streaming the interview.

"Oh my God!" she exclaims. "The numbers are through the roof!"

That's great for the network. Depending on what the Special Counsel has in store for Lee, it could mean a lot of people who feel betrayed.

Polly keeps scrolling through her texts. "Everyone at the network is ecstatic at how smoothly it went."

I wonder if that means Harold too.

BY THE TIME WE FIGHT TRAFFIC BACK TO THE OFFICE, WENDELL IS only halfway through his broadcast.

He's left a note on my desk:

Care to go out for a cocktail when I get off the air? Perhaps the

Metropolitan Club? The cliché is true: membership has its privileges.
    —WE

As much as I'd like to say yes, I write below it:

Rain check tomorrow? Am exhausted by the heady experience! 'Til tomorrow!
    —GD

The key and information on Harold's penthouse condominium was in the employee welcome packet given to me by Human Resources when I signed in this morning. The condo is on M Street near Logan Circle, a mere six-block stroll from the office. And since it's a beautiful evening for a walk, why not?

My mind turns to Jack and the children. When I called yesterday, he didn't ask to be put on the phone. Today he's in New York. Still no call.

I miss him terribly.

I pick up one of the free copies of Hart Media's daily D.C. newspaper, the *Washington Tribune*. It's folded into quarters and it fits in my valise. It'll give me something to read when I get to Harold's apartment.

I'm only a block from the office when I see them: the men-in-black-cars, creating a subtle but defensive wedge on all three lanes of K Street.

Slowly this mini-motorcade pulls over next to me. Lurch gets out of the front seat passenger side of the Cadillac Escalade.

Okay, yeah, I should have expected this.

Slowly, I make my way to the car. When I reach it, Lurch asks, "Where are you headed?"

I give him the address.

He opens the back passenger door.

Yes, I get in.

And no, I'm not surprised Lee is sitting there.

He waits until we're rolling before he declares, "Really, Donna? You thought you could fool me?"

LEE LOOKS OUT THE BIG PICTURE WINDOW IN HAROLD'S penthouse, which faces west. It is twilight, the Potomac is a green glistening snake coiling its way through the city.

Lee allowed his Secret Service detail to precede us in order to secure the building. But they were commanded stay in the lobby when we took the elevator to the penthouse.

To his credit, Harold has a decent wine cellar. I open a nice Chilean pinot noir and pour us both a glassful.

Lee sniffs and sips. Then he gets serious: "Tell me what this is all about."

So, I do.

Sort of.

"You must already know that Acme provided the intel that tied Wagner Klein to the Russians, and to Hart Media."

Lee nods.

"My mission team has four agents who have infiltrated Hart Media, following through on the CIA directive to investigate links between Randall Hart and the Russians."

Lee's right brow arches. "And it was Hart that broke the news on my blind trust."

"Exactly."

"And now it's a race to see if this bullshit indiscretion ends my presidency before the CIA gets the answers it needs," he reasons.

"Lee, Acme's tech-op has already done a full cross-analysis

between your various companies and those we found in the Wagner Klein database. Thus far, it's pulled up nothing. I've asked Arnie to keep searching." I sigh. "What is it that Reynolds thinks he has on you?"

Lee flops down on the couch. "Damned if I know, Donna!"

"It's obvious the whole investigation was fast-tracked," I point out.

Lee rants, "Tim Gardiner is a weasel. He'll do anything to make a name for himself."

I snort. "If you feel that way about him, why did you hire him as your attorney general?"

"It was the party's idea."

"Oh, I see. By that you mean Edmonton," I reply.

"Another one of my mistakes," Lee admits.

"Lee, if it's any consolation, I believe you're innocent," I say softly. "And I believe what you said in the interview will resonate with the American people."

"That means a lot to me, Donna. You know that." He leans back on the couch, shutting his eyes.

For the first time, Lee looks as if the job is aging him.

I glance down at the newspaper I tossed onto the coffee table when we walked in. Lee's photo is above the fold. The paper was printed prior to the interview. Naturally the picture of him, behind his desk in the Oval Office, was taken previously.

There is another photo below the fold, accompanying a story about New York's Fashion Week. In it, Babette is shown sitting front row center at the tent show for a hot new couturier named Jered Friedland.

Lolita Jamison sits next to her. Both are laughing conspiratorially. They hold identical purses: part of the designer's swag. Also in their hands are beautiful patterned silk scarves: a pink one for Babette; turquoise for Lolita.

The photo's caption points out that the scarves "are exclusive one-of-a-kind gifts for each attendee, signed by Mr. Friedland."

Lee opens his eyes. He follows my gaze and frowns.

Time to come clean. "I saw Babette this weekend in Hilldale."

"Then Janie got to see Trisha?"

"Yes. They were ecstatic. It was fun watching them together." I hesitate then add, "Babette intimated that she was moving back. She'd set up a look-see at Hilldale Elementary."

Lee doesn't say a word, which tells me I'm the bearer of bad news.

"She also said that she may be putting Lion's Lair on the market."

Lee's laugh is mirthless. "Donna, don't you find it ironic that I have to hear this from you? And *she doesn't even like you!*"

"Gee, thanks for that," I retort sarcastically. "Frankly, it wasn't me she told. It was Mary, who was interviewing her for the school newspaper."

Now Lee is laughing even harder. "Seriously? She broke her 'scoop' with a teenage reporter?"

"I guess it is funny, when you think about it," I admit. "I'm sure she did it because she knew I was listening."

His face falls into despair. "At least it wasn't the *Washington Tribune*." He puts his head in his hands.

"Oh, Lee! I'm so so sorry!"

I pat his arm.

He buries his head on my shoulder.

We sit like that while the sun sets.

THE KNOCK ON THE DOOR WAS TOO SOFT.

So was the key in the lock.

Why else would Jack be standing here, staring down at me?

At Lee and me.

When I leap up, Lee's head jerks back.

Jack is even rougher with him: pulling him up by the collar of his shirt.

But as Jack's fist goes back, I grab it and hold on tight. "Jack, what the hell do you think you're doing?"

Jack, breathing heavily, pauses. Lee's glare dares him to follow through.

Jack knows better. He drops his hand. "You're not worth a lifetime prison term."

Lee smiles at Jack's dilemma. Considering the week Lee has had, I'll say he's earned this small victory.

I wonder how he'd feel if he knew of Babette's proposition to my husband?

Lee straightens his shirt before picking up his coat and walking out the door.

Jack, still incensed, watches until Lee shuts it behind him. Then he turns back around to me.

At which point, I back-hand him across the face.

"You accuse Lee and me when you and Babette are—"

Jack backs me up against the wall so quickly that I'm taken off-guard. His hand is against my mouth. As I struggle, he presses against me and whispers, "This place is bugged."

Oh…

Hell.

My eyes search the room. In time, I can pick out the obvious cameras.

Jack points to his earbud and mumbles, "Thanks, Arnie."

Then he lets go of me so quickly that I drop to the floor.

Stunned, I whisper, "What the…*How did you know*?"

"Charlotte mentioned it when she offered me the company's

D.C. penthouse. She said to turn it off when I walk in. I flipped the switch. To play it safe, though, I've got Arnie to hack in and block the camera and audio signals. Otherwise, all your movements—including you and Sleeping Beauty snuggling on the couch—would have ended up in Harold's homegrown porn collection. I'll call Arnie back and tell him to scrub the last couple of hours."

"Harold is some son of a bitch!" Suddenly, I'm suspicious. "Wait a minute! Why did Charlotte offer *you* the condo?"

Jack sinks beside me on the couch. "Because I've been transferred here too. She wants me covering international news from the D.C. Bureau. Makes sense, since the morning show blew up and they're revamping it anyway."

"Oh." Yes, I'm happy about that.

I'm just not happy with *him.*

"I guess she didn't know Harold offered it to me," I reason.

"Hey, if we play our cards right, they'll never find out that we're sharing the place." He puts his feet on the coffee table.

I jerk the newspaper out from under them. Pointing to the photo with Babette on it, I hiss, "As far as I'm concerned, you can sleep on a bench in Franklin Park until you come clean about your little secret with Babette."

"Now that Ryan has approved my little scheme, I can," he retorts.

"What 'little scheme'?"

"To pull security cam footage from the lobby and elevator of Trident Union Bank in Netherlands Antilles. For that matter, on the streets and from the better hotels in and around the building."

"That's a brilliant idea! How did you come up with it?"

"Frankly, Babette gave me the idea."

"What? How? And considering how badly she wants to see Lee go down, why would she?"

"Let me start with the 'how.' When Babette pulled me aside at our house, she filled me in on what I'd missed in Mary's interview: that she's divorcing Lee. But she knows he'll fight her for custody of Janie and Harrison by trying to prove that she's an unfit mother. And with the prenup she signed, she'll probably run through all of her money trying to prove Lee wrong before she sees a dime of his." Jack puts his feet back on the coffee table. "Now for the 'what' part: Babette claims that the biggest part of her request for a divorce is his philandering—*with you*."

I shake with rage. "How dare she accuse me of that!"

"Then I guess you're relieved it wasn't her who walked in just now as opposed to me."

I raise a brow. "And found us 'sleeping together'? Give me a break!"

"I am, and it's a very big one." He leans in. "She asked if it upset me too, that my wife was quote-unquote, 'the president's booty call.'"

This time my anger actually lifts me off the couch. "Why that bitch! Well, I hope you set her straight!"

He yanks me back onto the couch. "Calm down. But yes, you bet I did! I told her, 'Hell yeah, I'm heartbroken,' and it disgusts me the way you fling yourself at him whenever he comes into sight. How I want to punch him in the gut, but that if his goon squad has me put away, no one will be there to raise our poor kids while you go traipsing off into the sunset with Lover Boy."

"You didn't say that! *Did you?*"

"Nah. Donna, get real! We were only gone a few minutes, remember? Okay, maybe the part about how seeing him moon over you breaks my heart. Because that is the truth."

I sit back down. "I'm sorry it hurts you. But Jack, I swear: Lee and I are just good friends!"

"I know that, Donna. But it would drive any guy crazy to see his wife so 'friendly' with another man who so desperately wants her," he says softly. "Just as, I'm sure, it hurt you to see Babette kiss me."

He's got a point.

"I'm sorry I ever doubted you," I whisper.

Jack kisses me gently—

But then he pulls back when I graze his cheek with my lips. "Ouch! Sorry! I'm still sore where you slapped me."

"I'm sorry for that too," I admit.

"You'll be even sorrier when you hear the 'who' part."

"Don't leave me in suspense!"

"I was tipped off that she was being less than sincere when she then added, 'In fact, I think he was also having an affair with his fund manager, Helen Drake.'"

"Ha! As if!" I exclaim.

"My thought exactly," Jack declares coolly. "He's so smitten with you that he never looks at other women."

I blush because I was thinking exactly that.

"All of that brought me to the same conclusion you've already drawn: she's doing her best to ruin Lee."

"Finally!" I yell. Looking skyward, I whisper, "Thank you, God!"

Jack scowls. "You're being overdramatic. To make a long story short, I agreed to play along. You know, do what I can to get the goods on all the whorish philandering going on."

Sarcastically, I ask, "And finding Lee and I curled up in the couch helps you prove it? Let me guess. You took a photo of us before you almost killed Lee."

"Even better, trust me." He grins supremely. "It got me thinking. She'd made her point by smearing you, and I know that's a bunch of hooey. So, why add the mysterious Helen

Drake to the mix? Then it hit me: she wants to make sure Lee falls hard."

"Of course she would. She's Quorum," I reply. "Do you believe me now?"

"Yes, Donna, I do. And now Acme has the proof to back up your claim. You see, after I got out of the shower, I called Ryan and asked that he get clearance to pull the Netherlands Antilles security cam footage. Arnie and I spent all day Sunday and Monday looking through it until we found Helen Drake."

My heart leaps in my chest. Will this woman be Lee's salvation or his downfall?

Jack opens the cell phone and scrolls to a video. It's not the best picture. It's too grainy and in black and white. Still, I can clearly see a woman walking through a lobby and into an elevator.

I'd know that saunter anywhere. It's Babette.

"Wow," I whisper.

"Yeah. Wow. And the elevator tracking shows that she got off at the same floor as the bank."

"So, she's controlling the account!" I sigh. "But we still have to figure out the account's bank number, and what name it's under."

"You should warn Lee," Jack says.

"I will." As much as I hate being the bearer of bad news, the sooner he hears this, the sooner he can retaliate before she does even more harm.

Suddenly, we hear the rattle of keys in the front door lock.

Stealthily, Jack and I tiptoe to the door.

From the peephole, I see Harold.

A woman stands behind him. She wears a beautiful new scarf.

A collector's item.

The woman is Lolita.

"I'll answer it," I mouth to Jack. "I know just what to say."

He nods then ducks behind the door.

I swing open the door before Harold can do it. He glances up, surprised. On the other hand, Lolita turns around quickly and walks down the hall so that I can't see her face.

"Mr. Hart! What...what are you doing here?" I frown.

"Oh! Ms. Durant! I'd forgotten..."

"What? That my new contract gives me use of this apartment for the next five years?" Smugly, I put my hands on my hips. "I don't remember anything in the fine print that said I must share it with you and..." I glance down the hall. "Is that *Mrs.* Hart? Or are you presumptuous enough to think I'd consider some sort of *ménage-a-trois*?"

Lolita is now running to the elevator.

Harold scowls at me. "My mistake. I'll see you at the office tomorrow." He makes it sound like a threat.

Not if I see you first.

I slam the door. "Sheesh! This is beginning to seem like an old Marx Brothers movie. I wonder who will walk in next?"

Jack is laughing. "So that's why Lolita quit! All Charlotte said was that she'd gotten a better offer."

"But...I thought you said she and Bev were fired!"

"Ironically, Lolita turned in her notice before Charlotte called her. She said she'd decided to cash in and leave the country for, as she put it, 'some desert island that can't get a TV signal.'"

"Ha! A better offer from that whore dog Harold? Well, I guess anything is possible!"

"After the stunt he pulled with you, I'd say they deserve each other."

"And sometimes I feel as if I don't deserve you. Like now." I pull Jack in for a hug. "I'm sorry, Jack, for doubting your ability to see through Babette."

He chuckles. "I'm sure you'll think of a way to make it up to me."

"I already have."

All sex with Jack is great, but make-up sex is the most fun of all.

Even in a twin bed.

14

Network

In television parlance, a network is a corporation that provides news and entertainment programming to stations that are either affiliated or owned and operated by it.

"Network" is also the title of a classic satirical film. Released in 1976, it starred Peter Finch. The plot revolves around a newscaster named Howard Beale whose job was on the line for poor ratings. Because he feels he has nothing to lose, he quits reading the teleprompter and announces he will take his life during the next day's broadcast.

Needless to say, the ratings soar.

Talk about prescient! Network news is still ratings-driven. Sadly, what drives it are still horrible tragedies.

Seriously, there is nothing funny about that.

JACK AND I LEAVE THE PENTHOUSE SEPARATELY, AND THROUGH different entrances.

We arrive at the Hart News Bureau separately, as well.

When I walk to my cubicle, Polly stops me. "Harold Hart is here! He asked to see you the moment you got in."

This ought to be interesting. Nonchalantly, I say "Thank you, Polly. Please tell him I'll be there in a moment, after I get off the telephone with the president."

It's the best way to make Harold cool his heels. His father made it clear to me that I'm not to serve as Harold's puppet. Randall also made it clear to the both of us that he'd prefer the truth from Lee rather than Harold's slant on Lee's presidency.

Hearing this, Polly's eyes widen. She nods fervently as she takes off down the hall again.

To document the call, I put it through the Hart News Bureau switchboard. Upon hearing my name, Eve puts me on hold for a moment before patching me through.

"Ms. Durant, how may I help you?" Lee's words are formal, but his tone is anything but.

"I hope you'll agree to accommodating me with a second interview. This time it will run in print, so no camera crew needed." This is my way of telling him that I'll be coming alone.

"Sure, okay. Can you be here in, say, an hour?"

"Of course. And thank you, Mr. President."

Now, to see what Harold wants. I made it clear that a threesome is out, so at least it won't be that.

WHEN I ENTER, HAROLD COMES OUT FROM BEHIND HIS DESK. HE'S not smiling. "Well, well, if it isn't the president's sympathizer-in-chief!"

I arch a brow. "Pardon?"

He tosses down a cheat sheet.

Just glancing at it, I recognize it because it's a replica of the one I was to have used in the interview.

I shrug. "I thought my questions were spot on."

"You don't understand your function here, lady!" He picks up my producer's identical copies of the prepared cards for the interview and waves it in my face. "You're supposed to stick to the script!"

"If you don't like my process, fire me."

He reels back from the taunt. He knows he can't break with his father's wishes. His lips curl into a snarl. "You must give great head."

"If I do, you'll never know it." I turn to leave.

The next thing I know he's got me pinned to the wall.

His hand goes between my legs. As it inches up my thigh, he whispers, "I guessed right, didn't I? Chiffray liked what he saw. It's why you're going over there now."

When my knee hits his groin, he doubles over.

I'm almost at the door when he gasps out, "Hey, if you want to, take him back to your place."

"I'm a journalist, not a porn star. By the way, sleeping in strange lands run by dictators has taught me one lesson: someone is always looking to own you. Usually via video surveillance. So, yes, Harold, I found your security cameras." As his face falls, I snicker. "Shall I warn your father that his little boy may have been naughtier than he thought?"

That shuts Harold up.

He waits until I've shut the door before throwing a chair against it.

Conversations stop. Heads raise from the cubicles.

At least, I know our noisy exchange won't make it into any Hart newspaper headline.

$\sim$

Eve shows me into the office and shuts the door behind me.

Lee comes out from behind his desk to greet me. He does so formally with a handshake.

I pull him in for a hug.

When, finally, we disentangle, he says, "I guess you don't have good news."

"I don't," I confess. "We should sit down."

Silently we watch the video from Trident Union's bank lobby. Lee's face falls in despair when he sees the woman. Even with dark glasses and a broad, brimmed hat, there is no mistaking Babette's walk: runway-worthy with a touch more attitude.

The video cuts to the elevator feeds, both in her rides up and down to Trident's floor.

"If she opened an account, why is it tied to me?"

"Acme can't figure that out. It's not in either of your names, and it's not being run through any of your subsidiaries." I shake my head, helplessly. "Still, somehow Reynolds has made the connection. Acme won't give up until it does too. In the meantime, you have to watch your back. She's setting you up to take a really big fall, Lee. She wants it all. And Edmonton and Congress are primed to let it happen."

Lee hangs his head. "I see that now."

"That's all I could have hoped for; that you'll do the right thing."

He doesn't answer. He won't even raise his head.

I leave him like that.

I'M BACK IN THE HART MEDIA TOWN CAR WHEN MY PRIVATE CELL phone rings. The call is from Trisha.

The privacy glass between the driver and me is up, but still I whisper, "Hello, sweetie!"

"Mom...I had to call you because...I...I just don't know what to do."

"I'm listening, Trisha. Always."

She takes a deep breath. "Janie just called. She's in trouble with her mom and dad because of a selfie she took with Madison when she went on her school tour."

"Why would that be a problem?" I ask.

"Madison and she were doing that thing! You know, with their hands? The gangster signs. I guess it was for MS 13, whatever that is."

I stifle a groan.

"It went viral! In fact, it got more hits than Mary's interview! And way more than her mother at Fashion Week."

I'm sure that's the real reason Babette is angry with her daughter.

Babette shouldn't have wed Lee. She should have married a Kardashian.

"Anyway, Madison dumped Janie. She told her she didn't want to be friends with someone whose father is 'going to spend all day and all night in a ghetto penthouse.' Mom, what does that mean?"

"It means your ex-friend, Madison, has been boning up on her prison slang." If this is any indication of her at ten, I think she'll soon have a reason to put it to good use.

"So...it's true? Mr. Chiffray may be going to prison?"

"As you know from your studies, the U.S. Constitution asserts that we are all innocent until proven guilty," I remind her.

"Janie called because she wants to be friends again...but I don't know."

"I can't make that decision for you. It's got to come from your heart. But keep this in mind. Janie has been your friend for five years. Your relationship has been tested by distance and time: half of your very young life. Janie is a lonely person who hurt her nearest and dearest friend. She had the maturity to say she's sorry."

"She called because she doesn't have any other friends. People either suck up to her because of who she is, or they make fun of her without really knowing her," Trisha counters. "Why do I always have to be the nice one?"

That's a great question.

I only have one answer: "Because it's the right thing to do."

"I don't know, Mom..." Grief causes her words to drop down to a whisper. "I think it's time that someone else be nice to me first."

Janie has never been humbled. Like her mother, she has always gotten her way. And because of this, it's more than likely that Trisha will lose Janie's friendship if she doesn't accept her friend's olive branch.

But that's okay.

Trisha is right. She is long overdue for a friendship that merits loyalty and trust.

"Darling, it is solely your decision to make."

My daughter hangs up with a sigh.

"Gwendolyn, have you met our newest correspondent?" Wendell is standing beside 'Grant.'

I tilt my head, as if trying to remember where I may have

seen him. "Ah, yes! In the New York office. Congratulations on your hire. Grant, isn't it?"

Jack grins as he shakes my hand. "And you're Gwendolyn, I know. I suppose the whole world does after your interview with the president."

"Grant has just returned with a very important get himself," Wendell informs me. "Vice President Edmonton spoke on the record regarding the Special Counsel's investigation of President Chiffray."

"With that in mind, I should join Arvin in his editing bay. I'm sure he's ready to show me the final edit before we upload it for tonight's broadcast." Jack waves as he starts off.

Wendell looks at his watch and grumbles, "Oh bother, I'm late for a production meeting. I shall see you tonight, though, eh?"

"The Metropolitan club, eight-fifteen. I wouldn't miss it," I assure him.

"Well, then, ta-ta until the cocktail hour." He heads off in the opposite direction from Jack.

And a good thing, too, since Jack has circled back to me. In a louder than normal voice, he says, "Ms. Durant—Gwendolyn—I could use your ear on my interview."

I feign curiosity. "How so, Grant?"

"The vice president made some curious statements that seemed less than supportive of the president than one would imagine. If you wouldn't mind giving a clean eye to my supporting copy so I can add some analysis to my soundbites, I would truly appreciate it."

"Of course. Any way I can help." I walk with him down the hall to the editing bay Abu has already reserved.

"YIKES! TALK ABOUT A SLAM JOB." DISMAYED, I SHAKE MY HEAD at 'Grant's' Edmonton interview. "The only soundbites he gave you are mostly backhanded compliments toward Lee."

Abu nods. "First, he declares Lee is innocent of all charges, then he backtracks and says Lee's interview might have painted him into an ugly corner."

"A corner in which Edmonton comes out the victor," Jack points out. "Edmonton's endgame is to run against Lee in the next election. That is, if Lee isn't impeached first."

"His biggest crime is covering up for his wife," I retort.

"No, Donna. His biggest crime was not putting his country before everything—*including* her."

Jack is right.

Suddenly, Abu does a double take at something he sees on the TV monitor playing silently in the corner of the bay. Awed, he shouts, "Hey! Look there!"

Our eyes follow his.

Jeanette is on the screen, standing beside the banks of the Potomac River. It's pouring rain, so she's reporting under an umbrella.

Over her shoulder, viewers can see a Bethesda CSI team looking over the covered body.

The copy scrolling at the bottom of the screen reads:

DEAD WOMAN'S BODY IS THOUGHT TO BE PRESIDENT'S MISSING FUND MANAGER

"*HELEN DRAKE?*" JACK AND I SAY IN UNISON.

Abu turns up the sound.

"...and the body was found this afternoon by a man who

walks his dog on this path at least twice a day," Jeanette proclaims into her handheld microphone.

The camera makes a quick cut to the man—mid-forties and balding—who pats his dog, a Labrador retriever.

"Eddie here started going wild! He almost dragged me into the river with him." The man shakes his head as though in shock. "At first I thought it was an old log. But then I saw her...her *foot*." He wipes away a tear. "The rest of her was pretty much a mess."

The camera cuts back to Jeanette. "Although it has not yet been officially confirmed, because of items found floating upstream from the body, the victim is believed to be Helen Taylor Drake. She was a person of interest wanted in the Justice Department's Special Counsel investigation of President Lee Chiffray's dealing with a German law firm known for laundering its client's funds in offshore bank accounts."

The camera zooms in on the crime scene. "To hinder her identification, the tips of the victim's fingers have been clipped off and her eyes were gouged out. However, a purse was found two miles upriver. Experts on the river's currents say that it is possible it might belong to the victim."

The camera cuts to another closeup: this time of a CSI investigator bagging the purse.

"All evidence must be examined by the county's forensic lab before there is a confirmation of the victim's identification. However, one of the officers on the scene has already confirmed that a cell phone and wallet bearing Ms. Drake's name was discovered in a secret pocket inside the purse."

The camera goes back to Jeanette.

"If indeed the victim is Ms. Drake, our viewers will know soon. The lead investigators say they'll be prepared to make an official statement later tonight. " Jeanette pauses before adding, "Back to you, Wendell."

Jack and I stare at each other. "How could that be?" I ask.

"Maybe it wasn't Babette in the tape," Jack reasons. "We'll know more as soon as Ryan gets ahold of the coroner's report." He stretches in his chair. "Hey, where do you want to go for dinner?"

"Sorry, you're on your own tonight," I announced grandly. "I already have a date. In fact, I'm going home now, to change into something more appropriate. And since I'm headed out anyway, I can take any cheat sheets you scrounged up and upload them to Emma from the condo."

Jack's brows rise. "If your bestie needs more consoling, I hope you're not implying a negligee under a designer raincoat."

I tweak his nose. "No, Wendell and I are going out for a drink when he gets off the air. He's a member of the Metropolitan Club. And by the way, that's only a look I save for you, because *you* are my bestie." I kiss Jack's cheek.

"Ah, sweet love," Abu grumbles.

"Is that your way of telling me that you're free to grab a beer after we get done with the Veep's hatchet job?" Jack asks.

Abu snickers. "You'll have to do better than that. Scotch. Neat."

"Damn! So much for those rumors about you being a cheap date," Jack retorts.

"Hey, it could be worse. Dominic could have been here instead," Abu reminds him.

Jack slaps his head.

On that note, I'm out of there.

I'M ABOUT TO STEP INTO THE ELEVATOR WHEN POLLY RUSHES UP.

"Gwendolyn! I'm so glad I caught you. Mr. Hart would like to see you."

Damn it! What does Harold want now?

"I'm sorry but please tell him I am predisposed. Ta-ta!"

I turn to leave.

Polly grabs hold of my arm. She looks if she's about to cry. After glancing around, she hisses, "Gwendolyn, please! I cannot go in there and tell Mr. Hart that you're...you're *predisposed*. He'll beat me with his cane!"

"Oh, *that* Mr. Hart!" Damn it! He's the one Hart I can't dodge. "You're right. We mustn't encourage public floggings in the newsroom! That won't do at all."

She's practically running to the elevator, which will whisk us up to the top floor of the Hart Media Tower.

My stride is a little more dignified, but not by much.

UNLIKE HIS SON, RANDALL HART IS STRAIGHT TO THE POINT. "Gwendolyn, have a seat."

No howdy-do. No please. *Hmm.*

Because Randall sits behind a massive desk, it makes him look all the smaller. I take a seat in one of the two chairs directly across from it.

"Your interview was our most-watched special news report in over a decade," he says.

I smile politely. "I'm happy to hear that."

"However, I am somewhat disappointed that you went off-point on some very specific questions for the president. May I ask why you decided to do so?"

"Yes, of course." *As soon as I can make up a plausible excuse.*

A minute ticks by.

"I'm waiting," he says.

His voice is calm. But his eyes can't shield his anger.

I sigh. "Sir, I was under the impression that the questions came from Mr. Harold Hart as opposed to you. And considering your very firm command that he allow me to work in peace, I thought it best to ignore his recommended questions and honor your directive: that I seek the truth while I have a glaring spotlight on the president."

He says nothing. Instead, he watches me. Is he waiting for me to betray my excuse with shifty eyes or quivering lips? If so, he'll be disappointed. As it is, I feel as if I've betrayed Lee and the office of the president with the interview's opening remarks.

If they were coded, I'll live with the guilt that I betrayed my country. I imagine every Hart Media reporter who has been duped into reading the cheat sheets would feel the same way.

So, yes, I hold my head high and say no more.

Finally, Randall growls, "You may go."

Because I'm still holding his gaze, I see the slight change in his demeanor. It's as if his skin has grown a bit paler and the light has gone out of his eyes.

But as I rise, he says, "Just one more thing. Did you happen to see Harold when he was here this morning?"

I nod. "Unfortunately, yes."

"I take that to mean he accosted you again."

"Yes, sir."

He shudders. "I hope I can count on your discretion."

I nod.

He turns his chair to face the window.

I have been dismissed.

15

Catch and Kill

Some tabloid magazines pay for interviews.

Some pay to kill interviews.

The latter practice is known as "catch and kill."

This occurs when an interview subject accepts a mutually agreed-upon compensation for the exclusive rights to any and all specific details of his or her story without any guarantee that the story will ever make it into print or broadcast.

It never does, for good reason:

Someone wants the story killed.

"Catch and kill" is a term that could easily describe the extermination business as well. (Not for bugs, silly! For a hitwoman!)

The only differences:

1: It would be the assassin, not the victim, who gets paid; and

2: An untold story is never missed. However, someone always misses a murder victim.

I work as quickly as I can to take photos of the cheat sheets and upload them to Emma's cloud.

When I complete the task, I only have an hour left to get dressed. Even via taxi, it will take at least fifteen minutes to get to the Metropolitan Club, so I've got to get going. I choose a gray cocktail sheath embellished with soft blue soutache appliqués: simple, yet elegant.

I'm about to put the cheat sheets in my valise when it occurs to me that too many others, all named Hart, have a key to this apartment, So I slip the intel back into my purse. It doesn't go with my dress, but it will have to do.

I arrive fashionably: that is to say, five minutes late. Wendell is already in the lobby. The gold marbled walls cast a warm tone to its Federal-era furnishings. The staircase to the second floor is bound in a thick berry-hued carpet. An American flag stands to the left of it.

Wendell beams when he sees me. "You look divine!" He points to the staircase "Shall we?"

I laugh. "We shall."

He may be in his early seventies, but he keeps pace with my climb up the staircase.

We walk through a large arched doorway into one of the club's many libraries. Deep floor-to-ceiling bookcases flank its walls. The bright, white, coved ceiling softens the light emanating from the room's numerous lamps into an intimate glow. Comfortable blue armchairs, paired off, are scattered about the large room.

Wendell has reserved a small alcove. It is private enough that our conversation won't be overheard, but close enough to watch the meanderings of the other members.

After a waiter takes our drink orders, we make polite conversation about the top news of the day: The discovery of Helen Drake's corpse.

"I feel this will reflect poorly on Mr. Chiffray," Wendell opines.

"Isn't that the point, especially when tried in the court of public opinion? If he's innocent, either of the tax fraud or Ms. Drake's murder, the forensic analysis will discover it."

"You like him, don't you?" He watches me carefully as I answer.

"I don't know him well enough to like him," I demur. "I've only met him once. But I felt he was forthright in his interview."

"Your questions were quite candid with him."

"I was just following my damned little cheat sheet."

He chuckles at my response. I'm about to ask him why when my cell phone buzzes softly. As I pull it out of my purse, Wendell reaches for my hand. "I'm sorry dear, but all calls must be taken in the conversation lounge downstairs. Club rules."

I glance down at the Caller ID:

DUMBLEDORE

A.K.A. Arnie. He wouldn't call unless it were very important.

"Will you excuse me? It's…a source."

He nods.

I try to slow my pace to the stairwell, but at the same time I don't want to lose Arnie's call.

When I reach the lobby, my frantic look and the phone in

my hand is all the shorthand the club concierge needs. He points me to a door marked CORRESPONDENCE LOUNGE.

I've just clicked onto the call when Arnie crows, "I'm a genius!"

I pull the phone away from my ear.

Others around me, all murmuring *sotto voce*, glare at me.

When I put the phone back near my face, I hiss, "Prove it. *Quietly.*"

"Okay, so listen! The offshore bank account linked to Lee is tied to an entity called JBC Holdings."

"How do you know?"

"Because it's the only account in Wagner Klein's database that isn't under GWI's umbrella corporation or affiliated with another owner. Not only that, it was the only account accessed on the same day and time Helen Drake appeared in the Trident Union Bank building. So, *BINGO!*"

This time I get shushed by some guy talking to "the Coast" in a voice almost as loud as Arnie's.

I shush him back.

"Great work," I whisper. "Call Jack with the news. Tell him I'll be back in an hour."

I feel it's an appropriate amount of time to spend with Wendell before I give him the bum's rush.

As quickly as possible I head back upstairs.

WENDELL IS READING SOMETHING AS HE SIPS HIS DRINK.

It's a Hart Media cheat sheet.

"Shame on you for taking that out of the office," I tease him. "But I won't tell on you. I think it's a silly rule anyway." I sit down. "Are you cribbing for tomorrow's broadcast?"

"Not at all. In fact, this isn't even mine." He allows me to read the assigned reporter's name on it:

GRANT LARKIN

I feel my face heat up.

He points to my now open purse, where I stuffed the rest of the cheat sheets.

"CIA or GRU?" he asks.

Nervously, I retort, "Why would you think I'm either?"

Before I can I reach for the purse, he hands it to me. "I took the liberty of relieving you of your gun."

Now I'm panicking. "And you are?"

"Can't you guess?"

I say what I'm hoping: "MI6?"

He nods.

"I'll need verification," I say.

He pulls out an ID. As I peruse it, I say, "I'll have my boss check it out." I sigh. "Oh bother! That means another damn trek downstairs…"

"Ryan Clancy? No need to do so, Ms. Craig. We're old friends. A pleasure to meet you. Your reputation precedes you." He holds out his hand. "May I call you Donna?"

I laugh as I shake it.

"I must admit I was somewhat wary of you from the get-go," he adds.

"Oh? And why is that?"

"Despite your spot on Mancunian brogue, you were tripped up by its regional slang." He winks broadly. "For example, when I invited you to 'dinner,' you suggested lunch instead. In Manchester, they are one and the same."

I wince. "Ha! I'll have to remember that. Still, better to be burned by MI6 than Moscow."

"Frankly, I didn't ID you until Acme's Regent's Park operation," Wendell concedes.

"Do tell!" *Wait until Jack hears this!*

"Because of the U.K.'s recent altercations with Russia, MI6 has also been investigating Hart Media's ties with the Kremlin. Charlotte's fiancé, Mikhail, set off all sorts of bells and whistles. Mikhail was always shadowed by one of our operatives. First Dominic Fleming popped up to comfort the grieving fiancée. Then, when Acme requested preferential treatment on Mikhail's autopsy, we realized Acme had been contracted to do the same for the CIA. Langley confirmed it." He grins. "I must say, I don't mind taking credit for Dominic's innate talents. He was one of the best honeytraps to come out of my class at Fort Monkton."

"Don't let him know that. His head is big enough as it is." I ease back in my chair. "Lucky you, to be able to hide in plain sight. From now on, I'll always assume that any foreign correspondent I meet is also a spook."

"I do," Wendell assures me. He leans forward. "Since we're on the same team, perhaps we should share leads?"

I tap my glass to his. "The more the merrier."

By the time Wendell and I get back to the condo, Jack is already there with Abu. Ryan has confirmed that his "old buddy, Wendell," is in fact a Cousin, which is the nickname MI6 and the CIA share.

And Wendell confirms that MI6 has already broken Hart's cheat sheet cipher.

"That news deserves one of the best bottles of champagne from Harold and Charlotte's wine cellar," Jack declares.

"I'd suggest keeping your wits about you," Wendell replies.

"Yesterday, I intercepted the office boy who delivers the cheat sheets to the newsroom. He divulged that they come via courier every evening. The sender's name is Cain N. Able."

"An interesting name," I say.

"And a rather obvious alias, as there is no one by that name within the organization," he says dryly. "Ironically, tonight, our target is to rendezvous with Mr. Able's GRU extradition handler."

"Do you have a location?" Abu asks.

"In a manner of speaking. What was clear is that the meeting takes place at midnight."

"What's the fuzzy part?" I ask.

"The location given was simply 'Lincoln.' It either refers to the Lincoln Theater or the Lincoln Memorial."

I frown. "They're three miles apart."

"I suggest we split up," Jack replies. "Wendell, why don't you and Abu take the theater? It's a dark night there, so whoever shows up is our target. Donna and I will cover the memorial."

Abu looks at his watch. "To have an element of surprise, we should take off now."

"Head out with Wendell," I say to Abu. "I still need to get out of this dress and heels."

"You're allowed another rain check on the club," Wendell promises with a wink.

It's Randall.

I know this because, like me, he's at the Memorial much earlier than the designated time. I would not have allowed him to see me except that the open plaza provides very little cover, and I wasn't expecting him to be here so soon.

He stands as opposed to sits. It must be a difficult endeavor because he is stooped over his ever-present cane.

He wears a long cashmere wool coat. A heavy scarf is wrapped around his neck and his hands are sheathed in gloves. A wool newsboy cap is on his head. Still, his ears are red from the cold that, even on a mild spring night, penetrates the thin skin of a man entering his ninth decade.

When he spots me, he waves as if he's been expecting me all along.

Does he know his handler? If not, does he assume it's me?

Well then, one of us is going to be sorely disappointed.

HE GREETS ME WITH A NOD. "I'M SURPRISED IT'S YOU."

"It's not," I inform him. "I'm sorry, Randall, but you're under arrest. The CIA has been aware for some time that Hart Media is passing intel on behalf of our nation's enemies, and we know how this is being done. It's how I knew you'd be meeting your handler here, tonight."

A gun springs from the wolf's head handle of his cane. It's small, but no doubt accurate and deadly too.

He holds it steady enough that, yes, I'm concerned.

"Please, raise your hands."

He pats me down and finds the Sig Sauer P229 in my appendix holster.

But he misses the Springfield XDE strapped to my ankle.

Still, I do as I am told, for now, anyway.

Jack may be hearing and seeing what I do, but he's far enough away to wait and watch because capturing Randall's handler, too, would be a feather in Acme's cap. Also, Arnie is watching via a ComSat feed.

"We'll wait together." Randall points to the steps in front of the mammoth statue of our sixteenth president. "Please, have a seat."

"Tell me about yourself," he insists. "Do you have a name other than Gwendolyn?"

He is not crass enough to put the gun to my head, but I won't test his aim with any sudden moves.

"Once a reporter, always a reporter, eh, Randall?"

He shrugs. "It's a hard habit to break."

"I'm up for a game of Twenty Questions. But you go first. Are you also Quorum?"

He laughs. "It's now a smaller but even more elite group, but yes. And now your name."

"Donna Craig."

"Ah! Finally we meet!" He squints and leans in for a closer look at my face. "The change was enough to fool our facial recognition scanner. Bravo to Acme on that!"

"My turn. Why is Babette selling Lee down the river?"

Randall chuckles. "Without his political power, she has no use for him. It's time she move on." He rests heavier on the stick of his cane, but his gun doesn't waver. "That is thanks to you and your colleagues, Mrs. Craig. When Acme exposed the connection between Trident's clients, Russia and Hart, it led to the revelation of Chiffray's connection to the bank too."

"You mean Babette's connection," I correct him. "Babette passed herself off as Helen Drake."

Randall's silence speaks volumes.

The memory of the body on the embankment suddenly comes to me. Then, like a bolt of lightning, I see the connection in my mind's eye:

The Jered Friedland pocketbook.

Lolita had an identical one.

"You killed Lolita," I declare.

"Yes." As he smiles, his skin stretches thin over his face creating the illusion of a living skull.

He is proud of his admission. I imagine he's thinking, *The old boy still has it in him…*

I hear something that Randall does not: footsteps.

Is it Jack, or is it the Russian handler?

No.

"But Harold doesn't know, does he?" I ask. "He thinks she left him. And you don't want Harold to know, either—about her murder, or about that part of Hart's business dealings. You're his father, but you never wanted him to take the fall for your treasonous acts."

Randall frowns. "Not to worry, dear. As always, Harold will go down his own clueless path for as long as he's alive."

"Maybe no," I counter. "Things are heating up, Randall. Isn't that why you reached out to the GRU and requested asylum after all these years?"

"Sadly, yes." He sighs heavily. "The weather is always so damnably miserable in Moscow! Still, there I'll die a hero."

I snort. "I guess you're proud of yourself for reigniting a worldwide nuclear arms build-up."

"You see? That is the advantage of a dictatorship!" he exclaims. "One person sets the course for the whole world's destiny! Everyone else picks up an oar and rows." He shakes his head in resignation. "But I won't see it in my lifetime."

"I don't plan on seeing it in mine, either," I declare.

"But you will, Mrs. Craig! Because, in the geo-political chess game between our two nations, democracy wins only when another dictator falls from his or her perch of power." Randall enjoys rhapsodizing poetically on something he has no choice but to believe. "Russia's way of cheating at the game is to whip up tribal or social conflicts. Pawns are collected when fascism replaces humanity; when denial and apathy smother common sense. My son and my daughter may suck at the teat of anarchy, but they don't realize how close they are to its source. They do know, however, which side their artisan bread is buttered. It's why they only do as I tell them."

"Say that to their faces," I dare him.

He laughs. "I have, in so many words. At least, to Harold. He is inanely weak. And like most weak men, he thinks his power—*the power I bestowed on him*—makes him virile." He shakes his head in disgust. "Lolita was just one more complication. Still, in the end, she served her purpose. She kept him entertained." He chuckles. "And me as well."

I feign horror. "You have no qualms taking what belongs to your son?"

Randall shrugs. "Tit for tat. He's taken enough from me over the years." He raises the gun. "So sorry, my dear, but one of us will not be attending my bon voyage."

He raises the gun—

Then his head explodes.

I duck, but I'm still spattered with his blood, brains, and skull shards.

THE FOOTSTEPS WEREN'T JACK'S BUT HAROLD'S, WHO STOOD JUST out of his father's peripheral vision. Perhaps if Randall's ears had been keener he might have heard Harold approaching us.

Just another way in which getting old is a bitch.

Harold is undone by the sight of his damage. "I...I loved her," he sobs, "and *he killed her!*"

I now realize that what he mourns isn't whom he feared but what he lost.

"Did you know that he cut off her fingers and her face so that no one would know it was her?" he asks.

"I don't understand. Why would you think her disappearance would have anything to do with your father?"

"Don't you understand? He'd done it before! He paid them off to go away! It's why I...*why I try so hard not to fall in love with them!* He always told me, 'Just have sex with them, Sonny! They're all whores! They're only after your money. Look at you! It's not your looks..."

He stares down at the gun.

Then he raises it.

Randall pocketed the Sig Sauer, so I only have a split-second to decide if it's dark enough that Harold might miss me if I duck and go for the XDE—

But I'm too late. Harold puts the gun to his temple and pulls the trigger.

Damn. What a night.

I drop to the ground, exhausted, lying flat on the cold marble walkway behind the monument.

Traffic noises tickle my ears: the swish of cars, freed of mid-day traffic congestion.

Again, I hear footsteps.

But then the person stops, having likely spotted the two bodies.

But by the time I leap up and follow, the person is running away.

I call out, "Jack! The handler took off between the trees! Do you see him?"

"On it!" I hear his breathing get heavier. I'm sure mine sounds the same to him.

Jack's breath gets louder.

Then I hear a gunshot.

Then another one…

Frantically, I whisper, "Jack? *JACK!*"

"I'm fine," he assures me. "The suspect is headed toward Constitution Avenue."

I run that way too—

And right into Jack.

We hear a door slam shut. A car veers off without lights.

Jack takes a shot.

"Too far away, damn it!" he growls.

"Arnie! Can you track the vehicle?" I ask.

"On it!" Arnie exclaims.

Jack and I don't hear back from Arnie until we get to our car. "Sorry guys. From Constitution, I lost the car when it jumped into the I-66 spaghetti bowl."

Jack shouts, "Did you get the make of the car or the license plate?"

"No, sorry," Arnie admits. "I've alerted the police about Randall and Harold."

A moment later we hear sirens coming our way.

Dominic should be prepared that Charlotte is going to need a shoulder to cry on.

TODAY, JUST TWO DAYS AFTER THE EVENT, CHARLOTTE IS overseeing a joint memorial for Randall and Harold.

It is taking place at Randall Hart's stately thirty-three-room mansion sitting on three verdant acres of prime McLean, Virginia real estate. The size of its grounds, along with an ornate twelve-foot wrought iron fence, roving Dobermans, and battalion of security guards, makes it almost as secure as Fort Knox.

The crowd of five hundred mourners is not only large but also varied. Besides the corporation's board members, executive staff, featured newscasters, and senior correspondents, a plethora of politicians and foreign dignitaries have come to pay their respects.

Charlotte's hastiness in coordinating the event has allowed her to muzzle all news about the true cause of death—murder and suicide—until after her father and brother are laid to rest.

By now, the CIA has informed her about her father's treason. It cut a deal with her: when she is eventually contacted by Randall's Russian handlers and blackmailed into continuing his endeavors, she is to pass along the covert messages. Should some eager reporter or inside whistleblower come across the scheme, Charlotte, along with Hart Media's unwitting newscasters and talking heads, will be indemnified against prosecution.

In fact, CIA operatives are here now, ID'ing and observing the mourners.

In the days prior to the memorial, Charlotte has rallied the sympathy of Hart Media's board in order to withstand any attempts of a company buyout.

By now, Abu, Arnie, Jack, and I have turned in our resignations. She also knows our true roles within the events. Surprisingly, she is grateful to us.

She makes this clear to Jack and me as we walk over to express our condolences. "I may have loved my father, but I never liked him," she admits. "How could I? Whereas I did everything I could to win his love, Harold gave up trying to please him. And yet, he disdained us equally." She wipes away a tear. "We were never allowed to see beyond the façade. At least, now I know why."

"You've already made the right decision to right his wrongs," I say.

"I hope so. I'll start by being the opposite of my father. In fact, I'll do my best to model myself after Katharine Graham." Charlotte shrugs. "I like her motto: 'If we had failed to pursue the facts as far as they led, we would have denied the public any knowledge of an unprecedented scheme of political surveillance and sabotage.'"

"She was right," I concede. "A story is only as good as the facts revealed."

Charlotte chuckles. "May I quote you, Donna Craig?"

I nod. "Better yet, put it under your byline. Something tells me that in the next decade you'll be one of the most quotable women in journalism."

"It won't be easy. It starts with cleaning house, top to bottom." She frowns. "Personally, that begins with ending my relationship with Dominic."

Her eyes scan the crowd of mourners, finally honing in on Dominic. He's chatting up the new *Good Morning Hartland!* cohosts—identical twins whose resemblances are only skin deep. The idea to hire these B-rated actresses was smart. One plays it sharp, witty and straight, while the other plays the show's ditz. The program achieves its mandate: great morning eye candy, but with none of their predecessors' petty jealousies and infighting.

Jack winces. "Dominic will be heartbroken, to say the least."

Charlotte snickers. "Oh, somehow I doubt that. He sweats anytime I bring up the 'm' word."

I sigh. "Ah yes! *Marriage.*"

"No, I mean *money.* Seriously, what kind of man makes the woman in his life pay for everything?" She glances skyward as if the clouds above hold the answer to her question. "Don't get me wrong. The sex is sublime! But one has to jump out of bed sometime, right?"

With a straight face, Jack replies, "He'll be heartbroken."

"I'm breaking the news to him this evening. He's stopping by for some 'mourning sex.' After Mikhail, I know he's good for *that*, at the very least." She smiles at the memory. "Dominic may be hung like a horse, but he's still a cheap son of a bitch! Mr. Craig, do me a favor. If he needs a shoulder to cry on, be there for him, okay?"

Jack dares not say anything. From the look on his face, he may burst out laughing.

"Every politician in Washington is here." She grimaces. "If you'll excuse me, I must comfort those most bereft over my father's passing and the end of his donations to their campaigns." When satisfied that the grimace on her lips passes as a smile, Charlotte waves, exclaiming, "Ah! Governor Jessup! Senator Gannell! Thank you for your very kind condolence cards…"

As we walk away, Jack nods toward the terrace. "The Chiffrays are here. Should we stop and pay our respects?"

I shake my head. "Let's wait. The reception starts in a few minutes."

By then, the Chiffrays will have left. An appearance means too many people asking too many questions.

We both know it.

EVEN A SIXTEEN-BEDROOM HOME HAS ONLY SO MANY BATHROOMS. Before the crowd moves into the house, I'll take my shot at one of them.

The three lavatories on the first floor are in use so I climb the curved staircase to the second floor. Most of the doors are closed. An unused bathroom's door would be left ajar so I keep moving down the hall.

When I pass a door that is only partially closed, I peek in to see if I'm in luck. It's not a bathroom, but a large office. It must have been Randall's.

Jeanette sits at the desk. She is downloading something off the computer.

She doesn't hear me come up behind her so she doesn't realize that I'm reading over her shoulder.

It's an email, written in Russian.

Well, what do you know...

She must feel my presence because her back stiffens.

I'm not carrying a weapon, but instead of taking a chance that she's packing, I slam her with the largest book I can find. Such irony: it's the latest edition of the U.S. Tax Code.

She ducks instinctively. Still, I hit her hard on the shoulder as she stumbles to her feet. As she attempts to train her gun on me, I grab her wrist with one hand and jerk it up high. By the time her shot hits the ceiling, I've elbowed her hard in the face before pounding the fist holding her gun against the edge of the desk. She is stunned enough to drop the gun to the floor but still struggles for her life, charging at me with all her might. I don't have time to move before she slugs me in the gut. As I fall back onto the desk, she scrambles for the gun. I roll off the desk in time to kick the gun beyond her reach. Angrily, she rises up, but my kick to her kidney puts her back on the floor.

I then pick her up by the crew-neck collar of her dress (a true shame, since this ruin its lines) and throw a punch that finally renders her unconscious.

By now, Jack has come to see what's taking me so long. As he peruses the situation, I explain, "She was his Russian handler."

"Jesus!" he exclaims. "Is there anyone in this organization who *isn't* a spook?"

"Beats me," I say as I wipe away the blood trickling from my mouth. "Hey, do you mind watching her for a minute? I still haven't gone to the little girl's room."

"Go for it," he says with a wave.

16

Fake News

Despite what one might be led to believe, the phrase "fake news" was not coined in America's raucous political environment.

This expression has been around for quite some time: at least since 1890, when the Cincinnati Inquirer *had a headline proclaiming "Secretary Brunnell Declares Fake News About His People is Being Telegraphed Over the Country."*

Somewhere deep in the dustbin of time lays the bones of Master Brunnell, who shook his fist at the lies and innuendo that was spread from one part of the country to another, appearing in local newspapers, perhaps over a month's time.

Had he lived today, the same untruth that plagued him and his clan would have:

1: circled the globe in a mere second;

2: been created in some political backroom;

3: been disseminated as a pithy soundbite to one or many talking heads;

4: been attributed to some bogus news source;

5: been quoted often by other journalists; and

6: been re-Tweeted or Facebooked or Instagrammed by the rest of us.

The twenty-first century's news cycle is instantaneous and 24-7. When it comes to fact-checking, it is still every journalist's cross to bear.

All over the Internet, it is claimed that in 1919, Mark Twain said, "A lie can travel halfway around the world before the truth can get its boots on."

Fact Check: Mark Twain died in 1910.

So, there you have it: FAKE NEWS.

I AM ME AGAIN.

Even before we left for Los Angeles, I'd gotten rid of the wig by tossing it into the Potomac.

Watching, Jack roared with laughter. Taking a handful of my hair, he held it to up to his cheek and exclaimed, "I missed the feel of this bittersweet chocolate."

Gwendolyn's field khakis and her sleek on-air dresses are already in a bag soon to be dropped at the local Goodwill. I need no reminders of this mission. I don't view it as a failure but a temporary truce.

Big Brother is always watching. Big Media's mandate may be to dig out the truth, but it is always espousing half-truths, or leaving out pertinent facts.

The truth may be out there, but do you really want to know it? Sadly, most people only want to hear what they already think they know.

Right now, Jack sits at the dining room table, helping Trisha with her math homework. From the sound of things, she's caught on to the tricks for measuring quadrilaterals. But from the sobbing I heard coming from her room last night, happiness now eludes her. Trisha's grief over her decision to end her most treasured friendship pains her greatly.

No one is spared this life lesson.

Jeff sits beside his dad and his younger sister, editing articles for an upcoming issue of the *Signal*. Mary is going through online fashion websites, pulling up trends then matching her finds with the pithy editorials.

And I'm doing what relaxes me most: I bake.

Tonight, after a meal of rosemary-lemon roast chicken, garlic mashed potatoes, and string beans, my family will devour the cherry pie now baking in my oven.

I love to watch their eyes widen as they sniff the scent of lush cherries. The first cut into the golden-brown crust will elicit wide smiles. The first bite will be accompanied by ecstatic moans.

Then will come the accolades. "Sweet!" "Yum!" and, "Delicious, darling!"

I live for their love.

I'm checking the timer on the pie. It's got another fifteen minutes.

Suddenly, Jeff shouts, "Mom...*Mom*! You've got to read the newspaper!"

"I thought your paper comes out on Monday."

"No, Mom! I'm not talking about the *Signal*! I mean *The New York Times*!" Jeff points to his iPad.

My eyes go to the largest headline on the front page:

SPECIAL COUNSEL TO SUBPOENA THE PRESIDENT

THE STORY INCLUDES A VERY LARGE PHOTO OF BLAKE REYNOLDS.

Trisha looks out the window. "Hey, isn't that the man outside our front door?"

Even through the sheers, I see she's right. Blake is standing on our front porch.

Ryan is with him. He presses the doorbell.

Jack nods toward the great room. "Thanks for giving us some privacy, kids."

The children don't waste any time picking up their notebooks and moving. They shut the door behind them.

Before Jack makes his way to the front door, I reach for his arm. "You knew it was coming down, didn't you?"

"By Edmonton's comment, I suspected as much," he admits.

I hold my head high. "Well, I guess now Lee will be forced to tell Reynolds what he knows about Babette's connection with Eric Weber, not to mention Salem and Carl."

"You're right. It should be interesting to see how Lee handles this."

I'm about to ask him what he means by that, but now our guests are leaning on the doorbell.

I motion for him to open the front door before they break it down. Our neighbors have enough issues with us without having to witness yet another SWAT team raid.

RYAN AND BLAKE PASS ON MY OFFER OF COFFEE AND PIE. "WE don't plan on keeping you."

Well, that's a relief. Any opportunity to avoid a perp walk works for me.

Jack is warier. I can tell because he frowns when they pass on my offer to take a seat. "Now that we know it's not a social call, what can we do for you, Special Counsel Reynolds?"

Reynolds attempts a smile. "Acme did exemplary work in

connecting the dots between the German law firm, Wagner Klein, and Russia. The fact that it also had the Quorum on its client list is a bonus because it proves that the organization is still alive and kicking, despite the deaths of its titular heads, Eric Weber and Carl Stone."

His eyes hone in on me when he mentions my ex-husband's name.

Instead of wincing, I stare back at him. I'll never give him the satisfaction of shaming me for Carl's acts of treason.

"To the DIA's great dismay, the Quorum's financial trail seems to be intermingled with that of the President of the United States."

"You mean, through the corporation that he left in a blind trust, Global World Industries? I assure you that it's clean as a whistle," I retort.

"Except for one subsidiary: Breck Industries." Reynolds looks sharply at me. "But of course, you already know this."

"Yes. We reported this to the CIA and also to President Chiffray. When he found out, he cleaned house."

Except for one skeleton in the closet. Carl blackmailed Lee into giving him the position of Director of Intelligence—for a while, anyway.

Until I killed Carl.

"As it turns out, he didn't 'clean house.' Otherwise, there would not have been a transfer of funds between the Russian accounts and Breck Industries."

Babette is still listed as its Vice President of Operations. More than likely, it is the position that controls the corporation's finances.

Once again, she has duped Lee.

"We want you to get POTUS on record admitting to collaborating and financing the Quorum."

There it is: Reynolds now cuts to the chase.

I snort. "Are you crazy? Lee was never involved with the Quorum! Bab—"

Suddenly, Ryan is talking over me. "Donna, Special Prosecutor Reynolds already knows about Babette."

I relax with a sigh. *It's about damn time!*

"And because she's turned state's evidence—because she's willing to testify against her husband—the Justice Department will be justified in charging Lee with treason."

"But *he* isn't... *She's*—"

"You have his ear, Mrs. Craig," Reynolds interrupts. "We'd like to reach out to him. You know, friend to friend. Offer to meet with him."

I don't know who's angrier, Jack or me. He's on the move before I know it—nose to nose with Reynolds. "If you're insinuating that my wife and Lee are—"

"I have no idea what Mrs. Craig's relationship is with President Chiffray!" For one second, fear flashes in Reynolds' eyes. Then he remembers who he is, and stiffly, he adds, "It's none of my business."

You can say that again.

Emboldened, Reynolds declares, "And for that matter, I would imagine you don't know its full extent either. For the record it's not important. What does matter is that, for whatever reason, he trusts her—and loves her."

Glaring, I snarl, "Let me guess. Babette said that."

Reynolds blinks at the ice in my voice. "Yes, she did feel you'd be our best chance to persuade him. Of course, when you do, you'll wear a wire—"

"I'll do no such thing!" I throw up my hands as I pace the room.

Reynolds pulls three envelopes out of his inside jacket pocket. He hands one to Ryan, and another to me. Jack gets the third.

"You've just been served a subpoena to testify in front of the federal grand jury. For that matter, all employees of Acme will also be subpoenaed. Needless to say, with the organization under such scrutiny, Acme's standing with the U.S. Intelligence Agencies and its allies will certainly be damaged."

I don't have to look over at Ryan to feel him deflate under the weight of my decision.

I shrug. "I'll think about it."

Disgusted, Reynolds storms out.

Not Ryan. When our eyes meet, I see his concern. He lays a hand on my shoulder. "Donna, your point is well made. Still, one way or the other, Lee pays for Babette's sins."

"He already has, over and over," I counter. "Can you imagine how much more he could have gotten done, now that the Quorum is..."

I was going to say, now that the Quorum is gone.

But that's the problem: it isn't.

Otherwise, the Justice Department would not be breathing down Lee's neck.

Ryan slides his subpoena into his inside jacket pocket. "We are scheduled to meet with the grand jury on Friday. The Acme plane will depart from Van Nuys at fourteen-hundred-hours on Thursday. However, if you wish to honor Special Prosecutor Reynolds' request, I'll pass forward the message. If anything comes of your conversation with Lee, I'm sure that Reynolds will then have our subpoenas withdrawn."

Request? Ha! More like a demand.

Without another word we walk Ryan to the door.

We are watching him drive off when Trisha cracks open the living room door. "I think I smell pie—and *not* in a good way!"

By the time I run to the kitchen, Mary is already pulling the scorched pie out of the oven. But it's so hot that it burns her through the mitt.

Yelping, she slams the pie on the counter. Part of the pie slips out of the tin, leaving a hot mess over everything.

It is an apt metaphor for my life right about now.

OR MAYBE NOT.

Case in point: when life serves up burnt cherry pie, scrape off the crust and make a cherry cobbler.

After removing any part of the top or bottom crust that hasn't turned to ash, I spoon it, along with the pie's filling into a glass casserole dish, sprinkle the top with brown sugar, and cover the top with tin foil. I'll warm it in the oven before serving.

Trisha is duly impressed. "I thought my favorite pie was a goner!"

"Everything in life is salvageable," I declare.

"Even friendships?" she asks.

"If both people want to put the time and effort into making it work, then yes."

Without another word she walks away.

A few moments later, she's back. She carries a plastic bag in her hand.

"What's that?" I ask.

"When Janie toured the school, I introduced her to Coach Middleton. Coach invited her to practice with the team. She was impressed enough with Janie's moves that she ordered this for her."

Trisha opens the bag. It holds a Hilldale Elementary School girl's soccer jersey.

"Since you have to go to Washington, will you make sure she gets it?"

I nod.

"And tell her…well, just tell her I'm here for her, anytime she wants to talk."

"I will."

As Trisha grabs me for a hug, tears dampen my cheeks. By the time she looks up at me, I've wiped them away.

"What do you think I should do?" I whisper.

From my bedside clock, I can see it's after two in the morning.

I hear Jack's steady breathing. His knees are folded behind mine, like a second skin. Still, I don't know if Jack is asleep or awake.

Silence.

Maybe it's for the best. He'll only tell me what I don't want to hear anyway.

Jack sighs as he wraps his arm around my waist. "This is politics, plain and simple. Edmonton and his band of merry politicians want Lee out because he doesn't bend over and sign off on all the policies that their lobbyist buddies pay them to cram down the throats of the rest of us. As for Reynolds, the only thing that matters to him is getting another scalp under his belt. Lee's would be the pinnacle of his career. With Lee out of the White House, both men have accomplished their goals."

"And with Babette willing to play ball, they win," I reply. "I'll bet there is something in it for her too." I flip over to face Jack. I can't see him in the dark but I feel his soft breath. It comforts me.

"Donna, I'm not going to make up your mind for you.

Here's the thing: Whether you agree or not to entrap Lee, our testimony in front of a grand jury is a given."

"He threatened to blackball Acme with the DIA and U.S. allies," I remind him.

"Covert Ops will always be a pinball in political gamesmanship. And Acme will always land on its feet." He strokes my cheek. "The only upside of playing ball with the Justice Department is that the questions you ask may not get the response Reynolds wants in the first place."

"But in the past Lee has covered up for Babette," I've point out.

"That doesn't have to come out in your conversation," Jack points out. "When you bring up Babette's duplicity, he is just as likely to express his frustration with it without admitting that he was aware of it beforehand. That way, you've done what was requested of you. It's all he can ask of you."

"Before tossing me in jail," I grumble.

"Not to worry, hon. While you're serving your twenty years without parole, I'll whip the kids into shape. Mary's already a great cook, and Trisha actually enjoys doing laundry—"

I snort so loudly that he puts his hand over my mouth so that we don't wake the rest of the house.

I lick his palm. As expected, he lets go.

What he doesn't expect is for me to pull him closer. When our lips meet, he is just as hungry for me as I am for him.

Our familiarity with each other's bodies allows for shortcuts to pleasure. Tonight, however, our lovemaking is deliberate. Why forego the surge of anticipation? Why miss out on the chance to be tantalized yet again with one or more memorable sensations? Suppose he thrusts deeper, or I clench tighter? If the appreciative gasp is worth it, why rush to achieve the inevitable rush of bliss?

The ferocity of our love shows itself in many ways. I rejoice in my husband's touch. I revel in his adoration. I am always in awe of his thoughtfulness.

I live for our passion.

But love cannot survive without trust. It is his greatest gift to me.

We won't talk further about this issue. He leaves it solely up to me.

By dawn, I know exactly what I must do. I slip out of bed in order to dress quietly in the bathroom before leaving the house. I'll be gone the whole day.

When Jack wakes, he will see the text I sent:

It is, simply, a heart.

17

Man on the Street

Usually identified by the acronym, "MOS," the phrase "Man on the Street" refers to a reporter who is on location in order to get off-the-cuff sound bites and genuine reactions to the story from members of the public. Another term for this is "vox populi," that is, "voice of the people."

There are times when a wife and mother would prefer not to hear public opinion. Like, say, when your toddler throws a fit in the grocery store because you won't allow him to have a candy bar.

No matter what you say to reason with him, eventually his screaming is going to have heads turning to observe you and your little hellion. If you aren't yet chastising him into silence, you are viewed as inconsiderate of the other shoppers. On the other hand, if you threaten him, either verbally or with bodily harm, your threats may become GIFs that embarrass you on social media or perhaps gives the local Child Services department a reason to knock on your door.

Solution: Next time, leave him at home with Daddy. That way, you can do your shopping in peace.

*Unless some other tired toddler is cranky enough to throw a
tizzy fit.*

*It is human nature to crane one's neck for a better view of the
ruckus. Just be glad that, this time, you're not the entertainment.*

I CAN ONLY IMAGINE LEE'S SURPRISE WHEN, ON HIS PRIVATE CELL
phone, he receives a text from "the New York Public Library"
telling him that his loan of the Tom Clancy book, *Executive
Orders,* is about to expire tomorrow. This is our signal to meet in
the Manhattan penthouse apartment, owned by a GWI
subsidiary.

As per our agreed-upon protocol, I've preceded him to his
beautiful pied-à-terre, located in a modern condominium building, towering high above the Hudson River overlooking the
Battery Park Esplanade.

I enter via the back entrance off an alley. By tapping the
correct six-digit code into the keypad that summons the express
elevator, I am immediately whisked into the penthouse's foyer.

With its golden walls, marble floors, intricately carved
molding, and silk brocade appointments I could be in the
Hermitage Palace, the home of Russia's notorious empress,
Catherine the Great.

As I walk through this massive home, I suddenly realize:
This is not Lee's style, but Babette's.

Catherine successfully conspired, and succeeded, in over-
throwing her estranged husband, Peter III.

Yes, I am struck by the irony.

I spend the next couple of hours prepping myself for what I
will say to Lee.

HE ARRIVES IN TIME TO JOIN ME AT THE PICTURE WINDOW JUST AS the sun is setting over the river.

As always, his Secret Service detail stays in the hall, silent and uneasy sentries to yet another mysterious assignation in this secret sanctuary of the man they are sworn to protect.

As the White House's living ghosts, they are already privy to the scuttlebutt surrounding the Special Counsel's investigation. If they believe he is guilty, they must wonder if our meetings are relevant to the charges. Should he not be cleared, then certainly they will be relieved when these rendezvous are no longer on Lee's agenda. Their loyalty is to the office, not the man.

As is mine.

I don't turn around when he enters. I don't want him to see that I have been crying.

I have good reason. Until now I've never been forced to betray him.

I've convinced myself it is why I'm here.

Through me, he now has the opportunity to redeem himself.

If he allows me, I will be his savior.

HE WALKS UP BESIDE ME. "THIS IS A SURPRISE."

"And I'm sure it couldn't have come at a worse time." I pivot to face him. "Hellzapoppin', eh?"

"Something like that." Lee shrugs. "Reynolds won't find what he's looking for."

"Yes, he will, and with Babette's help."

Lee eyes me sharply. "How do you know?"

"Because I was subpoenaed."

"You told him about her?" Each word crackles with anger.

My caustic laugh startles him. "My God, if only I had!"

"I don't know if I should be comforted by that," he growls.

I shake my head. "You shouldn't. You vowed to me personally that you'd clean house. You didn't."

"In fact, I am cleaning house. Right now."

"So you're ready to tell Reynolds about Bab—"

"You mean about the Quorum—*and me*." He places his palm between my breasts. Before I have a chance to say anything, he loosens the top button of my blouse.

Then another.

I stiffen when his fingers slip through the third button.

Yes, he sees the tiny audio recorder attached to my bra.

He nods, resigned. Nonchalantly, he says, "I can't live with myself anymore. I'm resigning. It's the only way to get out from the Quorum's hold on me."

Once again, he's taking the fall for Babette.

To hell with that! Reynolds needs to hear the truth.

"You?…and *the Quorum*?" I chuckle, as if his statement is some ludicrous joke. "But the Quorum is—"

"It's a scourge on our world!" Lee shakes his head, warning me to play along. "And on our political system. You know well enough that I'm not the only Washington politician or for that matter, head of state who's been tainted by it. With me out of the White House, I finally cut the tentacles it has around the neck of our country."

He's right. Once he's out of power, Babette is too.

"It will still be well-financed," I counter. "Thanks to Jonah's death, Babette was left with enough money to fund the Quorum through several lifetimes."

"I'll be giving that information to the Special Counsel. Its endgame isn't just my corruption. For the good of the world, the international intelligence community must wipe the Quorum off the face of the earth."

He's right. And if it means sacrificing his presidency, he's willing to do so.

Lee has never let me down.

I stroke his cheek with my palm.

He takes my hand. After kissing it, he mouths, *Goodbye*.

My smile is weak, but I nod, then I form the words, *For now*.

AS ALWAYS LEE LEAVES FIRST.

I wait several hours before doing the same. When I slip out, I make sure that my face is never captured on security cameras. I've been here often enough to have devised a lock-proof surveillance avoidance strategy.

The device I wore records conversations. It does not transmit them. Although my escape route takes me away from the Battery Park Esplanade, on impulse I circle back around to it.

This time of night I'm the only living soul on the path. I pull the recorder out of my jeans' pocket and stare down at it. Had Lee said what I'd hoped for, I'd be catching the next plane to D.C., collecting a brownie point from a man who lives to make my life miserable. But since Lee has already made up his mind that he's taking the fall for Babette anyway, it's of no use to me.

More to the point, it's no use to Lee.

I toss it as far as I can. A moment later, I hear a plop as it breaks the water's surface.

I care too much for Lee to be the one to put the noose around his neck.

18

Leading Questions

When conducting an interview, it is not unusual for a reporter to steer an interviewee in a particular direction, or toward a desired response. This is done through what are called "leading questions." Sometimes this is necessary if the respondent is close-lipped and giving just yes-and-no answers. (BORING!)

You too can use this technique whenever you find yourself in a situation in which you're not getting the response you seek.

For example, don't ask, "Were you out last night with another woman?" because that is sure to get you an emphatic "No!" Which may or may not be the truth. Instead, ask, "Where did you find that plug-ugly woman with whom you spent the night?"

The interviewee may be shocked enough to retort, "Who says she's ugly?" This informs you that he thinks otherwise. It also validates that he never came home. And if he actually answers with, say, "I picked her up at Smitty's Bar during happy hour," you've got all the information you need.

It's up to you to decide what to do with—or more to the point, do to—your two-timing guy.

Something tells me that whatever it is won't be fit to print.

It's D-Day. In this case, the D stands for deposition.

Jack and I have been placed in separate alcoves, and under the watch of government agents. We are waiting for our turn to give testimony in the Special Counsel's investigation.

Ryan is already inside the federal grand jury chambers. Reynolds isn't the prosecutor. It is another member of his prosecutorial team: a woman by the name of Tala Karami.

"She's Sunni Muslim from Lebanon," Emma informs us. Although we aren't supposed to hear each others' testimony, our earbuds allow us to do so, just like our lenses take in the chamber's video feed. "She graduated Harvard Law, first in her class. Edited *Harvard Review*. Clerked under Justice Kagan before she reached the Supreme Court. Tala has made a career of investigating and prosecuting terrorists.

"She's also quite stunning," Dominic comments. "Very tall, beautiful high cheekbones. Long dark hair."

Should he get called on the stand, I hope he doesn't dare ask her if the carpet matches the drapes.

Before proceeding, the grand jury, court clerk, bailiff, and recorder are asked to step out because they lack national security clearance to be privy to the testimony. After the court is cleared, we again hear the voice of Tala Karami.

"How long have you been investigating the terrorist organization known as the Quorum?" Tala asks Ryan.

"For over eleven years. Not only at the behest of the U.S. intelligence community, but for our allies' agencies as well," Ryan replies.

"What does the Quorum do, exactly?"

"For the most part, it finances terrorism all over the world. However, it also recruits assassins and covert operatives for specific assignments that include but are not limited to exterminations, drug running, slavery, arms dealing, corporate and state intelligence theft, and of course, money laundering."

Ryan then goes on to explain the role that Acme's government-sanctioned covert operations has played in uncovering the Quorum's existence; tracing its society-shattering crimes against humanity; tracking its financial sources; identifying its operatives (he leaves out the part of our role in their exterminations); and stopping many of its terrorist schemes.

"Have your operations led you to believe that the Quorum has had dealings with anyone within the executive branch?" Tala asks.

Ryan pauses, then answers, "Over time, Acme discovered a money trail between the Quorum and Breck Industries. The company was eventually acquired by Global World Industries, the international corporation that is now being held in trust for President Chiffray."

"Breck Industries produces military weaponry and ammunition, does it not?"

"Yes. And most of its other businesses not tied to the arms industry were used to launder its black market sales."

"Had the sale of Breck Industries to GWI taken place prior to President Chiffray's tenure in the White House?" Tala asks.

"Yes."

"Had Acme discovered if President Chiffray was aware of Breck Industries connection with the Quorum prior to the purchase?"

"He was not aware of it," Ryan replies.

"How do you know this?" Tala questions. "Was it Acme who informed him?"

"No."

"Do you have knowledge of who told him?"

"He divulged that information to one of our operatives,"

Ryan admits. "Carl Stone told him. Mr. Stone later became Director of U.S. Intelligence."

The judge grimaces at this revelation.

"Was President Chiffray already in the White House when Carl Stone shared this information with him?"

After a pause, Ryan answers, "Yes, but Mr. Stone did so *prior* to being appointed DIO. In fact, he used it to blackmail the president *for* the position."

This time the judge's eyes open wide.

Assistant Prosecutor Karami declares, "That will be all, Mr. Clancy. But I reserve the right to call you back on the stand if further clarification is needed."

The next thing we hear is her proclaiming, "I'd now like to call Jack Craig to the stand, your Honor."

I'M SURE THAT, LIKE ME, RYAN IS TUNED IN TO JACK'S TESTIMONY.

Tala's first question is simple enough: "You were assigned the position of team leader for the mission of tracking the Quorum, were you not?"

"Yes," Jack says. "That was ten years ago, a few months after the supposed assassination of the Acme operative who had infiltrated the organization: Carl Stone."

"How long did it take Acme to realize that Mr. Stone was in fact very much alive?"

"We became aware of it around five years ago," Jack replies. "One of Acme's operatives was exterminated in Hungary. The assassins were caught on camera. One was Carl."

Jack doesn't mention that the other was his wife, Valentina, who disappeared just before Carl. She too was presumed dead when an alias assigned to her showed up on the manifest of a plane lost at sea.

"Stone's former wife, Donna, is also an Acme operative, isn't she?"

"She wasn't at the time. She was recruited within a year of his disappearance."

"By you?"

"No. By Mr. Clancy. He felt she was...highly motivated."

"You didn't agree?"

"Not at first. She proved me wrong."

"In fact, she's proven to be quite effective in covert operations, hasn't she? Both as an assassin and a honey pot, is that not correct?"

Jack's pause is much too long. At least he hasn't leaped up and throttled her for that remark, so all is good. Finally, he mutters, "Yes. Among other things."

"And when Carl Stone resurfaced, he first approached her, didn't he?"

"Yes. Acme had intercepted intel that the Quorum was planning a terrorist attack that was to take place in the Los Angeles metro area. Once Acme knew he was alive, we felt certain that Carl's knowledge of L.A. would put him on the mission. If so, he might use it as an excuse to check up on her. To encourage this, Acme planted an agent in her home who pretended to be Carl. The plan worked. When he heard Donna was 'playing house' with someone using his name, he was angry enough to check it out."

"You played Carl Stone."

He nods.

Tala demands, "For the record, please answer."

"Yes. I took the name Carl Stone."

"You are now married to the former Mrs. Stone, aren't you?"

"I'm a very lucky man, yes." I blush when I hear the pride with which Jack states his feelings for me.

"Was Mrs. Stone forthcoming with Acme about her reunion with the real Carl Stone?"

Jack sighs. Then, warily, "Not immediately. Needless to say, his appearance was a shock to her. He tried to convince her that he'd spent five years in deep cover so that he could prove *I* was a double-agent and in fact leading the terrorist act to take place in Los Angeles."

"Acme was able to stop the attack, but Mr. Stone escaped, correct?"

"Yes. Donna shot and wounded him, but he killed a med tech on the way to the emergency room and got away. He resurfaced sometime later as part of the security detail accompanying then Russian Prime Minister Alexei Asimov to a summit hosted by the industrialist Jonah Breck. This gave him immunity from prosecution."

"Breck was eventually killed by Mr. Stone, am I right?"

"Yes. Breck was one of the Quorum's twelve leaders until Acme took possession of intel validating that he was selling WMDs to hostile nations. Russia traded slaves for some of their purchases."

"Upon his death, did his widow—Babette Breck, now the First Lady—put Breck Industries up for sale?"

"Yes. And Carl Stone brokered the deal between Babette and Lee Chiffray. In fact, they met through Carl."

"Interesting," Tala's reply is so soft I can barely hear her. After a moment she announces, "Thank you, Mr. Craig, for your testimony. I now wish to call Donna Stone Craig to the stand."

TALA DOESN'T BEAT AROUND THE BUSH. "DO YOU CONSIDER yourself a close, personal friend of President Chiffray?"

"Yes, I do." I am proud that my voice doesn't waver.

"How did you meet?"

"During a mission. Acme was asked to investigate the disappearance of an NSA scientist working on a top-secret chemical weapons project. He was last tracked to an island resort."

"Was then Mr. Chiffray a suspect in the scientist's disappearance?"

"No. He came on our radar only because his features were similar to the scientist's—and because he seemed to be racking up so many chips at the casino." I shrug. "By then, Mr. and Mrs. Chiffray were dating. As it turns out, they were vacationing at the resort, which was a property in the Breck Industries portfolio."

As I was soon to discover, Fantasy Island wasn't just about sun, sand, and eco-friendly tiki tents. For those who sought darker diversions, it had an exclusive hunt club where humans were prey of sport.

Ironically, Babette stalked Lee every bit as carefully as the wealthy hunters who chased down the prisoners released from the Plexiglas cages deep within the resort's bowels.

"The Brecks had been our neighbors," I continue. "My youngest daughter, who is a close friend of then Mrs. Breck's daughter, was invited as Janie's guest. However, since I hadn't met Mr. Chiffray prior to their arrival on the island, I didn't realize he was there with Babette until I, er...ran into her."

Really, I *walked* in on her as she was about to partake in some whipped cream-induced orgy with Dominic. He takes his job as an undercover agent quite seriously. I won't go into the particulars now. Dominic will be delighted to enthrall Tala with details of his conquests. Here's hoping he won't perjure himself with too many embellishments.

"Did you find the scientist?"

"Yes. Although it was presumed he left the NSA lab on his own volition, Acme learned that his disappearance was in fact a kidnapping by the Quorum. Unfortunately, we weren't able to save him before he was murdered."

"So, the island—the location of a Quorum mission—was an asset of Breck Industries, which was acquired by GWI. If all of this is true, President Chiffray's due diligence was lacking, to say the least."

"In fact, Lee was on a working vacation. He was considering pulling the financing from that asset. To that end, the trip was a success. He was lucky enough to have done so."

Tala lets that sink in. "I'm still not convinced that someone with Mr. Chiffray's business intuition and financial success could have been so blind as to the ties he had with the Quorum."

"I agree." I look her in the eye. "Sadly, love can do that to a person."

Tala stares at me, confused. "Would you care to elaborate, Mrs. Craig?"

THERE, IN A DARK MAHOGANY-PANELED CHAMBER, I PLAY Scheherazade to the mesmerized few permitted to hear my testimony.

However, my tale is not mythic lore but the cold hard facts as I know them, so help me God.

At this point, I don't care that it paints a picture of our president as a gullible suitor blinded by his attraction to a beautiful widow who wore the tragic circumstance of her first husband's death as if it were Dior widow's weeds.

I explain how Lee, even when threatened with Carl's blackmail, directed Acme to gather intel on the Quorum. We were to report only to him, bypassing the one person who could shut us down.

"During that time, the Quorum grew stronger," I explain. "Its acquired conglomerates similar to Breck Industries: all well-financed and publicly traded; a financial Rubik's cube with many moving parts."

"Where dirty money could be shuffled or hidden," Tala reasons.

"Exactly. They own a portfolio of companies that produces the tools or provides the services needed to wreak havoc with stable democratic governments."

"Similar to Hartland Media," Tala says.

"Yes," I confirm fervently. "You see, in today's world, an open tech-savvy media is a double-edged sword. It can bring us together or tear us apart. We have been taught to assume news is provided with journalistic integrity: fact-checked, and therefore based on history, reality, or the time in which it took place. But a mere phrase—especially one that provokes fear—can alter our perception of reality. It obscures the truth. In our recent past, Russia's troll factory, Internet Research Agency, provided the necessary wake-up call. But Russia's outright and surreptitious purchase of a far-reaching and supposedly legitimate news outlet—a bastion of the Fourth Estate, as it were—has had a far-reaching effect." I scan the faces before me. "Lee cleaned house. Carl is dead. The titular head of the Quorum, Eric Weber, is also dead. The Quorum has been his cross to bear, but its demise has also been his mission. As Hartland Media proved, there is still much to do. He can only do it, though, if he stays in office."

I take a deep breath.

The hero of my story is a devoted husband, a caring father, a strategic commander in-chief, a thoughtful president, and an inspiring statesman. Has he garnered enough sympathy to keep him out of jail?

It's a long shot since he's also the American president being blackmailed by foreign agents who wish to create chaos throughout our country by any means possible.

All I can do is pray for the judge's leniency toward Lee.

"Are you implying the means supports the end?" Tala retorts. "That the lies President Chiffray has told to stay in office justifies the actions that put him there?"

No, it doesn't. The judge knows this too. I see it on his face.

Before Tala can ask another question, one of her Special Counsel team members enters the courtroom. In five strides, he's at her side. He slips her a note.

No emotions cross her face as she reads it. Then, in a crisp, cool voice, she declares, "President Chiffray is resigning from office. Your Honor, the grand jury can be dismissed of any further duties."

It takes a minute or two for that to sink in.

When the shock subsides, the judge quickly brings the proceedings to a close. Stunned, I and those left to hear this unfortunate series of events filter out the chambers' heavy double doors.

RYAN AND JACK ARE WAITING FOR ME.

Before I can ask, Ryan is already answering the many questions reeling in my mind. "Lee and his personal attorneys have cut a deal with Reynolds. Bottom line: Lee will be censured and resign immediately to avoid impeachment for high crimes and misdemeanors. He will also avoid criminal prosecution."

"Thank God," I exclaim.

"He will leave the White House by noon tomorrow: by limousine and alone."

I frown. "You mean Babette and the children aren't accompanying him?"

"Her public statement is that she's mortified and heartbroken. She is also filing for divorce," Jack says. "In other words, she won't be there for his presidential perp walk."

That cowardly bitch.

JACK AND I MAKE THE GRAND DECISION TO ORDER ROOM SERVICE: steaks, mashed potatoes, a green salad, and a great bottle of wine.

Like me, Jack is ravenous. We devour the meal without talking. At first, I put it off to the fact that we're both dead tired and wrung out after our appearances before the special court. But when I reach for the salt and Jack grabs my hand, I can tell by the look in his eyes that it has nothing to do with his concern over my sodium intake.

"Okay, spill it," I demand.

I expect it has something to do with my testimony. Surely, he's going to tease me for my recital of the Quorum's greatest hits. Or maybe he's going to scold me for playing defense attorney for Lee.

In any regard, I feel no compulsion to apologize for anything I said. Jack will just have to live with that.

He starts with a sigh. "Listen, Donna, I owe you an apology for being jealous over Lee."

My mouth drops open because I don't believe what I'm hearing. Benjamin Franklin once said, "Never ruin an apology with an excuse." At this moment, I take the advice to heart.

I force myself to nod.

"I know there was nothing between you—well, except for his infatuation for you and your devotion to the office of the president." He looks intently at me. "And it heartens me tremendously to know he didn't really love you."

"What?" Wait! Lee...*doesn't*? "Why do you say that?"

"Because he loved Babette despite the fact she didn't love him back." Jack shrugs. "The poor sap proved it every step of the way. Hell, he was even willing to sacrifice his freedom for her. What a waste that would have been! He was a good president. Had she never come into his life, he might have been a great one."

"More than likely he wouldn't have been president at all," I remind him.

"Hey, knowing what he does now, I'm sure he'd have been fine with that." Jack crosses his heart. "So, on my honor, I'm okay letting bygones be bygones."

"As of tomorrow at noon, you can tell him yourself. I'm sure it'll make his day," I say with a laugh. "Seriously, Jack, I hope you'll give it a go. Hey, maybe you and Lee will become besties! You know, Hilldale's DILF-iest duo, breaking all the yummy mommies' hearts at the country club."

He chuckles. "You're on—*if* we ever see the Chiffrays again. Once Babette is through divorcing Lee, he may not be able to afford the largest mansion in Hilldale."

I frown. "Which reminds me! I promised Trisha I'd give Janie the Hilldale Elementary School soccer team jersey!"

So that I don't forget it, I roll out of bed, I dig it out of my suitcase, and stuff it in a hotel gift bag.

"This morning Ryan has a meeting lined up with Edmonton. He asked if we'd tag along. You can chase her down then."

"I'll certainly use it to get me into the West Wing, but I'll pass on the confab." The thought of seeing that creep behind the Oval Office desk gives me a shiver. "As far as Edmonton is concerned, I'm just eye candy anyway."

"He'll soon learn to respect you," Jack replies. "Someday his presidency—perhaps even his life—will depend on it."

He's not fishing for a kiss, but he gets one anyway, among other things that ensure we will both have a goodnight's rest.

19

Screamer

The banner encasing the headline across or near the top of all or most of a newspaper's front page is called a "screamer."

This type of layout is used when the newspaper wants to announce something very important has happened and the world needs to know about it.

Screamers are also known as "ribbons," "lines," or "streamers." (Meh. Not as EXCITING!)

You too are free to use screamers to get the attention of those you love.

(In fact, some sex partners actively look for "screamers"—but that's for another sort of book.)

Tip: To save time and effort, consider foregoing the paper, ink, layout, and newspaper press expenses. Instead, when the one who needs to hear you most is asleep, just get right down next to his ear and

SCREAM!

≈

At the appointed hour, Ryan, Jack, and I arrive at the White House. Before we secure our badges and are shown to the Roosevelt Room, my purse and gift bag are searched, as is Ryan's briefcase.

With the excuse that I must find the lavatory, I slip out to the staircase leading to the second floor of the Executive Residence, where I know I'll find the Chiffrays.

The family's Secret Service detail scan me. I smile and nod, but I am not stopped. The color of my security badge indicates I've got Intelligence Agency clearance. Besides, they recognize me from the numerous times they've seen me at Lion's Lair.

Janie's bedroom door is open. Before me is a tender sight: the poor girl is crying in Lee's arms.

"But why aren't you going with us?" She chokes out her words through her sobs.

"I'm sorry, Janie, but your mother is right. It would be best if you ride with her and Harrison in the other car. That way, when the reporters are too loud, you can help your mother calm your baby brother."

"I'd rather be with you! You're the one they want to hurt!" she argues tearfully.

"I promise you that as soon as we're off the White House grounds, we'll meet up and...and I'll get out and ride with you and the rest of the family." Lee's voice is husky. He's having just as hard of a time as Janie with Babette's directive.

"No, we won't!" Janie exclaims with an adamant shake of her head. "I heard Mummy tell Chantal that we'll never see you again—*ever*!"

Lee is silent. I imagine he is stunned by this new knowledge of his wife's true plan.

At that moment, Lee's head turns. He sees me.

I feel my cheeks redden.

He forgives my embarrassment with a stilted wave to enter.

Quickly, I step into the room and shut the door behind me. "Good morning, Mr. President. I'm so happy I caught you in time, Janie. I'd promised Trisha that I'd give you this."

I open the gift bag and hold up the jersey.

Janie's eyes open wide. Reluctantly, she lets go of Lee. I can't blame her. He has been the calm eye in Babette's maelstrom.

Gone is the spoiled, aloof ten-year-old whose sullen eyes and downcast pout made up her signature look. She walks in slow, measured steps until she reaches me. By now, a trail of tears is crawling down her cheek. Taking the jersey, she whispers, "Thank you, Mrs. Craig."

The next thing I know, Janie has her arms around me.

Frustrated, Lee bows his head.

"What the hell is going on!" No one heard Babette open the door.

She's ready for her public swan song: her sleek, fitted, black jacket over matching skinny slacks and four-inch stiletto heels send a formidable impression: she will leave as the victor.

She holds Harrison, but the infant squirms in her arms until he sees Lee. With a gleeful squeal he reaches for his father.

Lee smiles, if only for his son. When he walks over, Babette reluctantly lets go of the child but she only has eyes for me. "I asked what you're doing here, in our private quarters," she snarls.

Lee glances at a wall clock. "They're ours for another ten minutes, anyway."

"That's your fault, not mine!" she snaps. "You were a fool to resign!"

"You'd rather I hang in there to testify for the Special Prosecutor?" He takes a step toward her. "Aren't you the least concerned as to what I might have said?"

She blinks. Like magic, a tear falls. "You told me... You *swore*—"

"You took an oath, too, remember? At our wedding! Love, honor, cherish." His shoulders sag. "In sickness and in health. Well, Babette, I am sick of your lies and your games." Gently, he pats Harrison's dark curls. "You've already won. You'll be remembered as 'the good wife' who did the right thing—by *not* standing by her man."

Until now, I hadn't noticed that Janie has moved beside Lee and is cowering behind him.

Apparently, Babette realizes this too. She stalks over to her daughter. "What are you holding behind you, young lady?"

Janie stutters, "It's from Trisha. It's a soccer jersey, like hers."

Babette snatches the jersey from Janie's hand and holds it up. "'Hilldale Soccer'? As if! We are *never* going back to that odious town!"

Enough of this crap!

I grab the jersey. "This was a gift from my daughter to yours."

As I hand it back to Janie, I notice the embroidered initials under the team's name:

JBC

It stands for *Janie Breck Chiffray*—

And the offshore bank account.

Incensed at my audacity, Babette reaches for the shirt again, but this time the look on my face says it all:

Don't even try.

She stops in her tracks.

I hand Janie the jersey.

Even a beautiful woman's face is hideous when she screams. Babette's is no exception. "How dare you! Haven't you done enough to wreck my marriage?"

Lee's chuckle is mirthless. "You never needed her help,

Babette. You've done a great job all on your own—you and the Quorum. Now, if you'll excuse me, every network camera is waiting for me to wave my final farewell to the nation before driving off into exile."

Having witnessed Babette and Lee trade barbs, the au pairs are too stunned to move. But as Lee strides out, they shuffle to one side.

Babette points at the two dumbstruck women. "This isn't a sideshow, ladies! Put my kids in the car. I'll be there as soon as I take care of this last little issue." Glaring at her shaking daughter, she hisses, "Go with them—*now*!"

Janie runs out of the room.

The women nod. One of them has enough sense to shut the door. No need for anyone else to witness our argument.

And yes, I am ready for it.

Babette swings back around toward me. "This isn't over, Donna. When I get done with you, you'll wish you'd never met me."

"You're wrong, Babette. The realization that my life would have been better without you happened almost from Day One." I shrug. "It was inevitable, wasn't it? Let's face it. You've always been the steadfast power behind the Quorum."

The anger leaves her face. Triumph takes its place. "You finally figured that out, have you?" she hisses. "Men! All it takes is a few strokes to their egos, among other things. Well, a lot of good your great epiphany will do since you'll never be able to prove it. All roads lead to Lee."

She takes a scarf from her bag. Wrapping it around her neck, she adds, "As for me I'm on a different glide path, one that takes me far away from you, Donna Stone Craig."

I stare at her; not because of her declaration, but because of the scarf.

It's the one-of-a-kind Jered Friedman.

It's Lolita's turquoise scarf.

"There is still one road that leads right to you, Babette," I tell her. "It begins at Trident Union Bank, inside the account under the name of JBC Holdings—which *you* managed under the name of Helen Drake."

Babette scowls. "That Helen Drake person killed herself! It was all over the news!"

"It wasn't 'Helen Drake' who died," I insist. "It was Lolita Jamison—and you had her murdered."

"How dare you accuse me of such a thing!" she snarls.

"It's not an accusation. Lolita was Harold Hart's mistress. You commanded Randall to kill her, mutilate the body so that it couldn't be identified, and toss her into the Potomac. You put your fake ID in her purse. But then being the greedy little fashion slut that you are, you simply *had* to take her scarf as a keepsake."

I point to the one in her hand.

Babette's eyes narrow in anger.

Gotcha.

She backs away slowly.

"Lee got his pardon," I remind her. "On the other hand, you'll go to jail—not just for money laundering and treason, but for murder too. You can't run this time, Babette."

"The hell I can't!" She is close enough to the room's massive fireplace to grab the poker beside it. This time when she rushes me, it's to stab me with it.

Except for a few boxes and the furniture, the room is practically empty. I pick up Janie's desk chair, parrying her jabs at each turn with the chair's legs. Finally, she stabs the chair's upholstered seat dead center. It goes right through it, stopping an inch from my gut.

With all my might, I shove the chair onto her until I've backed her against the wall, pinning her between the chair legs.

But before I can kick Babette's legs out from under her, she ducks out and tackles me to the floor.

The wind is knocked out of me. It doesn't help that she's sitting on my ribcage. She giggles as I grunt. Suddenly, she puts her hands around my throat—

And snaps the chain of my necklace. Waving it over her head, she crows triumphantly: "Ah, the infamous silver locket!"

"Give me that! It belonged to my mother!"

"Like hell I will! It's my get-out-of-jail free card."

That piques my interest. "What makes you say that?"

"You silly fool! Carl hid a microdot with the access code to Acme's agent directory in there—the one he coerced Jack's first slut of a wife to steal for him." She slams down again hard on my ribcage. "And now it's mine!"

If he trusted Babette with the information, it meant he trusted her with his life. Carl never afforded me that privilege, and it cost him dearly.

Babette must have divulged his secret to Eric at one point because he too taunted me about it hiding in plain sight.

Boy, this bitch sure gets around.

There's a knock on the door. Babette freezes.

But I don't. My fist hits the side of her face with enough force that she slides to the floor.

I snatch my locket from her hand and leap up.

Just as Babette stumbles to her feet, Lurch opens the door. He stares at her, then at me. His eyes shift to her again as he murmurs, "Your car is waiting, ma'am. The President and the children have just taken off."

"What? No! *NO!* They were to go with me! I told the au pairs—"

He looks confused. "I'm sorry, but the ladies told me you'd specifically sent the children ahead." Lurch stares at her, confused. "Even Janie confirmed it—"

She runs past him.

Stymied, he takes off too.

Instinctively, I head to the window.

As Lurch confirmed, the other car is already moving down the long oval driveway of the White House's South Lawn. Although the presidential fleet has eleven very similar decoys, I assume it's the president's official car, a fifty-one million-dollar tricked-out mini-tank-designed Cadillac Escalade.

Eager to catch them, Babette leaps into the only other car in the driveway, a twin of the one driving away. By doing this, she's ruined her one chance to make the grand exit she's plotted for days. The media shouts its disappointment, but she has already slammed the door shut.

Lurch lunges into the driver's seat. Whatever she's said to him has him hitting the gas. Soon, he's blowing well past the White House grounds' posted speed limit of twenty-five miles an hour.

The first car has just reached the west security gate when the second car implodes.

The blast lifts the Escalade off the ground. By the time it lands again, the interior is an inferno.

The news cameras click away, but it takes a while before the stunned correspondents and their news crews find their voices.

The money shot happens when Lee and Janie jump out of their car. The sight of the horror-struck father holding back his inconsolable daughter will haunt the American public for a very long time.

20

Stay Tuned...

To encourage you to keep watching a television channel, sometimes you'll hear an announcer's voice imploring the audience to "Stay tuned!"

Before the technological advancement of remote control, the phrase you'd hear was: "Don't touch that dial!"

(Seriously, how quaint is that!)

Invariably, before this request is some plot twist or cliffhanger — that is, some action that has you on the edge of your seat and dying to know what comes next.

"Dying" is the operative word here.

Still, isn't it better if it happens on a studio sound stage than on the streets of your town?

As realistic as the violence may seem on your forty-eight-inch TV screen, even through the best Bose speakers the sound of computer-generated gunfire has nothing on one hundred rounds of Remington ammo spewing from a high power military select fire rifle on full auto.

And how can you compare a movie blood concoction of Hawaiian

Fruit Punch, corn syrup, food coloring, and corn starch to the bloodshed on a real battlefield? You can't, so don't even try.

In real life, not all heroes walk away after a shootout. Sometimes, bad guys get away with murder.

Still, we stay tuned in the hope that the good guy wins—

Even if it's only on TV.

"Mom!" Trisha comes running into the kitchen just as I'm pulling a pie out of the oven. Up until now, this most recent attempt at the perfect cherry pie has been incident-free. Although I jump at her shout, I'm able to slide the scalding hot tin onto the marble kitchen counter instead of slamming it down and cracking the crust.

Sighing, I turn to her. "Have you forgotten the rules? Unless the house is on fire or there are federal agents battering down the door, we use our inside voices."

"But...*but Janie just called! She's home!*"

Which means that Lee is at Lion's Lair too.

It has been three months since the accident that took Babette and Lurch's lives. From all accounts, the bomb, placed inside the vehicle, was set to detonate when The Beast hit the speed of thirty-eight miles per hour. Between the Beast's eight-inch thick doors and its bomb-proof windows and cabin—not to mention the two onboard oxygen tanks acting as additional lighter fluid —nothing could have prevented the engulfing inferno.

All remaining ashes were sent to Lee.

As they should be. Lurch had no family, and his loyalty to the president he served was matched only by his infatuation for Babette.

Mourning was handled with dignity and discretion. Frankly, Lee did the right thing in forgoing a public funeral or even a memorial service. There was enough drama surrounding Babette in life. No need to continue the circus beyond her death.

I have no idea where he had the ashes interred.

For the past few months there have been no signs of Lee or his children—not just in Washington or Hilldale but anywhere in the world. Even my calls and texts offering condolences and our family's love and support have been met with silence.

"She asked if I'd come over." Trisha eyes me hopefully.

"So, you girls have made up?"

"Yes. I reached out to her a couple of times since...you know, since the accident." Trisha blinks back her tears. "I wanted her to know that I'm always here for her." Hesitantly, she adds, "Would you mind driving me over?"

"Not at all." I'm just as anxious as Trisha to see our dear friends. "Grab the vanilla ice cream from the freezer and put it in the small soft cooler," I suggest.

When she sees me pulling out the insulated pie carrier from a cabinet, she squeals with delight. "Your cherry is Janie's favorite!"

Like daughter like father.

Ironically, it's something else Lee and Jack have in common besides me.

"YOU'RE A SIGHT FOR SORE EYES," I TELL LEE. HE HAS SAID THAT to me so many times that it's fun to return the favor.

His lips attempt a grin, but it is only a shadow of his signature smile. Still, he chuckles. "We've been hiding out in Mendocino County. A great spread. Eighteen acres of redwoods..." His voice trails off. "When you're standing beneath one of those thousand-year-old beauties, everything in the here-and-now seems insignificant." He tops his half-eaten pie wedge with another dollop of ice cream. "Wish you could have been there."

"Maybe next time. You know, a two-family outing!" I wink at him.

Hearing Lee's unfettered laugh, I realize how much I've missed it. "The Craigs—even the ones who might come kicking and screaming—are always welcome on any Chiffray expedition."

"Jack respects you, Lee." Sincerity causes my voice to tremble.

"Good to know, Donna." Lee shrugs. "I'll take that to mean that he no longer feels I'm a threat."

"I interpret that as he'd appreciate your friendship too," I insist.

"Done deal. And it's probably the easiest one I'll make this month. I'm in the process of divesting myself fully of GWI." He grimaces. "No need to go back to the corporate grind."

"I'm not surprised. As if anything could compare to being the leader of the free world."

"Only it isn't so free, is it?" When he swallows a bite of pie, he winces, as if it sticks in his throat. "GWI is an albatross. Considering its nefarious taint, I'll be lucky to get a decent price for it, either whole or broken apart. But at least I'll be free of the Quorum's noose, once and for all."

"Will you move out of Hilldale?" I hold my breath in anticipation that I won't like his answer. I only want what's best for Lee, but I will miss him greatly if confirms my fear with a resigned yes.

He thinks about that for a moment before giving a slow nod. "The last thing I need is to move Janie from Lion's Lair, or out of Hilldale. It's the only home she's ever known." He stares down at his plate. "You know, Janie blames herself for Babette's death. She thinks if we'd waited for her mother instead going on ahead in the limo that was already packed with Harrison's baby gear, Babette would still be alive."

I drop onto the couch beside Lee. "If you'd done what Babette wanted, gone by yourself in The Beast, you'd be dead. She and the kids would have remained alive."

"You think she knew it was rigged to explode." Lee isn't asking a question. He's making a declaration.

"Sadly, I do."

"Why so?"

"By insisting that she and the children leave in a separate car, she certainly did what she could to assure that your last drive away from the White House would take place alone, and that you'd head out first," I explain. "Lee, I'd never seen Babette so upset than when Lurch told her you'd gone ahead —*with* the children. She fairly flew downstairs and into the other Escalade waiting there."

"I guess she thought we drove off in The Beast." Lee has a catch in his throat. "If what you say is true and she realized we'd left The Beast behind, she wouldn't have ridden in it, no less insisted on speeding up to catch to us."

"From what I've heard, the investigators still don't know how the bomb got in there," I say. "It certainly shook up Edmonton. He's livid that such a thing could have happened."

"I've always wondered what she would have said had she caught up to us," Lee muses. "What excuse would she have given to persuade me to change places with her?"

"It was the one lie she never got to use." Hesitantly, I add, "Lee, before Randall Hart died, he confirmed that Babette was a Quorum operative. He also said you'd outlived your usefulness for her."

"You warned me. But Donna, I knew it even before you had. I guess I loved her too much to admit it to myself." Lee drops his head from the weight of this revelation. "She truly was a black widow."

His grief is painful enough to make me turn away.

I spot a photo on the end table. It must have been taken while Lee and the children were in Mendocino County. In it, Harrison and Janie are standing inside the cutout of a giant sequoia. The light behind them casts a halo. They hold hands and stare up, awestruck and smiling.

Lee is their sequoia. With him at their side, they will weather the loss of their mother.

In the hope of pulling Lee out of his anguish, I ask, "How is Harrison faring?"

Lee's grief softens at the mention of his son by name if not seed. "He's a champ. Babette never had the desire to breastfeed, so there was no separation anxiety there. He's had a few crying jags, so I know he misses her. I'm keeping on his au pairs. That way, he'll at least have some sense of continuity."

I pat his arm. "You're a good man, Lee."

Lee shakes off the compliment. "Despite his parentage, Harrison deserves my love. After all, he is Janie's half-brother."

And of course, the same can be said about his stepdaughter. "You've always been Janie's anchor."

"I'll be there for her until my last breath." He pats my hand. "It leads me to wonder if Babette had a role in Jonah's death. I know he gave her plenty reason to despise him."

"She was close to Carl, so it is possible. To Babette, the Quorum's leaders were her own personal chess pieces."

Lee flinches at this honest jibe against his dead wife but he knows it's true. Harrison's birth father was Babette's lover, Salem Rahmin al-Sadah, a Saudi billionaire as well as a Quorum member.

I don't have the heart to tell him what she divulged about

her closeness with Carl and what I suspect about her and Eric too.

Lee closes his eyes at the thought of Babette. When he opens them again, I see that they're damp. "Donna, I want to thank you for what you said during the special prosecutor's investigation. You are a real friend."

"I only told the truth. Frankly, I was surprised I was given such leeway to do so."

"Assistant Special Counsel Karami did the right thing on several levels. First, the longer you talked, chances were greater that you'd say something that might incriminate me. And I'm sure Reynolds instructed her to keep the proceedings going for as long as possible to allow him—and yes, Edmonton—to negotiate my departure." He grimaces. "I made it easy for them: none of the bullshit transition costs. No salary or other expenses. But I stuck to one demand: an immediate 'full, free, and absolute pardon,' which ended any possibility of an indictment."

"Considering that Reynolds was out for blood, why did he agree to it?"

Lee snickers. "He only did it at Edmonton's behest. And Edmonton only did it because it would leave a stain on Babette as well."

"Ah, let me guess. He was to be her next victim." I roll my eyes at the thought. "Well, he dodged a bullet there! Still, I can't think of a couple who deserved each other more."

Lee actually laughs at my declaration.

I join in—

Until I see the tears in his eyes.

"I'm sorry, Lee. That was cruel of me."

He shakes his head. "No, Donna, it was honest of you. On the other hand, I was never honest with myself about my rela-

JOSIE BROWN

tionship with Babette. My ego—pride, fear, whatever—ruined my life."

"You're wrong. The best phase of your life is just beginning. It's time to build a legacy that will make your children proud."

I look out toward the lawn, where Janie and Trisha, both in their soccer jerseys, hold Harrison's teddy bear just high enough for him to grab it. When he pulls it from Janie's hand, his joyous squeals send them giggling.

Lee follows my gaze. Finally, when our eyes meet, he says, "Thank you for always believing in me."

His appreciation merits a hug.

As my arms go around Lee, every memory I have of him converges into a montage of the emotions we've shared—awareness, suspicion, appreciation, concern, and yes, trust—before forging into a rock-solid allegiance.

I lied to Lee. I did not always trust him. But through his actions, he's earned my allegiance.

And, now finally, he's earned Jack's.

No more backward glances. Lee's future will be his redemption.

TRISHA BEGS TO STAY OVERNIGHT WITH JANIE. I SAY YES BEFORE I take off. They need this time to catch up, to enjoy being ten. Besides, Janie is anxious to talk about her new school.

"At least, I'll have one friend," she exclaims.

As assurance, Trisha puts her arm around Janie's shoulder.

I am walked to my car by one of Lee's Secret Service detail. Although Lee resigned, one will still be assigned to him for life. It's the blessing and the curse of having served as America's Commander-in-Chief.

I'm sad about Lurch. He will always be a hero in my eyes.

JACK IS MOWING THE FRONT YARD. I'M SURE THE NEIGHBORS, MANY of whom are piddling around now in their well-manicured gardens, are ecstatic about this. The grass has grown ragged during our far-flung travels.

When Jack realizes I've pulled into the driveway, he turns off the mower and walks over. It's a hot day and his tee-shirt is damp with perspiration. He must think I'll swat him away because he pulls it off and uses it to wipe down his chest before drawing me in for a kiss.

He's wrong. Neither sweaty abs nor stinky underarms keep me from jumping into his arms and kissing him as if I haven't seen him in a year.

Time with our loved ones is too precious to waste.

When I finally let him come up for air, he gasps out, "Well, hello to you too." Before I know it, he's carrying me into the house.

I tease, "Hey, He-Man, what do you think you're doing?"

"Taking you up on your very blatant invitation."

I glance around. "What will the neighbors think?"

With a devilish grin, he declares, "That you're one very lucky woman."

Hell yeah, they will. And they'll be right.

The End

Next Up for Donna!

The Housewife Assassin's Horrorscope

(Book 18)

Donna, Jack, and the Acme team must decipher horoscope tips that contain clues to imminent acts of terrorism.

Other Books by Josie Brown

The True Hollywood Lies Series

Hollywood Hunk

Hollywood Whore

The Totlandia Series

The Onesies - Book 1 (Fall)

The Onesies - Book 2 (Winter)

The Onesies - Book 3 (Spring)

The Onesies - Book 4 (Summer)

The Twosies - Book 5 (Fall)

The Twosies – Book 6 (Winter)

The Twosies - Book 7 (Spring)

The Twosies - Book 8 (Summer)

More Josie Brown Novels

The Candidate

Secret Lives of Husbands and Wives

The Baby Planner

How to Reach Josie

To write Josie, go to:
mailfromjosie@gmail.com

To find out more about Josie, or to get on her eLetter list for book launch announcements, go to her website:
www.JosieBrown.com

You can also find her at:

www.AuthorProvocateur.com

twitter.com/JosieBrownCA

facebook.com/josiebrownauthor

pinterest.com/josiebrownca

instagram.com/josiebrownnovels

Lightning Source UK Ltd.
Milton Keynes UK
UKHW020629271022
411161UK00011B/161/J